**Critical Accl**

"A fast-paced thriller, *Mother City* takes readers from Cape Town to Washington, Jerusalem, and the Persian Gulf in the fight against global terror. Well researched and provocative, readers will understand what policymakers and counterterrorism specialists already know: what newspaper headlines say and what the real world is are often two very different things."

—Michael Rubin, PhD
Foreign Policy Scholar
American Enterprise Institute

"Human trafficking is the slavery and women's issue of our time, and the great twenty-first century human rights issue. Defenders of the status quo who speak of 'sex work' are no different from people who spoke of 'servants' and 'field hands' when seeking to mask the evils of African chattel slavery. Starner Jones' gripping debut novel rips the mask from our eyes, and helps move us towards a spirit of abolitionism that will rescue tens of millions of the world's most oppressed humans. If, as should be the case, the hallmark of the twenty-first century will be the emancipation and empowerment of women, authors like Jones will lead the way to that goal. *Mother City* offers its readers yet further value. It highlights the extent to which radical Islam poses a threat to the hopes and values of us all—Christians, Jews, Muslims, and atheists alike. Bravo, Starner Jones."

—Michael J. Horowitz, LLB
Senior Fellow, Hudson Institute

"A deftly plotted thriller set in Cape Town's Muslim quarter, *Mother City* focuses on how a chance kidnapping of a special needs son of an international Jewish multibillionaire unravels a jihadist plot to use children to extort Israeli recognition of Jerusalem as the capital of a Palestinian state. Brutal realism, disdain for established political leaders, grievances long nurtured by those injured in past Israeli military actions, and skillful use of special forces recruited from around the world meld into a story that races to its satisfactory conclusion. But paradoxically, success leaves the victors convinced that unilateral actions outside state structures constitute the only way to protect the future of the West. This is *Realpolitik* thinking with an edge in a world where decisive action from governments is always problematic."

—Samuel R. Williamson, Jr., PhD
Member, International Institute for
Strategic Studies (London)

"Starner Jones has written an important and timely novel that illuminates the most pressing human rights issue of our day. Perhaps his greatest achievement in writing *Mother City* is to show readers how personal and dangerous the War on Terror has become in a world where global leaders are reluctant to fight radical Islam with the same force used by freedom's most capable foe."

—Paul A. Clarin
Publisher
*Key West Citizen*

"From the author of *Purple Church* comes an entirely different and more impressive yarn. *Mother City* is an espionage thriller and intense character study rolled into one. Tightly-woven prose and razor-sharp dialogue yield a novel as riveting as any I've read in recent years."

—Paul Ruffin, PhD
Publisher
*Texas Review Press*


"Outstanding insight, hard to put down."

—Major General Greg Gile
USA (Retired)

# MOTHER CITY

STARNER JONES

# MOTHER CITY

World Ahead Press is a division of WND Books. The views and opinions expressed in this book are those of the author and do not necessarily reflect the official policy or position or WND Books.

Paperback ISBN: 978-1-946918-06-2
eBook ISBN: 978-1-946918-07-9

*Printed in the United States of America*
16 17 18 19 20 21 LSI 9 8 7 6 5 4 3 2 1

# Acknowledgments

This novel would not have been written without the generosity of Dr. Robert Galli, Chairman of Emergency Medicine at The University of Mississippi Medical Center, whose department funded my first visit to Cape Town almost a decade ago. I owe enormous gratitude to Dr. Galli, for without him I know not what would have become of my career in medicine or the dream of becoming a novelist.

During my second visit to Cape Town, a series of unlikely events culminated in a fortuitous visit to Bo-Kaap. I was captivated by the place, its people, and their stories. Driven by a determination I had never known, I learned as much as I could about the locale and will never forget conversations with numerous Cape Malays who still call Bo-Kaap home. They were, and in many ways still are, pilgrims whose ancestors were trafficked from one continent to another. Today, descendants of Malaysian slaves live in peace along those gentle slopes at the base of Signal Hill.

Similarities between cultures ought not be overlooked, and in Cape Town I witnessed the best and worst of humanity. Its natural beauty, embodied by an unforgettable mountain and a meeting of two great oceans, provides inspiration that compels many novelists to write. The city's irresistible charm and breathtaking waterfront stand in contrast to its reprehensible and unalterable past.

As a native of Mississippi, I must say, Cape Town's history and implicit contradictions are not unlike my childhood home.

— Starner Jones
Houston, Texas

There can be no keener revelation of a society's soul than the way in which it treats its children.

— Nelson Mandela (1918–2013)

For Liberty and all who fight for her

# 1

It was Friday in Cape Town, noon on a warm New Year's Eve, and the call to prayer had just overcome a cathedral bell.

Excitement rippled across Victoria & Alfred Waterfront, where thousands of tourists gathered for a day of merriment. A majestic mountain and infinite sea framed splendid views of the sprawling metropolis and imparted a measure of charm to the Tavern of the Seas. Just north of City Centre, a steady wind blew over Table Bay. A flamboyant scene befitting a mural spanned the harbor: an armada of cruise liners and motor yachts, the *Jolly Roger* pirate ship, an international port that bustled with commerce night and day. Flyers posted on shop windows and light poles everywhere: Kaap Klopse, 2 January, Bo-Kaap.

Pylons on the boardwalk croaked with sounds of hungry drum fish as tourists edged closer to shore, smiling and laughing without a care in the world, tugging their happy children along. They stepped onto a concrete terminal to be greeted like members of some famed royal family, who graced the local peasantry and posed in front of vagrants who dreamed of an easy life. Bystanders enthralled with the uber-rich hung cameras over a metal rail, and regarded the moment as something to be treasured as a precious gem. The boardwalk moaned wearily again. In a few hours, it would bear its limit of weight from tired bodies that returned to their ships in the heart of the Western Cape.

An eternal south wind blew through the crowded terminal. A covey of seabirds took flight from a mooring toward the sun, then swooped down over a tattered fishing net held together with coarse twines and pulled by a sullen man into his dingy. Drops of bird dung splattered onto the bow of the tiny boat as a seabird hovered overhead. "Ay," the man mumbled gruffly. In his dingy was the Holy Bible and a knapsack tied to a walking stick two meters long.

A pair of strangers on the boardwalk peeped at the old man and chuckled at his plight, not knowing he could hear them. The fisherman peered surely up at them as the wind gusted slightly and kissed his gristly forehead. The old man pulled a drag from his cigarette, and then tossed the butt into the sea. Calloused hands gripped a splintered paddle as he cursed and swatted at the seabird before it sailed high into the air, squawking and spreading its wings to glide over the Dutch clock tower, busy merchants in their tiny shops, and excited tourists looking here and there for souvenirs. A covey of birds peppered a cloudless sky as they climbed higher toward the sun.

"Postcard for your kinsmen back home?" a child peddler asked. His accent had a soothing timbre when you heard it for the first time. A soft manner belied the urgency he felt inside. He spoke with the voice of a boy who knew too much. Courage flowed through his veins. Seedy streets had raised him.

The boardwalk eked its familiar sound as the boy showcased his stash of goodies in front of tourists who came from all over the world: a Sri Lankan with her designer hat and matching purse, a Thai couple conversing in their native tongue, stoic Russians who walked in silence, pale Brits who drew hasty conclusions about them all. The boy's face hinted a sense of purpose. He could not have been more than ten years old. His bony hands offered a box of religious icons in front of a Nordic man: cream-colored statues of the Blessed Virgin in repose, grinning Buddhas who sat with feet tucked under flabby thighs, burgundy crucifixes whittled from yellowwood. He shifted his hands under the flimsy box and beckoned a passing tourist. "Precious jewel for your lovely bride?"

But there came no reply from the chattering tourists, not even a courteous 'No' or a simple acknowledgement of the boy's earnest attempt at commerce, not even from blissful Hindus, who pranced by hand in hand on the boardwalk while savoring gelato.

Instead, the lucky crowd rocked on. They marched along Victoria Wharf and into the heart of the bustling waterfront, laughing and strutting with grinning faces fit for a leisurely stroll, and then turned and gawked in unison as the paparazzi sped by on Beach Road with blowing horns and revving engines rushing southwest toward Camps Bay—a Bentley, a Ferrari followed too closely by humble Asian makes. Children who looked on stopped their peddling as roaring automobiles raced by. Noise and bustle on the coastal highway seemed altogether natural in the Mother City, a necessary by-product in a burgeoning area that was poised to grow. Word of the entertainment boom spread like a fever. Sights and sounds of flashing cameras wielded by the paparazzi were entirely fitting in South Africa's unwittingly cooler version of Hollywood, and the opinion reached as far as the rolling hills in Durbanville.

A custom megayacht one hundred twenty meters long was in port following its maiden voyage from Italy, and so was its owner with his wife and son. Armed guards capped with maroon berets stood at attention in front of the stunning vessel that was equipped with a helipad and flanked on either side by two yellow skiffs. Envious gawkers smirked at the opulent ship's name that was plastered on the stern: *Royal Flush.*

Inside a massive stateroom, a khaki-skirted woman peeked at an oval mirror. Radiant cheeks still glowed from a romantic encounter with her husband a few hours before. The woman recounted a look of anticipation on his face as he drew curtains in front of a bay window in the owner's suite. "Worried someone will watch us from the sea?" she had said to him. Her voice welled with naked enthusiasm. She laughed as his arms fumbled in haste, but her husband regarded the woman's amusement as something he did not cause.

Fashionable waistcoats hung next to a black cocktail dress in a closet where luggage was stowed. Gracefully, she reached for a handbag and then raised a window. A sudden wind brought the woman back to her husband's chiseled face, and the hardy boardwalk on which they had often strolled as king and queen. His solid chest had led the way.

They sat in club chairs on the flybridge and peered over Table Bay. Jack wore a teal short-sleeve button down, loose at the shoulders, and slacks that fit just right. His wife placed her hand on top of his, then straightened the silver cross that hung from her neck. A scent of French cologne passed between them and her eyes lit with the expectation of another kiss.

On the clearest afternoon, Jack Goldwyn reclined on his company's finest vessel that had just arrived from the couple's primary home in Portofino. The flybridge afforded a view of Cape Town not often seen, even by the privileged few. A whiff of lit tobacco wafted up from his fingers as Mr. Goldwyn sipped a glass of sherry. His eyes tracked a cable car that was halfway to its station near the top of Table Mountain.

Life had unfolded as planned. At forty-two, Jack inherited a custom yacht line founded by his grandpa and taken to new heights by his father, whose financial acumen carried on the tradition of his family's success. His manner of business was a rare blend of congeniality, careful planning, and common sense. After managing Southampton Yacht Company for several years, Mr. Goldwyn relocated to Naples. There he existed in a world of luxury, leading a life of pleasure and intrigue, accompanied by his prized boxer and a few close friends.

Mr. Goldwyn held the back of his head with hands clasped together and lightly puffed his stogie. The slow, titillating scent emitted from burning tobacco seeped through his lungs and into his nebulous soul. An impression of honor was stuck on his face. His broad shoulders exuded valor and conquest. For a moment time held still.

He recalled the first time he saw his future bride. They met at a bar near a deserted beach on the Amalfi Coast. The scene was meant for a postcard. A perfect sunset framed the setting where Jack sought peace and rest during a lazy weekend. He wore a white tattersall dress shirt with the initials J.S.G. embroidered on each cuff. Carmen donned a lightweight coral blouse with matching chino jacket and grey Falmouth pants that fit snugly at her narrow waist, but fuller at the hips and thighs. He spotted her sitting at a table where she waited for her friends to arrive.

They drank and danced the night away, and awoke the next morning in each other's arms.

Jack Goldwyn was a happy man. There was no pesky phone or urgent meeting he had to attend, no whining clients or looming mess, just his new lady and her dazzling smile. After a brief courtship, the couple exchanged vows before family and friends during a private ceremony officiated by an aged priest imported from the Holy See. Jack had lived alone until he wed his much younger bride on a perfect evening in Venice near the end of spring. Their honeymoon in Nice was as he had expected. They romped and rolled for hours in bed, and thus was the couple's only child conceived. The addition of a baby boy brought more happiness than either of them had ever dreamed. His diagnosis of Asperger syndrome tried their nerves—at times he was impossible to manage—but a London pediatrician and little orange pills made life better for them all. Nathan would mellow with time, the doctor said. His mother prayed it would be so.

Religion did not divide them, nothing so trivial ever could. She was a lapsed Roman Catholic, and he a secular Rothschild Jew. He ascribed to no religious practice at all, not even on holy days. Faith, it seemed, was not meant for him, except the kind he placed in his wife. Her importance to him would not be outdone by any deity, clergyman, or adherence to an ancient creed. Love—their love—was all he would ever need.

A bus horn screamed across Table Bay. Mr. Goldwyn turned to his cigar. He gazed at the magnificent vista that was before him. A sense of accomplishment was melted on his face. He had paid his dues long enough. Adherence to simple lessons taught by his father spawned a trend toward success that made possible a life of leisure. "Dreams are like strange highways," Jack's father was known to say. "Both can take you to places you've never seen." *Memento semper.* His penchant for finer things in life was becoming of an educated and well-traveled man. His was not merely a privileged life that just so happened to be. It was molded long ago through sound reason and upward social mobility.

Jack's ethics were above reproach, even in an increasingly competitive business world. Any claim to the contrary was palpably false. At fifty-three, his fruitful career had come to an appropriate end. Retirement was planned long ago and earned by commitment to lofty goals and hard work that preceded a life of triumph. Already he was a multibillionaire. *Veni, vidi, vici.* The days that remained were meant for leisure. So what if he wanted to buy another home or even a fourth? So what if his next purchase happened to be in mellow Stellenbosch, where A-list actors often retreated following a busy day of filming? Mr. Goldwyn's timing was apropos. Never had he felt so alive.

Inside their suite, Carmen freshened her cheeks in front of a bathroom mirror. Her eyes fell on a diary by her suitcase. She recalled the day it was given to her by a friend in Paris as they sipped fizzing Moet. A smell of perfume blew away with the morning breeze. Lines of a poem raced through her head: *Something old, something new, something borrowed, something blue.* With her rounded chin and regal nose, her eyes mellow and loose, anyone could tell she came from wealth—from the pampered mother who never knew work, the accented nobleman who owned a thriving fashion chain. Her mother was not acquainted with the toil of hectic employment, and her father was always at play. She had searched everywhere for a deserving groom, for the spoiled man of leisure who lived like a king, and at last she had found him. She was entirely at ease about her marriage vow to Jack. "Carmen Goldwyn," she thought as she had rested on a canopy bed inside her father's Austrian estate. "It has a lovely ring."

Jack was raised as she was. His family reaped a tangible benefit from its patriarch's renowned custom yacht line that boasted international appeal. Wealth was the by-product of intelligence and hard work: they were rich and couldn't help it. Travel offered ample time for them to spend together—there was always someplace else to go. To be alone with Jack Goldwyn in a foreign land was to explore something different and entirely new, another culture of which she approved, another people to whom she was drawn. Carmen smiled when courteous customs agents stamped her passport, and she was inspired to visit orphanages in any city they decided to visit. She lent a hand to those in need—helpless souls counted on her. Her heart and mind were injected with joy in the form of a happy marriage, and with the birth of Nathan, her zest for life had been renewed.

Jack Goldwyn felt at home in the Mother City. Its coastal setting brought out the best in him. Cape Town was bold, its charm endemic. Life was better there. Even street peoples' faces were bathed with hope, in the city that sprang up from a beach.

After gaining an interest in South Africa, Jack and Carmen made several trips to the Western Cape. To facilitate docking of the *Royal Flush*, Jack brokered a deal with Parliament to construct a deep-water port, and his plan had been executed well. Contracts were signed and men were hired. At last, the project was finished.

Victoria & Alfred Waterfront soon became their favorite place to visit. Its panorama was peacefully composed. During a long vacation in the middle of summer, they purchased a home close to a golf club owned by Jack's brother just south of Cape Town.

Mr. Goldwyn blew a puff of smoke. The aroma from his cigar served only to augment the splendid scene that was before him, and magnify the beauty of his wife whose countenance exuded class. Carmen stepped onto the balcony and reclined beside Jack. As she kissed his cheek, they heard a knock at the cabin door, and then a sober Nigerian voice.

"Meesta Goldwyn, your escort is ready."

Jack rose from his chair as Carmen smiled and released his hand. A seabird hopped on the deck. Jack reached for the dark cherry door and heard the voice of the bellhop again.

"Sah, your . . ."

"Well, hello," Jack said.

The bellhop stood with feet close together.

"At ease, son."

A subtle breeze passed through the doorway. Twin seabirds squawked on a rail.

"Good day, sah," the teenager replied. "Would you and the Missus care for an escort to the shore?" His voice had a dreamy air.

"We would indeed," Jack said.

Carmen arrived beside him.

"Pleasure, sah. How about a refreshment for you and the lady?" He presented a tray with fruity drinks. "I have piña colada and lemon daiquiri."

A smile beamed from his face. His skin was black as lava. Only the whites of his eyes were visible when he did not speak.

"Why, thank you," Carmen said. She fingered a napkin around her drink.

"Pleasure, ma'am," he said. "Now follow me. I will take you to fetch your son."


Back at the boardwalk, the old fisherman peered up from his dingy. His face was marked with crusty lesions after years of labor in the blazing sun. A seabird hung over his head. "Ay, bloody birds," the old man grumbled. He reached for a paddle and froze.

The child peddler traipsed by on the boardwalk with his store of religious icons and petty trinkets. "Postcard for your kinsmen?"

the boy said. A cunning parlance flowed off his tongue, but it wasn't the mischievous kind. He cradled a colored sketch of Table Mountain in one arm, and with the other balanced a supply of Blessed Virgins, shiny menorahs, and necklaces made from local shells. Tourists who passed by him said not a word.

The old fisherman tugged on his haggard beard. Stubby cheeks came alive as his eyes settled on the tattered net submerged beside his dingy. His heart beat stronger than a few moments before. A tear made its way along a furrow on his sunbaked skin. The net was teaming with fish. A gust of wind scattered beads of sweat on the old man's leathery neck, and the boy, Jonas, went on peddling. He lifted a modest cross in front of Jack Goldwyn, who strolled by puffing a stogie with his wife at his side.

Rugged pylons sustaining the boardwalk moaned.

"Precious jewel for your lovely bride?" the boy pleaded. His bold, expectant eyes cased over the waterfront.

No tourist answered the eager boy.

The Dutch clock tower in Table Bay pealed quarter of twelve.

2

A *muezzin* bellowed out from the olive-green minaret on the lower end of Dorp Street: over the ceremonial cannon at Noon Gun, over brightly colored abodes and an empty café, a dusty graveyard where countless Mohammedans were laid to rest. Tawny-skinned men with flowing white robes crept toward a common destination as a sonorous wave of sound reverberated through Bo-Kaap. Leather sandals on lean, sinuous limbs scraped the shabby pavement in front of an idle museum and vacant realty, as hundreds of Cape Malays retreated to the quiet haven of Auwal Masjid.

Dutifully as soldiers, they formed a line on a sidewalk next to Dorp Street, waited patiently in single file, and then stepped slowly, reverently, through the narrow entrance to observe the obligatory wash in tiny stalls located a few paces inside the mosque. Requisite cleansing portended composure, and was done to enter the spacious prayer room that was decorated with imposing verses from the Qur'an. The sound of flowing water imparted tranquility to anxious souls, and contrasted sharply with the material world outside, a petty and frivolous realm seething with infidels whose immorality had no end.

Arabic calligraphy was etched on pale walls encompassing the prayer room. Soft curves belied pithy messages it conveyed: total submission matters most. *Salah* was a time of sober reflection on the important task at hand. A nervous hush permeated the room.

Personal strength was born of silence. A niche in one of the walls indicated the direction of Mecca, to which the faithful gazed before kneeling on lavish carpet equipped with exacting lines signifying order, and confining the believer to his rightful place of prayer. Hundreds of supplicants bowed in South Africa's oldest mosque. Plain white turbans covered their heads. Men of all ages prostrated before Allah in a show of strict obedience, planting their hands and faces on royal blue carpet that held not a shred of lint.

Calmly, confidently, the anointed one approached his lectern. *Kufic* on the minbar had ominous appeal. His folded arms disappeared under a long cotton robe. Imam Rauf studied the worshipers. He was a capable man, full of vigor, with salt and pepper hair over each ear, and a neatly trimmed beard attended twice weekly. Grown men sat in front of him as impressionable children eager to learn. To him they were the chosen few. An awkward silence filled the room. Vulnerability finds a place of refuge in the holy space. Each man was a clone of the one he knelt beside. Not a single woman was seen.

The men rose to their feet, and then promptly knelt and bowed again. With stoic faces and folded hands, they awaited instructive words from the anointed one. With trademark poise, he placed his hands on opposite sides of the minbar and said, "The story of Islam in Bo-Kaap is one of courageous sacrifice and collective triumph. It tells how early Muslims in the Western Cape, who first arrived as slaves from Malaysia, Bengal, and the Indonesian archipelago, overcame indignities, persecution, and forced labor. But their unfortunate circumstances did not result in disappointment or failure. Instead, adversity cultivated an environment ripe for intensifying Islam's struggle for legitimacy in a changing world. The quest began first at home, here in the Malay Quarter, and then spread as wildfire into the African bush. Just how far, no one can tell."

Rauf stepped away from the lectern. His message was clear, relayed by force and necessity from none other than almighty Allah.

"Who is a teacher from the perspective of Islam?" Rauf asked and turned in an instant toward his pupils, pointing a stern finger at them. "A teacher is first a seeker of truth. Second, a teacher is a disseminator and spreader of truth. Third, a teacher is an exemplar. It is he who sets the example."

Each man sat motionless as his leader spoke. Timidity soothes the distressed. A cluster of elders rested on a pew near the back of the prayer room. One of them nodded agreement. Nothing but faithful worshippers as far as Rauf could see. A pigeon cooed on a windowsill. A gentle breeze blew over stubby palm trees in front of the masjid. The anointed one lifted his arms shoulder high. Hostility welled in his soul. The pigeon preened its dirty wings.

Rauf stepped closer to the lectern. He held forth open hands with eyes gazing upward. Tension surged in his voice. He said, "Think of Tuan Guru. He built Auwal Masjid, which hosted the first *madrassah* that was open to Malay slaves and their descendants who resided in the Western Cape. How many of us are aware that the first Qur'an circulated in Bo-Kaap was handwritten by the highly literate, Tuan Guru?"

He spoke with the courage of a man who was ready to die. Islam informed his every move. Conviction beamed from his eyes. Darkness hid in his soul. Submission to Allah was his highest honor, and yet there was more work left to do. His words provided languid men with essential strength. To the lost he gave direction— to dejected souls, ambition and drive.

The prayer room was muggy, its air thick and stale. The men sat shoulder to shoulder as warriors ready for battle. Each man's deportment was mature, reserved. Their minds attended to an urgent message.

A petite man just shy of twenty years listened more intently than anyone else in the room. His appearance was frozen and vile, startling at first encounter. Sparse hair was combed tightly over his forehead. A thin, pointed goatee sprang from his chin. You saw his frosty eyes and speculated about what they had seen: Kidnappings? Child rape? Beheadings of Christians and Jews?

The young man sat motionless near the center of the room. From out of nowhere a sense of purpose germinated from years of neglected emotional and physical pain. Sermons at Auwal Masjid had an intoxicating flair to vulnerable and misguided youth— this the anointed one knew. His sermons were addictive as the purest drug. Islam was the cure for every pain, including the pain of loneliness. Grief? What grief? The more the young man with the goatee heard, the more he wanted to hear. He could never get enough. It was as though Rauf spoke only to him: *There is no God but God, and Mohammed is his prophet.*

Rauf's thick, dark brows tilted inward. His tight fist slammed down on the minbar. With a heated pitch he said, "The whole of the Qur'an is important, and not just certain aspects of it. You must wholly dedicate yourself to all its teachings. Islam is not meant only for chosen ones who hail from Sana'a or Bo-Kaap, but for the world at large."

A faint breeze wafted through the prayer room. The sermon grew more heated as minutes passed. Rauf rested a clinched fist on his hip. His staccato voice was stronger than a few moments before. Spittle ran down his chin as his oratory grew more intense. He said, "Yet it is the specter of losing in the here and now that haunts adherents to Jacobianity in the land of Abraham, Isaac, and Jacob. You see, my brothers, disaster and misfortune take place according to the perfect will of Allah. Life begins and ends as He sees fit. No force or power directs one's destiny or causes harm to anyone without permission from Allah. Evil is not forbidden by Him. In fact, it is ordained." He held open the holy book, and then turned to face the men. "No misfortune happens on Earth, nor afflicts your souls, but is recorded in a book long before you bring it into existence. This is truly easy for Allah."

The anointed one reached for a kerchief and held the Qur'an overhead as he stood beside the lectern. His eyes peered at the holy book, and then over the prayer room as he scanned each man's face. His height and form were as impressive as his practiced words, becoming for a man who craved political influence most of all. In his face was tireless purpose, as though a lofty goal and how to achieve it were ever present in his mind.

He said, "Hear these words from the Qur'an. Fight those who do not believe in Allah, nor in the latter day, nor do they prohibit what Allah saith." A thick finger turned the page. "Men are the maintainers of women, and as to those on whose part you fear desertion, admonish them, leave them alone in sleeping places and beat them. Surely, Allah is great."

A few elders nodded approval, another sat motionless and prayed. Rauf placed the Qur'an on the minbar, then clasped his hands together and turned to the faithful. Stout arms extended in front of his chest. A robust silhouette was cast on the wall behind him. Again, his eyes peered upward. The mosque fell deadly silent when he did not speak. His words breathed life into the quiet space. Soft, smooth hands rested on the minbar. He surveyed his flock and said, "This present life is only a trial, a preparation for the next realm of existence. Islam must be for you the only endeavor that matters."

He looked boldly at the young men who bowed before him and said, "To exert yourself to the utmost of your ability in every endeavor you undertake, that is the mandate of Islam. That is what Tuan Guru did."

A moment of silence came and went like the shortest prayer. The man with the goatee stiffened with resolve he had never known. Youthful muscles pulled tight as the anointed one spoke. His spirit was more enlivened by every word. The notion that he had not contributed enough to the cause of Islam had troubled his conscience for many years. For him, this thought, this interminable feeling, was more than a casual musing on Friday afternoon: it gnawed at his soul. The intensity of his conviction waxed strong in his chest and it did not wane. Religious obligation haunted him day and night. He was never at peace. Memories from his childhood constantly tormented his mind. He saw the world through the taint of excessive guilt and self-loathing. A pervasive nausea dampened even his desire for basic nourishment, and he had grown inhumanely thin in recent months.

Rauf said, "A day will come when the whole universe will be destroyed, and the dead will be resurrected for judgment by Allah. This day will be the beginning of a life that will never end. This day is the Day of Judgment, and on this day all souls will be rewarded or punished by Allah for what they did or did not do to serve holy Islam." Each man's countenance was calm and true. Rauf's words were potent as the brightest poppy. He said, "You see, Sharia law is the divine law sent by God to the Final Messenger, Mohammed salah allahu wa salam. It is justice for mankind. It will take mankind out of the shackles of man-made law into the perfection and beauty of divine law. Surely, this is a noble thing, to invite someone to a superior way of life."

Some of the elders sat dead still. A few of them rocked slowly back and forth. Another held his eyes shut and stroked his beard.

"If we believe Westerners are oppressed, why should we not bring them out of oppression through adherence to divine law? Most of the world lives under the law of infidels, and when we shine the light of Sharia law on them they do not like it."

The sermon concluded as powerfully as it began.

"From the lascars who sought refuge after the Grosvenor's shipwreck, to the fight for freedom in the Malay Quarter, Islam has etched a permanent place in the hearts of those who struggle. But too often I hear young people say, 'I enjoy going to mosque. I like going on hajj. I like to fast in observance of Ramadan, but do not bother me about jihad.'"

The young man in the center of the room fingered his goatee. Cold eyes stared into a distant place. Sharp words from the anointed one pricked his heart again. It was true. He had adhered to enduring tenets of Islam since he was a boy. He fasted during Ramadan and prayed the Namaz. Hajj was his favorite time. He had even touched the Black Stone. But his stagnant faith could turn into something more. Islam was not merely the still, small voice heard only by the chosen few. It was the unquestionable truth that bellowed in the heart of every man. Islam's best work did not occur in the dark of night. Rather, it happened in the light of day for all to see.

Rauf said, "So, my brethren, I must ask: How will you restore Islam to greatness in the Western Cape?" An elder at the back of the room snorted softly. "What mighty act will you do in the name of Allah? How will you serve holy Islam?"

The young man rocked back and forth with eyes tightly closed.

"Perhaps you are ready for jihad," the anointed one said. "Perhaps you are ready to fight."

## 3

He unlocked the door of his apartment and quietly stepped inside. The scene was as pathetic as his reticent heart. So was the offensive smell that permeated the gloomy abode. A stench of soiled kitty litter smacked him in the face each time he arrived home after a long day at the hotel where he worked. Aside from the Qur'an placed on a woven blanket in the center of the kitchen table, there was no attempt at décor. He set a bag of groceries next to the holy book and paused to survey his humble space.

A handmade palate occupied a corner of the living room floor. Nearly empty bags of dried lentils and fava beans were stacked on the counter where he prepared his meals. A faded rug covered most of a stain on the floor in the middle of the room. The closet was bare, except for a pirate costume and a cockroach turned belly up. He gazed at a shabby piece of furniture in the flat. *This is not my home. I am just passing through.* He scrubbed his hands in a sink that was stained with dark blue detergent.

His cat spent most days outdoors and returned in the evenings to feast on half-eaten sardines and week-old bread. The mangy feline served a purpose, catching rodents and preserving hygiene in the flat, but in his heart the young man with the goatee knew she was his companion too. He lit a stick of incense to temper the intolerable odor, and as he did, the cat, which he recently took in, gave a timid meow to announce her hunger. The young man pivoted and threw a wicked stare at his meager pet. "Hiss!"

The cat arched its back and tiptoed away.

He stroked his goatee and skimmed a recipe affixed to the pantry door. A jug of water and crusty bread rested next to a sack of apples and neglected mail. Homegrown spices were stowed in a drawer along with a bag of tomatoes. Directions for *mavrou* were scribbled on a piece of paper underneath his passport. Deep-set eyes scanned a list of ingredients for what must have been the thousandth time: five hundred grams diced lamb, two onions finely chopped, three potatoes cut in cubes, a generous heap of rice.

The cat took its place on a palate beneath a square table. Lint-covered blades of an oscillating fan whirred on the opposite side of the room. He lit another stick of incense and placed it on the counter. A smell of fresh apricot slowly filled the room. Hunks of lamb crackled on the hot plate. The young man sniffed a jar of nutmeg and froze.

A copy of the *Cape Times* was sprawled across the back of a wicker chair. Its headline read: "American Tourist Kidnapped in Langebaan." Tension surged in his chest. The young man had grown accustomed to constant pain and appeared much older than his age. He had the eagerness of a child, but a child he was not. His face was branded by years of heartache, but the smooth skin below his neck showed no sign of age. He drew a deep breath and shrugged his shoulders. Still, he felt no relief.

His eyes fixated on a dusty passport.

*Passport/Passeport/Pasaporte*
*Surname/Nom/Apellidos: Al-Munir*
*Given Name/Prénom/Nombre: Asram*
*Date of birth/Date de naissance/Fecha de nacimiento:*
*17 May 1996*
*Place of Birth/Lieu de naissance/Lugar de nacimiento:*
*Sana'a*
*Date of issue/Date de délivrance/Fecha de expedicion:*
*2 June 2008*
*Sex/Sexe/Sexo: Male*
*Authority/Autorite/Autoridad: Republic of Yemen*

He sat in a chair and his mind returned home again. He held the passport in one hand and dangled the other hand over his knee. Pensive eyes gazed dead straight. A photo from his parents' wedding rested beside a sack of flour. He fantasized about what had occurred between them on the night he was conceived. They met at his mother's family tent and went to the village hangout to eat and chat. One thing led to another and they engaged in the notorious act through which all people come to be. He thought of his mother's resolve to make a better life for her son who was fathered by the only man she ever loved.

Asram hovered over the hot plate and swatted a lazy fly. He gazed at the passport again. Specks of beige sand on the cover reminded him of the humble place where he was born and bred, the seedy nation that gained its independence first in the north from the Ottoman Empire, and later in the south from England. Life was nothing if not an endless show of conflict. He recalled the Marxist orientation of the government that was adopted in southern Yemen and the flight of fellow countrymen who sought a better life and headed north. Then came unification, followed briefly by a secessionist movement that was quickly and effectively subdued by paramilitary troops. The noblest of worthy endeavors, spawned by the purest dream, was bound to end in ruin. Hostility was the only way. Asram sniveled with indignation as he fingered his scant goatee. "The British," he mumbled, "always meddling."

His glossy eyes threw a murderous stare at the cat as she recoiled on a dust-stained rug. "Hiss!"

The animal snarled in a show of phony self-importance.

He lifted a box of *Playboy* magazines and placed them on a table. The fan blew open a magazine, exposing Miss October in a tempting spread eagle pose. The love of a woman was something he had never known. Intimacy with another mere mortal was intolerable to him. It was Allah whom he loved most, Allah who showed him the narrow way.

Asram returned to the hot plate and rotated a sizzling hunk of lamb. A crumpled clipping from a Yemeni newspaper lay on the kitchen counter. With sad, lonely eyes he began to read.

SANA'A—Terrified worshippers ran for cover yesterday after an Israeli missile attack killed scores of Shi'a Muslims here in the capital city. The blast at a shrine near a busy area of commerce left at least eighty-four dead and injured dozens more. The attack was the deadliest military action to date in a city that has struggled to find legitimacy in the eyes of a cautious UN, which is expected to issue a travel warning for Yemen later today.

Authorities say women and children were among those killed or injured in the blast that took place on the eve of Ramadan. A young mother lost her legs as a result of the blast and bled to death in her son's arms. His father also died. The boy, seven-year-old Asram al-Munir, was taken by rescuers to a nearby hospital where he remains at this hour.

He replayed the attack again in his mind. Indelible memories danced in his head.

It happened at night, as tragic events often do. He saw beads of sweat on his mother's face as she labored over an open fire in the family tent. Heat wafted from boiling curry as she stirred it in the pan. Thick, grey smoke engulfed her face. Cracks in a curtain admitted the soothing *adhan* from a mosque at the end of their street: "*La Ilaha Ill Allah*" (There is no God but Allah). Calmly, Asram's father knelt to pray.

And then, it happened.

He jerked with memory of the fatal explosion. The strike came out of nowhere amidst a dead calm, and then moved closer with a sound no one in the village had ever heard. Dozens of tents caved in when a missile landed by an ancient Muslim shrine. Whirling trash and debris slammed onto sandy streets. Seams in every turban were rent. His mind flashed to a sight of his mother dying in his arms. Her forehead had been turned into goo. He stretched out his hands and recalled sadness he felt while holding his mother as vitality slipped away from her lips. Blood pooled at his feet as her eyes rolled back in her skull. He watched as her cheeks changed from pink to white, and then to a shade of grey he had never seen. Horror was etched on his face as he wept and wept and wept. At last, his mother lay dead in his arms. Her final words echoed in his mind. "I love you, son. Always be faithful to Allah."

Asram was kept in intensive care at a military hospital for several months, and adopted following discharge by a local imam and his wife who nursed him back to health. Flies had landed on his face and the gauze dressing that encased a three-centimeter hole on the front of his neck. He had sweated day and night in the imam's tent that was hardly different from the one where he was born and raised. A look of misery was sealed on his face. He carried marks from his childhood with him as a man: a contracted burn wound on one hand incurred as he cradled his dying mum, a tracheostomy scar from the procedure that saved his life, the permanent limp from polio, which made life a constant challenge.

*Damn the Jews*, he thought as he peered at his right hand that was missing its thumb. *Those bloody pigs—they did this to me.*

He folded the newspaper clipping and placed it in his pocket—wherever he went, it went with him.

A line of transfer trucks idled on South Arm Road overlooking the port at Table Bay. Drivers leaned against their cabs as they smoked cigarettes and chatted about the day. Somewhere in the distance a siren wailed.

Ali eased his cargo van to the curb and waited. His frumpy attire and scruffy face made one think he was content to remain a single man. He had been under the direction of the anointed one for many years, first as a student in the Madrassah at Auwal Masjid, and now as a tour guide at Bo-Kaap Museum. He got out of the van, sat on a mooring, and lit a cigarette. He watched with eager eyes as a crane hoisted huge metal containers into the air. The *Maersk Mandela* was in.

Fangs of a forklift dispensed a row of boxes onto the cargo deck. Ali watched as a stocky man stooped to load a forty-kilogram sack of rice onto a flatbed truck. He had a sturdy build and made the task look effortless. The forklift operator lowered a large wooden crate into the back of the cargo van. As the man hoisted another sack onto the truck, he said, "There you go, mate. That ought to do you for a while."

The stocky man received his customary tip and heaved a bulky sack as wheels on the van began to turn. "There we go," he said to Ali, "just like always."

The stocky man bent over again. Ali did not look away.


A chauffeur opened a rear door of his dark sedan.

"Mr. Goldwyn?" a voice said.

"That's me."

"Welcome to Steenberg. My name is Niels."

"Pleasure to meet you."

"Thank you, sir. Please follow me."

They walked through a corridor that led into a lounge where Jack's brother and three other men played cards. A bottle of scotch stood in their midst.

"Gin!" a man exclaimed as Jack and the club manager approached. Niels said, "Sorry to crash your party, gentlemen. I would like to introduce our newest member of the club, who is familiar to at least one of you."

The men rose.

"Keep your seat," Jack said.

"Pleased to meet you, Jack," one of the men said. He offered a hand. "Joe said he was expecting you."

"Your reputation precedes you," said his brother, Joe.

Niels stepped forward a pace. "May I arrange a tee time for the group?"

"Already done," a man replied.

"I'm afraid I can't stay," Jack said.

"Are you sure? We'd be delighted for you to play," said Joe.

"You're kind to offer, but we have a meeting in Bo-Kaap. I stopped by to sign a document and say hello. Must be going soon."

"Buying more real estate?" a man asked.

"Purchasing another vineyard?" another chimed.

Joe said, "What's the matter, bro? Is one not enough?"

"No," Mr. Goldwyn said. "Nothing like that, I assure you."

"What gives, Jack? Why are you in such a rush?"

"A meeting with a prospective au pair. She was recommended by Carmen's friend who teaches at the University."

"UCT?" Joe asked.

"Yes."

"Sounds promising. Where is she from?"

"Netanya. Her uncle holds a seat in the Knesset."

"You don't say."

"I do. We're meeting her at five o'clock."

"Where is the meeting?" his brother asked.

"Noon Gun."

"Surely you can make room for a quick nine," one of the men said. "We'd really love for you to play."

"No, I'm sorry. Another time, but not today. Our agenda is just too full. And besides, Carmen is waiting in Bo-Kaap."


Two-dozen tourists chatted at the lower end of Dorp Street as they waited for the guide to arrive.

"Do you really want to do this?" said Jack.

"Of course, babe," his wife replied. "It's just a short walking tour. Nothing to worry about."

"I thought we were meeting the au pair."

"Not until five thirty. Her meeting at a bank ran late."

Jack's expression didn't change.

"Come on, it will be fine." His wife nudged him and smiled. "We're going to see a madrassah. Besides, our guide was recommended by the hotel concierge."

Inside the mosque, a group of schoolboys sat in a half circle and read the Qur'an. Their daily routine was dictated by the anointed one.

A not-quite middle-aged man with a dingy turban and matching smock appeared in the doorway. He was pudgy, his girth not entirely hidden by long, flowing robes.

"Good day, my friends," he said with a narrow grin. "Welcome to Auwal Masjid. My name is Ali. I will lead your tour of Bo-Kaap." He stepped down from the entrance, careful to avoid a sleeping cat. "Looks like we have everyone here. Let's begin."

Tension surged among the tourists. One by one, they peeked at each other and fell in line. Jack and Carmen walked behind the group up the gentle slope next to Dorp Street.

After a few meters, Ali turned and faced the tourists. He said, "Located to the south of Victoria & Alfred Waterfront, at the bottom of Signal Hill, is a mystical enclave with its enduring revival of shops, markets, art galleries, and cultural museums, where visitors find a place bustling with young professionals unwinding after work in the evening. Bo-Kaap, as the locale is called, is quintessential Kaapstad."

Men and women gathered around him as he spoke with hands clasped behind his waist.

"Bo-Kaap has a unique culture, which has developed over the last three centuries. There are definite influences of Western culture here, and the people of Bo-Kaap have adjusted to the ever-changing world around them. The peaceful enclave is home to a population of just over six thousand people. Bo-Kaap is a delightful treasure to many holidaymakers. Its character emerged during the period from 1790 to 1840. The earliest people who settled here became known as Cape Malays, which is an incorrect historical term, as most of Bo-Kaap's residents are not entirely of Malaysian descent. Present-day residents are mostly descendants of slaves who hailed from Africa, Indonesia, Malaysia, Java, and elsewhere in Asia. Slaves were sold by their own people to the Dutch during the sixteenth and seventeenth centuries. Imported slaves, who were abruptly cut off from their kin and native cultures, had no place to turn and were suitable for conversion to Islam, which is the predominant religion among today's residents of Bo-Kaap."

The visitors were a hodgepodge of mankind. Carmen moved a step closer to Jack, who stood motionless with his eyes glued to the speaker. Ali said, "There are still traces of Indonesian vocabulary in the Bo-Kaap dialect in such words as *trim-makaasi*, which means 'thank you,' and *kanalah*, meaning 'please.' Many other commonly used words have been substituted with Afrikaans." He gave a wry smile to Carmen, who held open a street map.

"Bo-Kaap is the place where East meets West, and the rest of the world should take note of happenings here. Although Muslims far outnumber Christians in this quaint locale, the two religions mesh quiet well. Christians embrace their Muslim neighbors in Bo-Kaap, for it is the place that forms the hive where the Cape Muslim community began. After all, we Muslims were here first, but not by choice."

He wiped a moist stain on his smock and offered a feeble grin.

"Let cobblestone streets serve as your guide as you explore this lively village filled with brightly colored houses dating from the seventeenth century, and silhouetted against a clear blue sky made even brighter by hand-sewn blankets draped over front porch walls. You mark the difference between older Dutch buildings from English ones by their lines of ornamental arched roofs, and distinguish them also by straight gutters, or the absence thereof. Take note of Muslim shrines, known as *kramats,* which dot hilly landscapes along with many beautiful mosques, including one situated at 43 Dorp Street. This mosque has an intriguing history and is known as Auwal Masjid. It was the first mosque established in the country."

The Goldwyns stood near the back of the group as Ali's presentation went on.

He said, "Be sure to visit the Cemetery of Muslim Saints, not far from Noon Gun at the top of Wale Street. Among the *auliyah,* or Muslim saints, buried at Tana Baru, is Imam Abdullah ibn Kadi Abdus Salaam, also known as Tuan Guru, who is by far the best known and most important. It was he who was the prince from Tidore in the Trimate Islands and traced his ancestry to the Sultan of Morocco. It was he who established the first masjid, where your tour began. Tuan Guru was captured by the Dutch for conspiring with the English, banished to the Cape, and imprisoned on Robben Island, where he lived as a prisoner until 1780. During his incarceration, he wrote a book on Islamic Jurisprudence and transcribed several copies of the Qur'an from memory. One such copy exists to the present day in a glass case inside Auwal Masjid. His other handwritten works on jurisprudence became the main reference texts for Cape Muslims in the nineteenth century.

"The year was 1792. After twelve years of imprisonment on Robben Island, Tuan Guru was released and went to reside in Dorp Street, which was then the main residential area of Muslims in Cape Town. It was during his stay in Bo-Kaap that he recognized the need for a Muslim school, or madrassah, where students could learn to read and write. This was his primary concern. So, acting as the Blessed Servant of Allah and his prophet Mohammed, May Peace Be Upon Him, the Dorp Street Madrassah was established. Thus, it is because of Tuan Guru that many freed blacks and Malaysian slaves learned to read and write Arabic.

"In madrassah, children learn from highly educated teachers and imams about the tenets of holy Islam. Daily lessons are carefully planned. Curricula encompass the breadth of those taught at the most respected institutions in the secular West, while at the same time adhering to honored traditions set forth by Tuan Guru and the holy prophet, May Peace Be Upon Him. This environment fosters a healthy atmosphere in which intellectual capacities of students are undergirded and challenged in preparation for college and the professional world beyond. So the Madrassah at Auwal Masjid is not just a madrassah that doubles as an orphanage, but rather fertile ground for intellectual and spiritual growth for children of all races whose parents are not around to see after them. You see, my friends, we Muslims take care to raise our children in preparation for life in a free, civilized, and democratic society."

Ali continued. "Iman Abdullah was both saint and learned professor. Hence, his nickname, Tuan Guru, which means Mister Teacher."

"His second major concern was to acquire a venue where *Jumu'ah* or Friday prayers could be performed. Tuan Guru's application for a mosque site was flatly refused by the Christian magistrate in Cape Town. Nonetheless, Imam Abdullah led early Cape Muslims in an open-air Jumu'ah at the abandoned quarry in Chiappini Street. In 1794, one of Tuan Guru's students, Achmat van Bengalen, gave one of his properties to him. The house had been owned by a freed Muslim slave named Corydon van Ceylon. Tuan Guru recognized the property's suitable locale and it became Auwal Masjid. Today the building looks very different than it did at its inception, with only two of the original walls remaining intact after it collapsed in 1930. As you may presume, Tuan Guru was the first imam at Auwal Masjid. All this he accomplished while the practice of Islam in the Cape was a criminal offense."

Jack shifted his feet as huge palm leaves waved overhead. Ali extended his arms before the tourists as they stood in front of the mosque. A placard above the entrance read, "Auwal Masjid, Est. 1794."

The group formed a circle around Ali.

"And now we will have a look inside," Ali said with a narrow grin. "Follow me, and remember to remove your footwear."

His whisper emerged as incense from his lips.

"To grasp the extent of Allah's Throne, imagine a platform raised on eighteen thousand pillars. The distance between pillars is a journey of seven hundred years. Allah buried each pillar under the seven layers of heaven, and to carry His throne, Allah created four gigantic angels with distinct shapes. The first one appears as a human being, the second as a tiger, the third as a vulture, and the fourth is in the shape of a cow. Their respective sizes are beyond anyone's imagination, save Allah. Their legs reach the bottom of the seven heavens, and, with a single step, angels travel seven thousand years."

"How was the provision of five prayers ordained?" a tourist asked.

"Good question," Ali said. "From the blessed light of Muhammad, Allah created a peacock and placed it atop a *Sajaratul Yakin* tree. Sitting atop this tree, the peacock prayed to Allah for seventy thousand years. Then, Allah fashioned a mirror of shame and situated it in front of the peacock. The peacock was overjoyed to witness its extraordinary beauty so much that it prostrated to Allah five separate times. Thus began the tradition of five compulsory prayers offered by the faithful."

Schoolboys sat cross-legged on the floor in the prayer room. Some of them rocked back and forth as they chanted verses from the Qur'an. Another stood next to the minbar and turned his face toward Mecca, "Assalatu khayrum minan naum" (Prayer is better than sleep).

Ali said, "As a faithful adherent to holy Islam, Tuan Guru was moved to see the masses educated and lift themselves from the bondage of slavery." The tour group gave a collective smile. "And now, behold the fruits of his blessed labor, which hath wrought literacy to generations of children in Bo-Kaap, who would otherwise have remained in bondage and illiteracy, making it impossible for them to study the Qur'an."

"Where are the girls?" an English woman asked.

Ali turned to face her head-on. He said, "The Madrassah is reserved only for boys and girls are kept in a separate locale. You see, in the days of Tuan Guru, girls were thought to be a curse for society. No one bothered about them and they were neglected for centuries by imams. The plight of girls pained Tuan Guru deeply, but he was powerless to change the system overnight. However, he was not discouraged by regrettable circumstances and took steps to level the gender gap. Unfortunately, he did not live to see his dream become a reality. Today, orphanages for girls are alive and well at numerous locales throughout the Middle East. Thus sayeth the holy prophet, 'Do not hate the girls. I am father of girls myself. Daughters are passionate and worthy to prosper.' A pious woman gives birth to a pious generation, for it is from her cradle that children are raised. It is impossible to organize a holy and pious society without cooperation of pious women. Our ancestors were raised by dedicated mothers who were filled with Islamic vision. Islam had been observed by them since childhood, so their progeny developed into proud Muslim men who lead us today."

Jack's face was devoid of emotion as Carmen smiled sweetly beside him.

Shadows lengthened over Büitengracht Street. A car horn blew in traffic held up by a broken-down bus. Wind from the southeast blew stronger, lifting the South African flag on a pole at the center of a busy roundabout.

A few blocks west, the bell at Saint George's dinged quarter of five.

## Interlude in Tel Aviv

In a fortified building north of Tel Aviv, Abel Reuben waved his ID card in front of a detection unit and a sleek glass door slid open. Third floor at headquarters was reserved for the director, his immediate staff, and select agents whose missions required continuous supervision. His dark suit, striped tie, and neatly combed hair were becoming of a man who was in control, just as the spring in his step had the effect of an articulate leader, a general, an important political figure whose strategic mind was seldom at ease.

A stately corner office had served as his base for several years. He leaned back in a leather chair and propped one foot on a mahogany desk. His work space was cluttered with official memos, an empty pack of Marlboro, a half-used book of stamps, a pocket knife, and an invitation to a cocktail party he had marked on his calendar but did not attend.

Reuben's eyes were drawn to a reflection beside his desk. His dress shoes glared back at him from glass covering a portrait of his late father that hung on a wall.

The phone buzzed.

"Reuben."

"Good morning, sir," Melanie said in a neutral tone.

"Morning, Mel."

"We intercepted new terrorist chatter between Yemen and sub-Saharan Africa last night. Washington is aware, but the memo we sent to the president fell on deaf ears."

Through the years, Reuben's assistants had always benefited from a firm, guiding hand. He unfolded his arms in front of his chest. "It would be helpful to have boots on the ground."

"We have a set close by," Mel replied.

"Good. We need an asset with fresh legs in the region, a real local."

"Ascension Island in the South Atlantic has the closest air base. We can mobilize an asset from there if you would like."

"Ah, yes." Reuben sipped his coffee.

Mel said, "A thousand British Royal Air Force and US naval officers are stationed there. Tactical operations and linguistic capabilities are limited, but there is a GPS augmentation antenna on base and a sparingly operated missile testing facility. The State of Israel funds part of the lab."

"Your taxes at work," the director said.

"It was Washington's idea to keep the base open."

"Such a waste," Reuben said. "Put the United States in charge of the Sahara Desert and in six weeks there won't be any sand."

"This is no time for games, sir."

He knew Mel's thoughts as well as his own. She said, "Other assets are available."

"Does the one you mentioned speak Afrikaans?"

"Yes. Should I notify dispatch?"

"Right away," he said, rapping his knuckles on the shiny wood. "The asset will be more useful to us on the mainland."

Mel did not speak.

"Are any memoranda ready for review?" Reuben asked.

"You said by Sunday, sir. Today is Friday."

"Okay, Sunday it is. We will convene at 0800."

# 4

Asram stood at a waist-high table in the hotel laundry where he worked. He reached for a bottle of detergent as the lazy afternoon dragged.

On the far side of the room a door slammed shut. Mr. Cilliers, the hotel manager, entered without warning. His protuberant belly was impossible to ignore. It was no wonder his wife had left for someone else.

Asram twirled his head.

"Mo, what the hell are you doing?" Cilliers asked sternly. His disposition had never been gracious.

Asram didn't answer. He peered longingly at a clock on the wall. Months earlier he had decided never to argue with his employer again. It was no use. Cilliers always won. As the minute hand approached the bottom of the hour, his scarred fingers sorted through a pile of soiled linens. He could have gagged when his hand touched a freshly used condom that was stuck to a pillowcase stained with dark rum and strawberry jam.

The manager stood next to him. A blend of body odor and stale beer emanated from his pores. "You were to have all linens finished by three o'clock. What happened?"

Silence.

Cilliers smirked. His eyes were glazed from too much booze. He said, "What have you done all day?"

Asram rotated a faucet knob and snatched a bar of soap.
"Answer me!"

The second hand ticked on.

"We had the party. That's why so many linens."

"Oh, is that so?"

Asram held a vacant stare.

"Is that your pathetic excuse?"

"It's not an excuse. This pile of sheets is all that's left."

"Don't talk back to me, Mo." Cilliers' head was flush with rage.

"It's almost done. Chill out, okay?"

"I am your superior."

"You should be kinder to your workers."

"Shut up and do your job!"

"Treat me better and I will!"

"Why, you little . . ."

Asram gasped as the vicious man clutched his neck and squeezed.

A tour bus roared passed the corner of Longmarket and Burg, where the old fisherman napped in a cardboard lean-to. He had no place to call home, save the infinite sea, and no pillow on which to rest his head. Calloused hands cradled a shallow wastebasket that held his morning catch. Wide shoulders pinched blades of grass that poked through a rusty fence, which surrounded an abandoned industrial site. As the old fisherman dozed in the sunlight, his belly groaned for lack of bread. Heavy eyelids cracked open as the summer sun began to set.

Outside Cape Town Lodge, a sport coupe idled at a traffic light. Asram paused on the sidewalk and looked askance at the driver. Rap lyrics blared from speakers that rattled the gaudy ride.

> *Now I ain't got no kids yet*
> *but this right here's for practice*
> *I hate to get the seats in the Benz wet*
> *but that's how good yo' ass is*

Asram peered over his shoulder as he trod on. "Hideous bloke," he whispered.

A blind beggar sat on a street corner next to a trash bin. Water from a hydrant provided cheap entertainment for schoolchildren who loitered in front of a bakery. A pile of sandals had formed upstream. They ran and jumped with bare feet into a puddle next to a motor scooter that was propped up by its kickstand.

A sour taste oozed in Asram's mouth as the rap song played.

> *She said, 'I heard you got a main chick*
> *A mistress and some hoes*
> *You be up to no good*
> *And everybody knows*
> *My homegirls tried to warn me*
> *They tried to let me know*
> *But what you got, I need a lot*
> *So I can't let you go'*

Advertised on an electric pole: "Mavericks—Cape Town's Most Distinguished Club and Revue Bar, 68 Barrack Street, Ticket price R200, Thrilling Fantasy Shows Every Night." A separate ad boasted:

"Decadence has a Name—Teazers Cabaret, Free Admission, Open 7 p.m.—Late." Photos of a nubile babe suspended in arabesque were displayed in a store window a few steps away.

Asram growled and reached for his goatee. Nausea churned in his stomach, abhorrence surged in his gut. Rejection of worldly pleasures was a chief mandate of Islam. The more extreme his self-effacement, the more fervent his belief would be. He recalled Atta's final words. To sacrifice was to obey.

His brow was moist with sweat. A clinched fist hung at his side. He was far from Sana'a and the humble village where his life began. He saw his reflection in a hotel window. His chest was numb with disgrace. A scar on the front of his neck reminded him of agony he felt during months he had spent in hospital when he was a boy. With only part-time work and little money, he yearned for a place of refuge, a chance to start anew. He peered at the minaret near the lower end of Dorp Street and yearned for the comfort of Auwal Masjid.

The coupe squealed tires when the light turned green.

"Ignorant pig," Asram mumbled.

A man wearing a yarmulke passed him on the sidewalk.

"Bloody kike," he said.

"Pardon me?"

Asram turned. His face held an expression of utter contempt even as his stomach dropped at the sight of Rauf. *Had he heard?*

Rauf said, "Just now I thought you . . ."

"I enjoyed your sermon today," Asram said, "especially the part about jihad."

"Ah, my good boy. One never knows the blessings Allah has in store for those willing to give their all."

"I'd like to hear more, Imam," Asram said.

Across the boulevard, on Dorp Street's gentle incline, Ali heaved a wooden crate onto a dolly at the basement entrance of Auwal Masjid. Big block letters stamped on opposite sides read: HOLY BOOKS—HANDLE WITH CARE.

Carmen and Nathan sat on the veranda of a hillside café. They occupied a table decorated with fresh lilies and prepared to dine with Jack. A wooden sign over the entrance read, "Welcome to Noon Gun." Jack returned from the washroom. He peered down Wale Street as Asram sauntered alone up a rocky incline.

A waitress approached their table. She said, "Welcome to Noon Gun. May I take your order?"

"What kind of beer do you have?" Jack asked.

"There is no beer at Noon Gun, sah," the woman replied.

"How come?"

"The café owners are devout Sunni. They do not allow any beer."

"Are you Muslim?" Carmen asked with a smile.

"No, I am not," the waitress answered. "I pray to a merciful God, and they to a vengeful Allah."

A gentle breeze refreshed as incense in a tropical cathedral.

"Good for you," Jack said.

The waitress grinned.

Asram placed a basket of linens on a nearby table and sat on a bench.

Jack chuckled.

"Are you a Muslim?" the waitress asked Jack.

Asram spun his head.

"Hell no," Jack replied.

Carmen tapped her husband's leg beneath the table. "Now, honey," she said, "Islam is a beautiful religion."

Her assertion stopped Asram cold.

"Mrs. Goldwyn?" a young woman said.

Carmen turned.

"Hi, I'm Suri."

She was a stunning young Jewess, a brunette in her mid-twenties, with terra cotta skin and fine, wavy hair just passed her shoulders.

The Goldwyns stood to greet her.

"Delighted to meet you, Suri. This is my husband, Jack, and our son, Nathan."

The boy smirked and made an awkward gesture with one hand.

Suri stooped to meet him. She said, "Hi there, handsome."

Nathan held out a juice-stained hand. "Hello, ma'am," he said with a chuckle.

"You stinker!" His mum tickled him.

"Mommy, look at that funny man." The boy pointed at Asram.

Something about Nathan was off. He was an ill-tempered kindergartner, immature for his age, and given to public displays of distasteful opinion.

"He's goofy," the boy declared.

"Ja-cob," Carmen chided. She reached for her son's hand.

Asram's chest pulsated with fury.

"How old is he?" Suri asked.

"Five."

"Are you having fun in Cape Town?"

"Look at that man," Nathan said. He ignored the young woman and stared at Asram.

"That's enough," Jack implored.

Asram's blood boiled hotter. Even little children laughed at him.

"How did you find the au pair agency?" Carmen asked.

Suri sat in a chair. "A post at University Commons. I inquired about an opening in Windhoek that had just been filled, and then I was referred to you."

"I see. How long was the application?"

"Ten pages, not including a background check. I submitted three references, underwent a psychological evaluation, and appeared before a panel for an interview."

The waitress delivered their food and Nathan dove in.

Asram hated the way the boy conversed with his imaginary friend and ate his meal in utter bliss. Laughter came easily to Nathan. In the midst of a scrumptious dinner that someone else had prepared, freedom-loving people smiled and laughed in a manner that was carefree. Asram turned away from them. He brooded over his unfortunate lot in life as the Goldwyns chatted with Suri over a table filled with delectable Malay cuisine.

"Are we going to see zebras tomorrow?" Nathan asked.

"Yes," Carmen said. "We'll see them."

"What about leopards and monkeys?"

"Yes, sweetie."

"Will there be lions?"

"Yes, honey, lions too."

"Mommy, are zebras black with white stripes or white with black stripes?"

Suri laughed. "So cute."

"I don't know, sweetie," Carmen said. "What do you think?"

42

The Goldwyns were unknown to Asram—a nonentity a few minutes before—but he hated them just the same. Life in Sana'a was short and grim. Such was not the case for the Goldwyns and their spoiled-rotten son. To be sure, their lives were easy—this, Asram knew. He heard the collective laughter that came from their table next to his and could not help but imagine what might have been, if only his parents had lived.

Again, the boy pointed at Asram. "Is he a monster?"

"Nathan," his father said.

Carmen felt obliged to interject. "No, son. That's just a scar on his face."

"A scar?"

"Yes, but it's not polite to point. Remember?"

"What's a scar?"

The boy was insufferable.

"That's enough, son!" his father declared.

Carmen peeked at the stranger.

"What happened to his hand?" Nathan asked.

Asram burned with rage. Again, he was under attack from intruding Jews. His mind wondered back to the decade before. Gunfire rang out in his head.

"Look at his hand." The boy raised a finger at his subject. "His thumb is gone. I wonder what happened to him." Nathan got up from his seat.

Carmen cradled her chin with a palm and turned away from Asram's accusing stare.

The boy stepped toward Asram. "Sir, what happened to your hand?"

"Nathan!" Carmen chided. She grabbed him and pulled him close.

He did not relent. "Are you a Muslim?"

Asram did not budge. His small fists were tightly clinched. Islam was not something one discussed with infidels in the light of day. The conversation would be more fitting in the comfort of a shadowy mosque.

Suri was pensive and did not speak. She had seen Asram before, but did not recall when or where—a store, a sidewalk, the madrassah where her roommate Leyla worked? His appearance was memorable to say the least. One could not forget the tracheostomy scar on the front of his neck or the right hand that was missing its thumb.

"I'll hear no more of that," his father said.

"He looks like a monster."

"We'll be leaving now," Jack insisted.

Carmen turned to Suri. "He does this sometimes."

"He's just a boy," Suri replied.

"Yes, but it's still embarrassing."

The waitress smirked as the call to prayer bellowed out from the minaret at Auwal Masjid.

"What is that?" Jack mumbled.

"That's the adhan," the waitress replied.

"The what?"

"The call to prayer," Suri answered.

"Sounds like a wounded beast," Jack said.

The waitress giggled.

Asram lingered. His face turned pale. To him the call to prayer was soothing and true, but to hordes of infidels it sounded more like a dying warthog taking its last breath in the African bush.

"Can we meet another time?" Carmen said.

"How about Sunday?" Suri replied.

"Sure. We'll be free most of the day."

Asram tarried by the stairs.

"We're going to the Kaap Klopse parade at noon," Carmen said. "Shall I ring you when it's done?"

"Yes," Suri replied. "I'll await your call."

She turned to where the young man with the goatee had been. A moment later Asram was gone.


The kramat of Tuan Guru was creamy white, rectangular, with a quarter moon and star atop the building that was flanked by stubby flora.

Halfway down Wale Street, the Goldwyns came to a dusty path that led to the iconic shrine. Nathan stayed close to his mum.

They approached the kramat and saw a young man who sat alone on a bench. It was Asram. For him, the kramat of Tuan Guru was a symbol of Islam's struggle for recognition and legitimacy in a fallen world. Countless men had devoted their lives to securing the modern Muslim's freedom to worship and escape oppression through adherence to Sharia Law.

Asram held the Qur'an in front of his face and kissed it. He recalled names of faithful men who lived before him. The first imam who lived in Cape Town was Said Alochie of Mocha in Yemen. Sentenced to work in exile on Robben Island in 1747, Said Alochie later moved to Cape Town where he worked as a police constable, an occupation that afforded opportunities for him to visit slave quarters where he taught from the Qur'an. Asram meditated in silence, his eyes closed as he rocked back and forth. He was inspired by sacrifices of Muslim martyrs who gave their all in the name of

Islamic jihad and often recalled Mohammed Atta's defiant epitaph. *We have some planes. Just stay quiet and you will be okay.*

He remembered the comfort he felt during Friday prayers at Auwal Masjid. Rauf's most recent sermon echoed in his mind. "The whole of the Qur'an is important . . . wholly dedicate yourself to all of its teachings . . . Islam is not meant only for the chosen ones who hail from Yemen or Bo-Kaap, but for the world at large."

The call to prayer rang in Asram's head. *Alhamdulillah. Praise be to Allah. Allahu Akbar!* His eyes cased slowly over Bo-Kaap, and then homed in on the minaret at Auwal Masjid. The mosque was the focal point of Muslim life. Its doors were open to frustrated and recalcitrant youth. Amid uncertainty, Rauf offered encouragement, guidance, and moral rectitude. For the first time in his life, Asram found hope in the face of sin and compromise. "Until we destroy Western institutions and all their negative influences that plague our culture, we will continue to suffer their shameful effects: corruption, social decadence, famine," a famed Mohammedan had said from the minbar.

As the Goldwyns approached the sacred shrine, Nathan pointed at Asram and said, "Look at that ugly man. See, there he is again!"

"Yes, sweetie, I see him," Carmen said, "But please don't call him ugly. He's probably sightseeing like us."

"Sightseeing?" Jack muttered. "In his hometown?"

"Maybe, I don't know," Carmen said.

"Not a chance."

Asram was silent inside his adopted country's oldest kramat, where Tuan Guru was laid to rest. He knelt beside the dusty grave and sang loud enough for the Goldwyns to hear.

*There is no god but Allah.*

"I don't like it here," Nathan said. "That man scares me."

"Shhh," his mother said, "He's praying. We're leaving soon."

"No, this is weird. We're leaving now," Jack said.

Asram heard every word. His eyes peered straight ahead. The Goldwyns turned as he rocked back and forth and whispered, "There is no god but Allah, and Mohammed is his prophet."

A man in a sports car went on peacocking as though his activity were entirely expected of someone with his pedigree. Lyrics of a rap song blared up the hill to the sacred shrine where Asram kneeled to pray.

> *She said, 'I heard you got a main chick*
> *A mistress and some hoes*
> *You be up to no good*
> *And everybody knows*
> *My homegirls tried to warn me*
> *They tried to let me know*
> *But what you got, I need a lot*
> *So I can't let you go'*

Asram rose from his place of meditation. He peered through a window as the sports coupe headed west. "Bloody pig!" he shouted.

The voice of a muezzin echoed through Bo-Kaap, calling the faithful to evening prayer.

Asram watched as the Goldwyns retreated along a dusty path. The boy's words had scorched his soul. Wounds borne of suffering when he was scarcely older than Nathan were opened again.

He sat on a bench with his head hung low. As his stomach croaked for want of food, he kneeled once more on the dirt and prayed.

Dorp Street was drab, except for Leyla, who stood on a street corner and filed her painted nails. She was an old soul. Vitality lived in her eyes. Willpower pumped in her veins. Inward charm was manifest without effort. She was not a princess by pedigree, her countenance was the portrait of wild beauty—it radiated from every curve. Her physique was slender yet defined. Ample breasts caused even ascetic imams to stare when her nocturnal attire was spotted by wandering eyes.

Rauf straightened his turban as he approached her. He said, "What poor life decision led you to this place?"

"Excuse me?" Her face held a subtle grin. If not for a mandatory veil and niqab worn inside the masjid—a dictate of the anointed one—she would have been spoken for long ago by any number of eligible men, and given birth a time or two.

His inspecting eyes rushed over her face. "You've got something in your lip. What is it?" the imam asked.

"A jewel," the young woman said. Soft pink rouge covered her cheeks.

"A jewel. What for? Why did you do that?"

The two spoke only to each other.

"I don't know," she said with a half wink, not thinking. Her expression was not insincere.

"What do you mean you don't know?" He did his best to indict her with a disapproving stare.

"Love of pain, because I wanted to, I guess." Her eyes danced as she spoke.

"What do you mean, you guess?" His lips quivered. "You know exactly why. You said so just now."

The summer air was sticky and damp. A tour bus roared passed the corner.

"You did that because you wanted to be different, but now thousands more have done it too and you are no different from them."

Leyla shifted her heels on the pavement.

"You say you are a nonconformist, but now you are the same as an infidel. Now you must think of something else to do to your body, so it will shock curious men who pay you to pleasure them at night." Rauf adjusted his headpiece.

Leyla did not flinch.

He held a pointed finger in front of her face. "Your lip jewel is ugly. I don't like it. Take it out."

His tone was biting and cruel.

"What else have you done to your body?" he said.

Her eyes darted away from his stare.

"Let me guess, pierced your privates?"

"You are a sick man," she said.

"And you are a disgrace to Islam."

Leyla shrugged. Her eyes cast a smug conceit at him. She said, "So what if I have a liking for worldly pleasures your Qur'an patently warns against? It's what's in the heart that matters."

She scanned the space around them. Not a living soul in sight. They were as alone as Adam and Eve. She jerked her eyes away as his rant continued.

"Young people these days, they don't know how to be normal. All they know is how to be weird."

"Oh, is that so?" she said with a mocking tone.

Her petulance annoyed him even more.

"Tattoos and body piercings—that's how one gets AIDS, you know."

It had been his habit on Friday afternoons for more than a decade.

Rauf sat alone in his basement office. He clasped his hands together and leaned forward on the desk. He recalled the severest verses from the Qur'an. Edicts read to him by his father were fresh on his mind. He thought of Sana'a, an unshakable memory, the place where his life began. After a moment of reflection, his mind returned to Bo-Kaap.

South Africa was replete with political corruption. Little had changed in the post-Apartheid era. Millions of youth, disillusioned by poverty and moral decadence, were ripe for conversion to Islam. They were not born rats and thugs. Life had turned them that way. Christendom had let them down, but Islam could lift them up.

Rauf opened a large wooden crate and beheld his newest loot: two thousand neatly packed copies of the Qur'an, a dozen semiautomatic assault rifles and smuggled contraband—the lifeline of enterprising imams—lay before him. A hundred bags of highly coveted liquid were tucked neatly between holy books stacked four feet high. To Rauf and his legion of complicit imams, black tar heroin was as precious as salvation itself. He reached for a bag as a rat leaped off the crate.

The concrete floor was cool and damp, a prayer rug its only décor. A small wooden desk and aluminum chair stood in a corner. On the desk was an old laptop computer and beside it a mouse, the Qur'an, two notebooks, and a plastic cup filled with matching pens.

Outside Auwal Masjid, close of day drew near. As dusk fell over Bo-Kaap, its gentle slopes were quiet and still. A south wind rustled palm trees that dotted slopes at the base of Signal Hill. Cobblestone streets called to mind a fairyland, a nursery rhyme, enchanted life from another realm. Lines of well-kept houses glowed as colorful toys that reflected light from a setting sun. The long summer day ended with delicious meals and fervent prayer. An aroma of mavrou cooking on a stove brought a smile to every Malay face. A widow opened the door of her home, peacefully humming the adhan as a half-dozen children shed their shoes and stepped inside for dinner.

And then it came, the familiar voice of a muezzin who bellowed the call to prayer.

5

In Hout Bay, restaurant owners bid on slabs of Galjoen piled high at Mariner's Wharf. Moments before, twenty kilograms of the day's catch had been sacrificed. Fish that had flopped in a tattered net suffocated and wound up hacked into small pieces on a chopping block before landing at last in a huge frying pan.

Asram watched with envy as thoughtless men persisted in their menial work. He admired their stoic expressions and reckless movements, the mind-numbing labor by which they made a living. A worker raised a machete overhead and peered at him with eyes void of emotion. The rhythm of work resounded deep in the butcher's chest. Death had a certain tempo—a predictable, sequential cadence—like the beating of a tribal drum or a harsh edict handed down by a radical imam. The worker's blade slammed down again. Blood splattered over a giant wooden palate as he chopped and chopped and chopped. Hacking sounds bellowed deep in Asram's soul. The gruesome scene made him grin.

He left the fish market and made his way to Büitengracht Street. Along the way, he stopped at a convenience store for a half-liter of milk and a pack of smokes. His eyes were drawn to the lead article on the front page of *Al-Qalam*.

President Ali Abdullah Saleh, who was in Riyadh yesterday, decided not to attend a meeting of world leaders and boarded a return flight to Sana'a. Upon hearing of an alleged Israeli military attack, he condemned the action, saying, "What we witnessed today in Sana'a was an unimaginable assault on innocent Muslim life, the worst kind of civilian atrocity perpetrated by the predatory Israeli regime."

The attack marks a new low for heinous Zionist Jews in their resistance to de facto Shi'a Islam. Sources close to the matter say Jerusalem denied any involvement in the attack, which left seventeen dead and dozens injured.

Asram lit a cigarette and pulled a lazy drag. He cocked his neck backward as his thin lips blew a cloud of smoke.

Two blocks west, rock music blended oddly with chimes from a cathedral. To Asram, no sound was as soothing as the adhan, that mysteriously elusive impulse that passed through the air on its journey to every sinner's heart and soul.

An outdoor bar hosted humanism's altar call. A singer's supple lips nudged the microphone as an unruly crowd began to cheer.

*Hey there, all you middle men*
*Throw away your fancy clothes*
*And while you're out there sittin' on a fence*
*Get off your ass and come down here!*
*'Cause rock 'n roll ain't no riddle man*
*To me it makes good, good sense.*

*Rock 'n roll ain't noise pollution*
*Rock 'n roll ain't gonna die*
*Rock 'n roll ain't no pollution*
*Rock 'n roll it will survive!*

Malice seeped in Asram's veins.

A brutish wind gusted from the south, stirring a covey of pigeons as they strutted in front of a dentist's office. Outside the building, a vagrant snored at close of day. A mess of fish lay beside him. The old fisherman often shared his afternoon catch. He lay face down in his lean-to and made not a move in his dreamless sleep. The vagabond was acquainted with the noise at hand.

A woman wearing a business suit walked by and paid him no mind. The man awoke as an executive carrying a briefcase dropped a few coins beside him. One of them bounced into a pile of brush. His sun-beaten face bent toward a rattling manhole as a taxicab sped. Heavy eyelids squinted in the final light of day. Weary eyes held the gaze of a broke and benevolent man who lived and died by the sea.

"Thank you, sir," said the fisherman. Hope dwelled in his soul.

He wiped a tear and began a futile search for the coin.


Back in Bo-Kaap, Asram prepared his evening meal alone. He cared not how it would taste. By now he was accustomed to his nightly routine: a predictable meal prepared on the hot plate, the call to prayer echoing through Bo-Kaap from the minaret at Auwal Masjid, tourists beaming pretty smiles and laughing as they tarried outside chic cafés, lamb curry consumed in sober solitude. Never had he enjoyed the pleasure of casual fellowship with other blokes his age. Fate imparted to his life disappointment and fear. Happy times eluded him. It seemed his luck would never change. Someday, he would die and no one would care.

He propped open the tiny window facing east. Sounds of Bo-Kaap trickled in: Malay children playing stickball, taxis speeding, busy tourists chatting about whatever they pleased.

Asram plopped down on the shabby couch in his flat. Frail, dry lips were cracked from scurvy. His eyes were injected and red. The sound of sizzling curry took him back to another time and place. He recalled the sight of his mother as she cooked over an open fire inside his family's tent in Sana'a. They were not unlike their ancestors from centuries past. The smell of zesty rue brought a grin to his face. Asram crossed his legs like a dainty girl. He remembered his mother's soft skin, his father rocking back and forth as he read countless verses from the Qur'an. He had often recited those comforting words. *There is no god but Allah, and Mohammed is his prophet.*

It had been Asram's custom to do things quickly. Even meals were a frantic rush. Sunni life was devoid of the simplest pleasure. Nervous, smacking lips made the only sound he heard. His tongue protruded as he devoured slices of roasted lamb. A stream of spicy curry trickled down his chin.

Insomnia plagued him always and food brought no pleasure to his tongue. Raised eyebrows offered an impression of heightened awareness, if not permanent surprise. His tremor was made worse by mounting fatigue and constant stress. His scarred face amused many a stranger. They laughed at his beak-like nose as he passed them at cafés during Happy Hour on Longmarket Street. The hardscrabble life of the lower class could have weighed even heavier on Asram's mind were it not for devotion to Islam. Nevertheless, he felt a connection to untouchables, derelicts, and ne'er-do-wells who roamed seedy streets in the Mother City at dusk.

He had spent countless nights alone in his apartment befitting an ascetic. This night would be no different.

As he plotted his next move in front of the bathroom mirror, he fingered his goatee and whispered, "Have I done enough to serve Islam?" If for no other reason than to feel the sting of indifference, he sneered at his reflection and said, "No, you have not, Asram."

A siren crooned on Büitengracht. He yawned and reached his hand into a paper sack, forgetting for a moment what was inside. A newspaper clipping drew his mind back to Sana'a.

Twenty-three people perished in a religiously-motivated suicide bombing elsewhere in the city today. Sources close to the matter say the bomber blew himself up in a manner strikingly close to that of his brother who sacrificed his life during personal jihad last year. The bomber detonated himself after strapping explosives to his chest, then halted amidst a growing crowd of Muslim pilgrims who gathered at the Shi'a festival of Ashura, commemorating the seventh-century death of the Prophet Mohammed's grandson. Around the same time, a bicycle bomb hit a convoy in Mazar-i-Sharif in the north.

Attacks on the Shi'a sect by majority Sunni Muslims are rare in Yemen, although such terrorist actions are quite common in some places.

Asram peered through the lone window in his lair. A three-quarter moon hung over Bo-Kaap, illuminating a row of peaceful houses near the base of Signal Hill. The call to prayer bellowed through a labyrinth of narrow streets. *La Ilaha Illa Allah* (There is no God but Allah).

His thoughts returned to a horrific scene inside his family's tent when he was a boy. He questioned Allah for the millionth time, "What have I done to deserve this miserable life?"

The siren crooned louder as moments passed. No answer to his query ever came.

Asram paced back and forth in the kitchen. It was a place where no woman had been. Every second or two a drop of water fell from a leaky faucet into the sink. An oscillating fan whirred on a table opposite the window. Weak rays of sunlight illuminated dust particles scattered by the fan. A stench of rotten plantain wafted up from a trash bin. A cockroach crawled over his foot, another scurried up a wall. Asram's face held no emotion. He leaned back on the couch and extended his neck.

"Why me, Perfect One?"

Again, there came no reply.

His inquiry to Allah was swallowed up by a sudden breeze.

Most Friday nights he entertained tourists on the *Jolly Roger* pirate ship in Table Bay. It was at night that he felt most alive, and this night would enliven him even more, but not because of any pirate ship. With a look of resolve planted on his face, he closed the door of his apartment and left for the serenity of Auwal Masjid.

The most powerful force in the world was not love—no, not by far—it was hate.

**6**

Car horns blew behind a stalled transit bus. A stiff north wind hoisted the South African flag high on a pole in front of Parliament as automobiles scurried into a roundabout decorated with fresh flowers and a sign that read: Coon Carnival, 2 January, Bo-Kaap.

The old fisherman relaxed on a street corner a few meters down from a swanky bistro. He cradled a half-eaten snoek in his hands as headlamps from a taxicab spotlighted his face. The old man leaned against a brick façade to escape notice and reached for a kerchief to wipe his face.

A businessman passed and dropped a few coins into the drifter's bucket. One of them bounced off the rim and into a sewer drain. A woman in high heels clipped by without looking at him. Another jeered and flipped him off as she mumbled an imperceptible curse.

"Get a life," a drunk man said as he walked by.

The old fisherman smiled and reached for a coin.

The chimes at Saint George's sang seven o'clock.


Asram turned a corner just south of the masjid, and as he did, tawdry images of scantily clad women on a poster tainted his conscience. Guilt surged as his eyes feasted on a tempting woman's face festooned with glitter and luscious rouge. Disgusted, he trekked a few meters, then stopped cold at the sight of another lovely woman–but this one had a pulse and feelings.

Her form and aura he could not resist. It was Leyla. Nubile, succulent Leyla. She wore tight athletic pants and an even tighter white shirt, sans brassiere. Silver loops dangled from her ears. Her alluring makeup had been deftly applied. She dashed into an alleyway to escape his merciless stare.

"Whore!" Asram screamed. Women always had the upper hand with him. He sighed and wiped his brow.

A young woman and her daughter glanced at him. He looked back, blinked nervously, and turned away.

"What did he say, Mama?" the girl asked.

"Never mind, honey. He's not fit to speak to."

Asram tarried on a corner. He looked inanely into the looming night. Why did Allah grant women such awesome power? To test the strength of men.

A Catholic priest trailed him. "Hard day, my son?" the aged man said mysteriously.

Asram did not yield. He pivoted sharply and confronted the man. "Mister, I'm not your son."

"It's a term of endearment, my boy."

"I don't need or want your affection, and I'd rather not be called boy."

The priest spared no effort in counseling him. "A hostile man needs plenty affection."

"How do you know?"

"Anyone could see. Tell me. Are you a man of faith?"

"Of what?"

"Do you believe in God?"

"I serve Allah, no one else."

"These differences are subtleties, my son."

"I'm not your son."

"Why did you insult that woman just now?"

"What business is it of yours?"

"I'm in the people business. Did she offend you?"

"Did you see her attire?"

"Yes."

"And?"

"Her activity is not something I celebrate, but she's not hurting anyone and hasn't broken any law."

"Which law?"

"Man's law."

"Allah does not approve."

"How do you know?"

"Allah does not love whores."

"God is loving. He loves all his children, and I saw no whore."

"The way she was dressed, ducking into an alley like that. Clearly, she is a whore."

"What if she is? There's still hope."

"You priests are all the same. Imam says forgiveness breeds indulgence."

"Ah, my son. Question your imam. Question all authority, not just his. Mine too, if you so wish."

"You have no authority over me."

"That's true." The priest rested a hand on Asram's shoulder. He said, "Suppose you had another chance to speak to the young lady. What would you say?"

Asram thought of his mum. Beautiful, yet humble, she lived as a woman should live. But a woman who lacked humility to conceal herself was hardly better that a beast.

He surprised even himself with an earnest reply.
"I don't know."

Captain Lou supervised Nathan as he explored the *Jolly Roger* pirate ship. The captain had the patience of Job. Powerful tranquilizers Carmen always kept on hand had helped as well.

Jack and Carmen held hands and smiled amidst a symphony of sounds on a portico outside Sevruga. They sat on a wooden swing with Nathan in plain view between a luxurious hotel and passenger terminal. Faint sounds of bush music floated across Table Bay. The tune evolved into a chorus that came from a dozen tribes. It seemed that all musical genres were represented. A black lady dressed as Ruby Elzy crooned a famed Gershwin tune. Folks gathered around as she sang.

> *Summertime, and the livin' is easy*
> *Fish are jumpin' and the cotton is high*
> *Oh, your daddy's rich and your ma is good-lookin'*

A paper menu listed an offering of vintage wines. The seasoned waiter knew just what to say. "Our Riesling, Cabernet, and Pinot Noir are all made from native grapes, and each goes well with a carefully selected cuisine."

Carmen looked up from her setting and smiled.

The waiter held forth a menu. He said, "A wine is measured by assessing the fullness of its lines, but the more important and nebulous test of its quality belongs to the way it moves your soul. If Cape Town were a wine, it would have to be a Shiraz."

Carmen agreed.

The waiter said, "Judging from a multitude of languages spoken in elegant cafés and espresso bars, Cape Town is a cross-cultural experience. The city's rainbow of ethnicities and cultures combined to produce a fusion cuisine with enough variety and flare to please even the most discriminating taste. For centuries, black Africans maintained a healthy balance of wild game, fresh fish, greens, millet, sorghum, and maize."

Jack and Carmen watched as he poured Chardonnay into a shapely glass.

Fresh culinary ideas were on display. There was something for every taste: cured capriccios of warthog, ostrich, and springbok, toasted garlic bread, roasted pistachio chips basted with cinnamon.

The waiter said, "Enterprising sugar farmers brought indentured servants from India to slash cane, and with them came recipes from their native Mumbai or Delhi. British and German immigrants added European embellishments to the South African fare. Workers from Malaysia brought unique servings of various foods showered with spices from the most remote locales. Malay and Zulu slaves offered bush meat consisting of all manner of wild game. French Huguenots landed just after the Dutch and introduced vineyards that sparked South Africa's love affair with fine wine that persists to this day."

Carmen lifted her glass as a pianist danced on the keys.

"Compliment your entrée with a lingering indulgence of dark chocolate paired with a fine Cabernet." The waiter cradled a bottle as a delicate bird. "We also have a Zin that suits the palate of even the most discerning connoisseur."

A street person played a clarinet by the portico.

The waiter returned with a platter displaying their entrées. He said, "Cape Town is a location as rich in culture as the people who call it home. Mother City exudes an airy charm unmatched by any other."

Jack reached for a napkin. Carmen patted his knee. The waiter delivered more words about his beloved city, and as he did the setting sun cast its last rays over an elegant waterfront and spirited people who drank and ate at close of day.

The woman dressed as Elzy donned a green fedora and crooned into a microphone. *So hush little baby. Don't you cry.*

Jack and Carmen gazed into each other's eyes. The restaurant had an intoxicating appeal. A batch of fine wines and liquors stood on a shelf made of cedar. Paintings by native artists were showcased next to traditional African faces that hung on tan sheetrock walls. Collections of fish bones were neatly displayed in a case next to the bar. This was no place for Monet. Gaugin would have been out of place with his charitable degree of restraint, for works of art highlighted in the Mother City are meant for the bold and daring: a Kriedemann here, a Pierneef there, a Thomas Baines with its gritty depiction of an aboriginal brute going about his life as many a primitive man was known to do.

Mother City was ripe for a relaxing holiday. The essence of Cape Town wafted into the balmy January air, over the waterfront with its tranquil sights, sounds, and smells: squawking seabirds gliding over a pirate ship and trading post, fresh lobster served by a cute Dutch waitress at Quay's Four, the smell of burning oil in an aged cargo ship, wet planks of a boardwalk bathed by an infinite sea, a shipyard cramped with dry-docked boats, a line of glimmering motor yachts with flags from all over the world, the burgundy clock tower connecting the present era to all centuries past, a Ferris wheel that afforded views of happenings below.

Jack and Carmen fit naturally in the romantic scene. Before them was a magnificent life waiting to be explored.

The waiter pulled a small box from his apron and struck a match. A candlelit dinner was next.

The worship hall boasted refinement that stood in contrast to the decadent world around Asram. During Friday prayers, he was part of something great. In South Africa, Islam traced its roots to the Dutch importation of slaves from Indonesia and Java some three hundred years ago. He was not unlike his forebears and the nineteen chosen ones, who rose above their plight to reach the highest level of stardom in jihad. *In somnis veritas.*

Inside the prayer room, a sense of peril permeated the air. Islam and its edicts were centuries old, fashioned by ancient men who sat on the ground to eat. The practice was learned from endless readings of the Qur'an and a study of history itself. In the place where Tuan Guru had taught and preached, many a soul found strength. Mercy was obliged to penitent sinners who had no place else to go.

Asram thought of many virgins that await those who sacrifice their lives in jihad. The promise of spiritual purity and fame rustled in his chest. He would enter a global society whose leaders take orders from none other than Allah.

Inside the mosque, the air was warm and damp. Asram inhaled deeply as heavy tears streamed down his cheeks. Existence was a terminal disease. His hands were moist and callused. He exhaled putrid breath. Emptiness betrayed what little joy he had ever felt in his soul. Desperation swelled within him. He was overcome with fatigue, but on the present night he could not sleep.

Asram knelt on a prayer rug and cried tears of anger, rather than fear. His chest was tight with worry. He wiped his cheeks with a rag and planted his face on the decorative floor. With head bowed and eyelids swollen, he began to pray. His cracked lips vibrated with each whisper. He had the same recurring thought each time he bowed: *I have not done enough to serve Islam.*

The anointed one stood over him. Rauf said, "My son, to understand jihad, you must first understand Islam."

Asram prostrated before his master. Was this the intervention he needed?

"I'm sorry. What did you say?"

"My son, Islam is a commitment to live in peace through submission to the will of Allah. This is what it means to be Muslim, to live each day in total service to Islam."

"I'm ready to commit, Imam."

Rauf said, "Do you know the meaning of your name?"

"I don't," Asram said. "May I hear it?"

"Brilliant one who was cut off. This is the meaning of your name. This is what you are."

Asram prostrated on the plush carpet as though he were dead and buried.

"I feel you are destined for something great."

Silence fell over the worship hall.

"Take heart, good lad. All is not lost. Your journey has just begun."

"My journey?" Asram said.

"Your journey in jihad."

"Please, Imam, tell me. What is jihad?"

"What is jihad?" Rauf asked rhetorically. "Well, what does jihad mean to you?"

Asram did not move. He sat cross-legged on the floor and rocked slowly back and forth.

Rauf said, "Jihad is our constant struggle against evil—evil thoughts, actions, and aggressions of every kind. It is the fight to defend one's self, one's honor, assets, and homeland. Jihad is a justifiable conflict. Anyone who engages in jihad is known as a *mujahid*. Those who give their lives in jihad are met in the life hereafter with lovely Companions of Paradise, whose beauty far exceeds any mortal being and whose number is too many to count."

The room was quiet and still.

With a measure of restraint, Rauf said, "Young man, we've had our eyes on you. So too has Allah. We know you are committed to Islam. But do you have an insatiable appetite for jihad?"

"I do, Imam," Asram said with a determined stare.

"Are you ready to join the fight?"

"I am, Imam."

This was an innocent man's introduction to jihad: in the midst of doubt, a firm resolve.

"Well, then, let your journey continue." Rauf grinned.

"What can I do to serve Islam?"

The anointed one stood over him as a master directing a helpless slave. His answer was practiced and sure.

"Bring more troubled youth into our fold to save them from infidels, both Christian and Jew."

Asram hung desperately to every word uttered by the omniscient imam. "What do you mean?" he said.

Rauf lifted his robe at the knees then danced a circle. "Remember the *Hand of Fatima* inspired by a daughter of the

Prophet Mohammed. Call to mind Allah's providence as the unifying force in your lonely and difficult life."

His head hung low, yet Asram fixated on every word.

"What dominant motif do you most embrace to further the mission of holy Islam?"

Asram prostrated before Rauf.

Rauf smiled. "Auwal Masjid has a tradition of service. There are opportunities for you here."

In the stillness of Auwal Masjid, and without waiting for an answer, the anointed one turned and marched away.

The prayer room was silent. Asram stood in front of the minbar then bowed his head on a rug and prayed. Electricity coursed over his skin. No longer was he bound by man-made law. He was different from men and boys he worshiped beside. Did they hunger as much for jihad? Surely, they did not. His head was light and numb. He had never experienced the feeling before. Was it the manifestation of mental illness, or religious illumination for which he had often prayed?

A wave of tranquility came over him. It tickled his fingers and toes and spread into his chest and back. Consciousness faded with each shallow breath. Time passed as a fever from which he had almost died. His body contorted wildly and gave a sudden jolt. Minutes later, he awoke to a smell of urine mixed with fecal waste. His tongue was muted, his face grotesque and thin. Asram's neck arched back as his blood turned ice cold. Fear raged in his veins until at last he was engulfed in dastardly pride topped off with an evil grin.

A muezzin stood on the balcony of the minaret and sang. "*Bismillah ar-rahmaan ar-raheem*" (In the name of Allah, the Beneficent, the Merciful).

Asram faced the minbar. His life on Earth was only a trial, a test of unproven belief.

A wall clock nudged ten o'clock. Asram stood in the center of the prayer room. He kneeled on the floor and whispered, "There is no god but Allah, and Mohammed is his prophet."

Back at Seruvga, Jack and Carmen viewed an assortment of desserts.

"I'll have crème brûlée," Carmen said.

"Good choice," the waiter replied. "And for you, sir?"

"Cappuccino and an extra spoon."

"Excellent. I'll bring them right away."

The waiter turned and made for the kitchen.

"Did I tell you Leisel called?" Carmen said.

Sibling relations are either hot or cold. Seldom do those who are close in age drift so far apart as to rarely speak. But such was the case for Jack and his sister who had married the prime minister of Israel.

"No. What did she say?"

"She found results of a paternity test in Reznik's briefcase."

"Sounds suspicious. But why did she pry in his space?"

"It's something all women do."

"All women?" The billionaire's face retracted.

"Most." Carmen grinned.

"So you've inspected every drawer and dusty box in my office?" Mr. Goldwyn's eyes spun way. "I've nothing to hide from you, dear."

"I know, honey."

Carmen nursed her Chardonnay.

"What else did Leisel say?"

"She said the test was from October '92. He was just out of law school at that time."

"I see."

"I'm not surprised he's kept it a secret, but it's something a wife should know. Don't you think?"

"I do. But he's a politician with motives of another kind."

"What do you mean?"

"He would be defeated handily in the next election if results of a secret paternity test were suddenly made known."

"No doubt."

"Any word on the child?"

"None. She said he became very upset and wouldn't talk."

A man doesn't forget his lifelong friend. In years past, Goldwyn and Reznik had made a formidable team. As a young lawyer, Reznik helped Jack negotiate a mining agreement with some of the industry's shrewdest execs. During the Gulf War, they exploited Jack's relationship with a private security firm and gained access to sensitive data that included estimates of crude oil volumes held at critical sites near the Kuwaiti border. Both men reaped untold fortunes after their joint sale of Iraq's largest untapped oil field to key players in the West.

Despite his acquisition of modest wealth, Reznik's lust for power could not be tamed. Though Jack pleaded with his best friend not to enter the political sphere, his oratory skill and proclivity for leadership made him likely to succeed in any venture he undertook. Charismatic as he was, not to mention his apparently clean personal life, he had a trusted friend from childhood who was now a multibillionaire to fund any campaign, or so he thought.

But when Goldwyn denied Reznik $100 million to fund his campaign for prime minister, the two men separated immediately, as a husband and wife embroiled in a bitter divorce. A simple misunderstanding led to a shouting match, and suddenly the scene turned violent. Insults were made, blows were hurled, and thus did their friendship end. Not since their drunken fight ten years before had they spoken to each other, and both wondered if they would do so again.

## 7

Morning broke over the Western Cape. Seabirds sang the first sound of day as sunlight seeped through matching windows in a cozy tenth floor apartment where Leyla and Suri lived.

Suri awoke and checked the time. A hot shower felt good. She dressed in a hurry. Her schedule for the day was jammed with activity.

Handsome retirees from Adelaide entertained themselves while chatting and walking about the waterfront on New Year's Day. They sipped mimosas on restaurant patios and inspected the exterior of the *Royal Flush* that was moored in Table Bay. A collection of thirtysomethings stirred tropical drinks with miniature umbrellas that doubled as straws. Sundry musicians marched over the boardwalk and played for grinning tourists who arrived at a passenger terminal. A pigeon squawked on a fountain and submerged its head. A Nigerian blew in tiny holes of his Oja flute as a thin-bearded Spaniard plucked delicate strings of his petite guitar. All the while, a cheerful bushman thumbed his bamboo reed.

A Caucasian gentleman approaching forty studied those around him on a busy sidewalk downtown. He was a regular man, fitly dressed, yet something was mysterious about his appearance. He might have been any ordinary bloke as he tarried without notice on a bustling corner next to Longmarket Street. His khaki pants and blue button-down gave the impression of a salesman, a British professor on sabbatical, a man of leisure out for his morning stroll. With his dapper attire and slim physique, he blended seamlessly with business types, something every confident man aspires to do.

Longmarket teemed with commerce. Not a single parking space remained unoccupied. It was Monday, and cafés and bistros sprang back to life.

A glass carousel spun a quarter turn and the ordinary man entered ABSA Bank.

"Good morning, sir," the teller said.

The mysterious man nodded assuredly. "Good morning." He slid his identification across the counter.

"One moment, please." Agile fingers raced across a keypad. "All right, Mr. Bloom."

Bloom. It might as well have been his real surname. His childhood and next of kin were a distant memory. Since making the final cut, the agency had become like family.

"I'd like to withdraw two hundred thousand rand," he said with a guarded pitch.

"Two hundred thousand. All right," the teller replied. She reached for a telephone.

"Hello," a man said.

"Good morning. Mr. Bloom is here. He would like to withdraw two hundred thousand rand from his account."

The sun shone bold in a cloudless sky.

A double-decker bus made its way through airy streets in Cape Town. Tweeting birds tickled the ears of tourists as they strolled along the waterfront at Table Bay. Polished windows and swept sidewalks gave the scene a distinct measure of worth: mankind attends activities and places it values most. The bus stopped by a tiny old-world café, where affluent locals drank espressos. They sat on chairs fashioned from woven sugarcane and chatted with bright faces that mirrored immutable happiness they felt within. Contentment is the default emotion of the fortunate few who have not seen desolate places in the world.

Tall folding doors of the tour bus drew in. The mysterious man took a seat on the upper deck. His eyes fell on a woman with short black hair who spoke to an acquaintance near the entrance of ABSA Bank. The traffic light turned green and the bus driver shifted the engine into gear.

The tour guide stood and faced the tourists on the lower deck. She said, "South Africa, with nine provinces, is comparable in size to England."

An easy smile lived on her face as she spoke.

"Located at thirty-three degrees south and eighteen degrees east, with the same latitude as Santiago and Perth, stands glorious Cape Town—the Tavern of the Seas—the Republic of South Africa's treasured gem. Founded in 1652 by settlers from the Dutch East India Company, Cape Town comes from the word Kaapstad. That's K-a-a-p-s-t-a-d in Afrikaans."

Her face beamed with pride.

"Cape Town is like London, except it is clean, warm, and friendly. Its people have a style as hip as the place they call home."

The tourists agreed.

"To the right you will see Trafalgar Market, another Cape Town tradition, where for some three hundred years flowers have been sold by their growers." The young woman spoke without hesitation. Cape Town was not merely her home. It was also her first love.

The mysterious man surveyed the locale around him. He folded his arms in front of his chest and peered down from the upper deck. His eyes were steady and clear.

The young woman continued her monologue. There was a certain innocence in her. Her tone implied a cute naïveté. She spoke with a kind of excitement that belonged to an intelligent child. "With its Mediterranean climate and four distinct seasons, the Mother City exudes its motto: *Bona Spes*" (Good Hope). Curiosity bloomed on the tourists' faces. The bus ascended an incline. "To your right you will see the Houses of Parliament and a colorful South African flag out front. The flag may be understood as a symbol of the long way from separation to unity for South Africans." The young woman jolted slightly as the driver adjusted his bowler hat and shifted gears. She gripped a rail to keep her balance. Her speech went on as the bus turned onto Church Street. "The South Africa flag has six colors, like no other national flag in the world. The colors green, black, and gold are also present in the African National Congress flag, while blue, red, and white colors refer to Dutch and English influence." She jerked again and gripped the railing above her head tighter than the second before. "There are important rules for presenting the *South African flag*. When presented behind a speaker in meetings, the flag must be to the speaker's right, but elsewhere in the meeting place it should be always to the right of the audience."

The mysterious man leaned back in his seat. No one sat beside him. He stretched his legs, adjusted his arms in front of his chest, and peered down sidewalks on either side of the bus.

The tour guide went on. "The flag was first flown on the day our nation's hero became inaugurated as the new president of South Africa on 27 April 1994. Can anyone name this honorable man?" The tourists answered in unison. "Yes, that's right—the hero from Transkei by way of Pollsmoor—President Nelson Mandela. This is where he gave his famous address in 1990 to tens of thousands who gathered to hear him speak: 'Friends, comrades, and fellow South Africans, I greet you all in the name of peace, democracy, and freedom for all.'"

An assorted crowd applauded and smiled. The tour guide offered an expression of gladness as she spoke. "This was the first time free elections were held in South Africa. Freedom Day, as the twenty-seventh of April is now called, is one of South Africa's public holidays."

The mysterious man absorbed an unforgettable panorama of the Mother City as he sat in a trance on the upper deck. He had been there once before on furlough, but only for a day or two.

He scanned the sidewalk on Rose Street and eyed a mixed-race couple who made their way to a lemonade stand. With lucid eyes and a sober head, he thought, "For once, people were granted the right to choose a political leader and they opted for freedom in the form of Nelson Mandela." Apartheid had been a low point in the continent's human experiment. Families were torn apart. Many innocent lives were lost.

The mysterious man rested his arms on the seat in front of him as he reflected on the life of a man whose name was synonymous with courage. Freedom is the chief desire in the heart of mortal men. The mysterious man leaned back in his seat. He imagined a twinkle in the speaker's eyes when she said, "South Africa owes eternal gratitude to Mr. Mandela, who was jointly awarded The Nobel Peace Prize in 1993, along with F.W. de Klerk."

The tour bus stopped at a traffic light and the mysterious man listened attentively. Men and women swiveled their necks as the tour guide continued. "The duo received the award, and I quote, 'for their work for the peaceful termination of the apartheid regime, and for laying the foundations for a new democratic South Africa.'" The tourists nodded approval. "Mr. Mandela had a decidedly positive impact on our country, and for that we are indeed grateful. Perhaps you will pay a visit to his home in the Eastern Cape."

He thought, *Freedom is anything but free.*

The bus idled in the shadow of a tall building with huge tinted windows. A group of Asians sat on the front row of the lower deck in plain view of the speaker. "Opened in 1885, the hallowed halls of the South African Parliament have seen some rather startling events. This is where British Prime Minister Harold Macmillan made his 'Wind of Change' speech in 1960, and where President Hendrik Verwoerd, chief architect of apartheid, was stabbed to death a few years later."

The mysterious man recalled the legacies of Tambo and de Klerk. He was reminded of Sydney and San Francisco, but was content to have arrived in Cape Town, for there he saw an iconic portrait of a once fragile nation where people were determined to live in peace.

A worn engine sputtered next to a roundabout. The tour guide said, "From Bo-Kaap's hilly neighborhoods dotted with peach, yellow, and lime-colored houses to the blissful V&A Waterfront,

Cape Town accepts praise from visitors of every creed. A temperate climate, friendly folk, and beaches that stretch forever await excited tourists in South Africa's vibrant coastal city."

The open-air bus was packed with sophisticated travelers. They were the serious kind who craved learning as much as entertainment. Is it not within the framework of an unchartered place that strangers confide in strangers? Invariably, conversations turn to mutually shared affections and they become as old friends without exchanging names. The bus was a microcosm of the modern world: an old, native-born driver greying at his neck and ears, tipsy coeds whose exciting lives still lay ahead, a European couple with their inquisitive child unable to remain still, smiling Asian people with astonishment stuck on every face.

The mysterious man drew a deep breath. His mind was staid, subdued. The tour bus was a place for abstemious reflection. He cleared his head of petty distraction—he was there for a purpose, and a noble one too.

The tour guide said, "From sophisticated Cape Town to the mountainous wine country, South Africa has something for everyone. Any family that visits is sure to be entertained. If it is hunting you are into, try Elandsfontein Private Nature Reserve in Langebaan or the rustic Bontebok Ridge in Wellington. If history suits your fancy, pay a visit to Robben Island, a World Heritage Site and South Africa's rendition of Alcatraz, a former prison perched on limestone rock in Table Bay, where Mr. Mandela was incarcerated for almost twenty years. Tours are led by former prisoners who were part of the struggle against apartheid."

The bus came to a stop where the tour began. A German couple held hands by the exit on the lower deck. Men and women rose placidly from their seats. Their faces were a collage of mankind.

The tour guide said, "If it is fun in the sun you are looking for, make your way to Camp's Bay, best known for white sand beaches, bars, and bronze-bodied babes who are eager to be seen. Lastly, be sure to check out Table Mountain, which towers more than a thousand meters above the Mother City as an unmistakable symbol of Cape Town. As the Statue of Liberty for New York, Big Ben to London, and the Eiffel Tower to Paris, so is Table Mountain to Cape Town. There are many ways to experience the mountain, from helicopter tours to guided hikes—all may be scheduled through your hotel concierge. Our time zone is UTC. We are one hour ahead of London and an hour behind Tel Aviv."

Asian tourists reached for their cameras and travel bags. An elderly man sat in silence near the front of the bus. Serenity was caught on his face as he eyed the tour guide whose speech drew to a close.

"And here we are at Victoria & Alfred Waterfront, the quintessential place for relaxation in Cape Town. Ladies and gentlemen, we hope you have a delightful stay in our charming Tavern by the Sea. Thank you. Enjoy." The tour guide smiled as visitors shuffled by.

The mysterious man got up from his seat on the upper deck. He drew a notepad from his waist pocket and turned a page. His agenda was carefully planned: one o'clock to two, bus ride in Cape Town; two o'clock to three, Waterfront and Beach Road; three o'clock to four, Farmer's Market; four o'clock to five, Longmarket and Bo-Kaap.

On a sidewalk by a coolly lit store on Adderley Street popped the pointy heels of a woman who knew how to walk. Her stilettos clopped on the sidewalk as a thoroughbred eager to race. Suri carried herself with shoulders back and forehead high. Men could not help noticing the way her toned legs and round buttocks moved. Her shoulders were magnetic and taut. She oozed beauty *au naturel*. A little vogue mirror was always within her reach. She did not leave her elegance in Milan or Paris—it was with her wherever she went. You saw her and dreamed of lying beside her at a picnic on Clifton Beach, or drinking with her at a chic bar overlooking Twelve Apostles on Friday afternoon. A fruity drink was her chosen delight.

She marched by a fruit stand and travel agency. A street person blew a familiar tune as locals passed his mat. He lifted a clarinet to his lips and played with emotion from deep inside his chest. In a soft voice, the old fisherman began to sing, "You are my sunshine, my only sunshine."

Suri sat opposite her roommate on a café terrace. She said, "I miss Tel Aviv. Every day I miss it more." A stiletto dangled from her foot beneath the table. "People there are educated. They don't care what you wear, what you smoke. It's a fantastic place."

The smell of cut lemons drifted from the bar as their conversation went on.

"I see," Leyla said. "Do you wish to move back?"

"I suppose so, one day." Suri went for her drink.

"Have you met a man here?" Leyla said.

"No," Suri replied. "It seems men everywhere are interested in only one thing."

"Agreed." Leyla took a sip of her drink as a motorbike whined on a nearby street.

Suri said, "We should go to Coon Carnival in Bo-Kaap tomorrow. I'm sure lots of people will be there."

"Sure thing. I'd love to go." Leyla swirled her drink.

Suri straightened her ponytail.

Leyla said, "Do you see that man walking on the sidewalk, the one wearing a camel-colored sport coat?"

It was expected that Suri would remember him after the confident approach he'd made at a coffee shop that morning. Her mind flashed to an inscription carved into a plank of stinkwood in the foyer: *Bona Spies.* Two hours had passed since their meeting and the words he spoke to her still echoed in her head. He had spoken to her over a latte. A soft tune played overhead. She had hoped he would notice her, perhaps ask for her number and ring her up someday. Her supple lips gripped him like an adder—he would not soon forget her desirable cheeks and neck, the firm nipples peeking through her blouse and staring into his soul—no, not if she could help it. Beauty was a habit she could not shake. She had always hungered for love.

"No," Suri replied.

"He's passing by the money exchange. Do you see him?"

"Yes, now I do." A lone finger traced the rim of her glass.

"He's rather extraordinary. We met this morning."

Suri appeared surprised. "How did he approach you?"

"He asked for a match to light his cigar."

Suri went for her drink and crossed her legs.

"Then he asked if I had ever been to Pretoria and if life was peaceful there."

"I see. What did you like about him?"

A bottle of wine stood next to a bouquet of roses on the table between them.

"He impressed without meaning to and I thought it grand."

Suri reached for her glass.

"Did he make a pass at you?"

"No. He was all business. A bit stilted, really. He asked about Bo-Kaap and if Malays ever raise a fuss."

"What did you say?"

"I told him we keep to ourselves. Then he inquired about Windhoek and Gaborone, and I said, 'What have you done, memorized capitals of every country in the world?' But he didn't answer. Instead, he looked straight ahead—a most interesting man. I feel I offended him though."

The waiter returned, and as he did, Suri recalled an admonition displayed in Bascule Bar.

*To those merry souls of other days*
*who again will make drinking a pleasure*
*who achieve contentment long before capacity*
*and who, whatever they may drink*
*prove able to carry it, enjoy it*
*and remain forever gentlemen*

Sunlight beamed over Bo-Kaap: a patchwork of colorful bungalows reminiscent of a rainbow, appealing cafés where excited tourists sipped assorted drinks and nibbled on pastries made from scratch. A Malay man wearing a turban climbed the steps of a minaret at Auwal Masjid and bellowed the mid-day call to prayer. His voice was solemn and low.

The mysterious man adjusted his pith helmet and stepped onto a pier at Den Anker in the epicenter of Table Bay. He strolled by the restaurant as a familiar ballad was sung.

*Mister Sandman, bring me a dream (Bum bum)*
*Make him the cutest that I've ever seen (Bum bum)*

An early afternoon sun migrated west. The mysterious man paced back and forth. A waitress led him to a table under a portico. She picked a piece of lint from his herringbone blazer and received his order for sparkling water.

He studied the scene around him. The rear door of a delivery truck was open, allowing a look inside. "Twenty-four bottles a case," he thought, softly cracking a knuckle. "Must be fifty cases there." He examined the space around him again. "Ten times twenty makes two hundred. Ten times four makes forty." In the distance, a siren blew. "Two hundred forty times five, that's twelve hundred." The waitress set a bottle on his table. He peered at the cases of beer and whispered, "Gonna be another rowdy night in the Cape."

The mysterious man had often fantasized about a lovely woman who might someday be his wife. She would have silky blonde hair like the waitress at Den Anker, and deep blue eyes. They would meet while sunning on a beach, cross paths again at a local bar, and maybe exchange a quick hello. Perhaps he would see her again, and not only in a dream. Perhaps they would meet at Bascule Bar and chat over drinks. Her name would be Maddie or Bri, and she would be of Dutch descent. His eyes would meet hers, and on a warm summer night in the Western Cape he would kiss her for the first of a million times. A first date would turn into another, and thus would their romance begin.

It had been his dream to grow up and marry well, maybe assume the role of an attentive and loving dad—something he never knew. But such had not been the case so far. For him, it seemed marriage was not in the cards. Loneliness dwelled in his soul. He longed for his emptiness to be obliterated by love, but was prepared for a life of solitude.

At thirty-three, he abandoned a thriving surgical practice in Jerusalem and was inducted into Mossad, being swiftly promoted to a pivotal role. With espionage his natural forte, the director valued him more than any other asset and reserved his kind of talent for only the most covert missions.

He appreciated Cape Town for the amiable city it was. A host of pleasurable activities lay before him: Clifton Beach with its pristine white sand and tanned bodies in search of fun, beaten rocks as old as time, checkered umbrellas over tourists who sipped mojitos in a world entirely different from their native lands, delightful Asians with cameras and passports dangling from their necks, a bushman playing his three-holed flute and never expecting tip.

As night fell over the Western Cape, the mysterious man was on the prowl.

8

It was dawn on Sunday, the second of January.

Asram spared no time as he dressed in his apartment. He faced a mirror and buttoned the collar of a ruffled shirt. The design was striped and imbued with primary colors of his adopted land. He paused to gaze at his wrist and arms. His skin was not accustomed to the texture of expensive silk. He pulled the sleeves back with each hand then adjusted the collar. Gold spangled earrings accentuated margins on his narrow face. Dark linen trousers stopped halfway down his legs. He affixed a solid black patch over his left eye. A tri-corner hat with an ostrich feather completed his pirate costume for the festive day.

Still before the mirror, his mind replayed the boy's searing insults at Noon Gun two days before. "Nathan," his proud mother had named him. *Calling me a monster. He will pay, and so will his infidel parents.*

He marched through the kitchen and closed the door of his apartment. *Damn the Jews.* He peered at his right hand that was missing its thumb. *The bloody pigs did this to me.* The brim of his hat was stiff and lean. He descended steps that led to a sidewalk and recalled the words of the anointed one. *Evil is not forbidden. In fact, it is ordained.*

Moving southeast along Büitenchracht Street, he came to a vendor accompanied by a talking bird that was perched on a stand inside a cage.

"*Raaack!* Time to party!" the parrot sang.

Asram's shoulders jolted with surprise. His feet turned to stone as the bird spoke to him again.

"Having fun?" The parrot raised its feathers in the back. "*Raaack!* Allahu Akbar! *Raaack!*"

Asram cast an infatuated stare at the bird. *Perfect.*

The vendor approached and entreated Asram with a tempting drawl. "You like?"

"Is this bird for sale?" Asram said.

"Everything is for sale, you know."

The vendor moved a pace closer to him.

"How much?"

"Five thousand rand."

"That is too much," Asram said impatiently. He looked at the bird. "I'll give four hundred."

"Ay, too little. I cannot sell for less than three thousand."

Asram turned. He took a step away from the bird and the vendor seized his arm.

"*Raaack!* Allahu Akbar!" the parrot sang.

"Sir, wait. Two thousand rand and the bird is yours."

Asram stared at the parrot's colorful feathers. "What need have I for a talking bird?"

The man stood quietly and waited.

Asram jerked his chin. "Two hundred," he said.

Sunrays bounced off Table Mountain, over brightly colored houses and cobblestone streets, across the waterfront and infinite ocean waves. Under a cloudless sky, there was no hint of shade as far as the eye could see.

STARNER JONES

Carmen Goldwyn perused a display of magazines and Malay cookbooks as she inhaled exotic aromas from goodies offered by street people who bartered with tourists. The Goldwyns held hands as they moved in their leisure up an incline on Dorp Street en route to a parade like none they had seen. Infinite frivolities lay before Nathan as a new toy he yearned to touch: a corn dog stand and carnival rides, a freak show starring a contortionist, the house of mirrors where throngs of children laughed and played.

"There's nothing quite like a parade," Carmen said to Jack. "Everyone is invited."

It was true, and such is the case every 2 January in Cape Town. Various purgatives have attempted to rename the festival 'Cape Town Minstrel' to assuage sensitive types who find the old term offensive. But the old innocuous name is insulting only to those who deem it so—rudeness lives in the paltry minds of those who revel in it. Contempt for tradition is a way of life. Never mind if it means sacrificing the traditional name of the oldest celebration in the Western Cape that was itself started by Malay slaves. A banner with giant red letters hung in a dress shop window. It read, 'Welcome to Cape Town's Coon Carnival and Parade.'

Bo-Kaap sounded as festive as it looked. The scene on Dorp Street had eclectic appeal. A street vendor wearing a fútbol jersey offered an assortment of enticing curry as a lost kitten rummaged through week old trash in an empty lot close by. A souvenir peddler loitered on a busy sidewalk dotted with cigarette butts and bottle caps from native beers. The brat vendor failed to distract excited tourists from the playful scene. "Lamb curry for you, sir?" he asked.

86

"Ma'am, would you care for spinach roti?" No tourist bothered to answer him. Around them beat the delectable sound of homemade drums from the Eastern Cape. Bo-Kaap was a hospitable amalgam of thespian taste and grub.

The old fisherman snored in his lean-to as a fire whistle blew on Chiappini Street, signifying the start of the parade. An empty-bellied customer chomped on a samosa. He shouted his elation in breath spiked with rum. An elderly man wearing a turban peaked through a window of his colorful bungalow to keep watch over the annual party as it unfolded. His home, like most others in Bo-Kaap, had an entrance as unique as the lives of those who dwelled within. Steps were made from stone and lime mortar fetched from Signal Hill. Porches were finished with tile and corrugated iron. Courtyards were paved long ago with Malmesbury shale harvested by Malay slaves. Dwellings were separated by small alleys and adorned with molded cornices and parapets raised to a central point. Tallow or oil was considered essential for sturdy walls at the time the houses were constructed, a worthy lesson learned from Dutch masters who sought fortunes in the Cape. The builder's work was meant to last.

Schoolchildren from Maputo gathered on a corner. They swayed back and forth and sang in their native tongue. The old fisherman hobbled passed a turquoise mosque. He peered at the bustling street party, a sophisticated convergence of old and new that took place against a backdrop of towering banks, the clatter of slapping sandals, a motor scooter propped up by its kickstand, and a convoy of Japanese sedans—smaller cars for smaller people—a collection of fishing boats sitting motionless as little toys in Table Bay. Flags from every African country were displayed outside the Dutch Manor House on Büitenchracht Street. Ensigns and pennants whipped in the wind and the children from Mozambique went on singing as if they were at home: "Kum-ba-ya, my Lord, Kum-ba-ya." Hillsides dotted with mosques and graves stood as sacred relics for visitors to see.

A double-decker bus screeched to a halt and a dozen tourists emerged in twos. They scattered as industrious bees in search of something sweet. In a corner café, a halaal butcher seasoned meats and reached for a rolling pin. Tantalizing aromas of spicy chicken and lamb tempted taste buds of Gentiles and Jews in Bo-Kaap Bazaar. It was a transcendent scene, sublime, fit for a Kriedemann inside a custom frame. What could be more authentic than *Victoria Basin Circa 1950* hanging in the lobby of a grand hotel in Table Bay? Only Bo-Kaap's Coon Carnival and Parade.

Time slipped away with the coolness of a mid-day wind. Samosas and spinach roti, those flat, crêpe-like niblets that start life in a tiny ball of dough, washed down with a nutritious mug of boeber sold by a grinning Zulu. The spiced drink brought refreshment to one's face. No flies tarried on Church Street. A steady breeze made sure of that.

A dwarf adorned with a rainbow wig exclaimed, "Step right up, step right up! Ladies and gentlemen, step right up! Come and see the World's Smallest Horse!" He lifted his cane as a wand, and stabbed to and fro in the air.

"Look at that little man!" Nathan said. "Over there, he's really short!"

"Yes, honey," his mother said. "He's a little person, but remember, it's not polite to point."

"He looks funny in that suit!"

It was true. The little man was nattily attired. He wore a white cotton guayabera shirt, tangerine paisley ascot, and natural linen slacks. His face, partly shielded by a sun umbrella, suggested a feeling of permanent surprise. He had short, sandy-blond hair with ample amounts of grey. Sunlight glistened on his cigarette-roasted skin, which stood in sharp contrast to a freshly pressed white collar on his loosely buttoned shirt. As an achondroplastic dwarf, his habitus gave one the sense that he always leaned forward. With a shock of hair protruding from his prominent forehead, he proceeded down the cobbled street at a clip slightly faster than necessary to keep up with the procession. A soft breeze lifted sun-bleached hair that lay too long over his neck.

Citizens of the Rainbow Nation were accustomed to cultural diversity, but the festive Irish dwarf dressed as a leprechaun amused even them. He traipsed up and down streets in Bo-Kaap, lit pipe in hand as he led the annual parade. Soon he was overcome by the rest of the raucous pack, and in the long line of bizarre characters he no longer managed to stand out. A few revelers fell into cadence behind the nameless little man, and he became a pied piper of sorts, leading them on toward further debauchery.

*I've been a wild rover for many a year*
*I've spent all me money on whiskey and beer!*

"I'm small but sexy!" the little man said. He danced on a cobblestone street and spoke loudly, as those under the influence often do. He was accustomed to public attention, the role of party animal he happily obliged. Eager to captivate, he sang a vulgar limerick and the joyous crowd gathered around the man. He ambled down the street to steal the show, flaunting his custom-tailored suit. The sight of the dwarf drew the boy Nathan away from his mum. He was intrigued by the dwarf's short, stubby fingers and painted face, the bright orange silk cravat that hung over a protuberant waste, the sound of his sidesplitting laugh.

Bo-Kaap was filled with revelers drunk on spirits of every kind. Tourists stood shoulder to shoulder as the parade moved south on Chiappini. A marching band stopped to play by Noon Gun. A drummer rolled a snappy cadence on his snare as French horns blared a tune soon lost amidst a cacophony of the annual celebration. Firecrackers tossed from a float exploded over excited crowds as the marching band played.

*Nkosi sikelel' iAfrika*
*(God bless Africa)*
*Maluphakanyisw' uphondo lwayo*
*(Raise high Her glory)*
*Yizwa imithandazo yethu*
*(Hear our prayers)*
*Nkosi sikelela thina lusapho lwayo*
*(God bless us your children)*

Asram stood on a corner. The parrot hopped on his shoulder.

"*Raaack!* Time to party! *Raaack!*"

The parade marched by to the amusement of natives and tourists. At last, the boy Nathan came near.

"Hey, little sport," Asram said with an inviting tone. "Are you Nathan?"

"Yes. I'm Nathan. What's your name?"

"Why, I'm Rollo the Pirate."

"Hi, Rollo!"

The parrot lifted its wings. "*Raaack!* Are we having fun yet?" the bird chimed.

"I like your bird!"

"Thank you, Nathan," Asram said.

"He's funny!"

"Yes, he is. Do you like clowns?"

"Of course! Do you like them?"

"I do, and I know where they live."

"You do?"

"*Raaack!* Allahu Akbar!" the parrot sang.

"Where?"

"Want me to show you? I can if you'll be my friend."

"Sure! Take me there!" the boy cried.

A pigeon squawked on a sidewalk.

Carmen sat opposite Jack at a table outside a café. A waitress served their drinks.

"Quite a scene," Jack said.

"Honey, where is Nathan?" Carmen asked. Her voice had a serious tone.

"I thought he was with you."

Carmen rose from her seat and screamed. "Nathan!"

Bystanders froze and stared.

She raced a few meters on the sidewalk. "Nathan!"

The boy did not answer.

"Oh, my god!" She ran farther still. "Nathan!"

Jack's eyes cased over Chiapinni Street. There was no sign of the boy.

Time was the resource they could least afford to lose. Carmen scurried up a staircase that led to the second floor of a realty. Nothing but strangers as far as she could see.

"Nathan!" she screamed.

Seconds stretched into minutes.

Jack tapped a button on his phone and the screen appeared. He scaled a list of contacts in search of Captain Lou.

Carmen panicked more as moments passed.

The call rang twice.

"Captain Lou," a voice said.

"We've lost Nathan."

"Sir?"

"We've lost Nathan!"

"You what?"

"He slipped away from us at a parade."

"Where are you?"

"Chiappini and Wale."

"What happened?"

"We lost him in a crowd."

"When?"

"A few minutes ago. Carmen thought he was with me."

"Is she with you?"

"Yes. Alert Foster, and tell him to call me right away."

"Will do, sir."

Jack knew something was amiss. Beyond a troubling suspicion, Nathan's disappearance was more serious than him simply wandering off. Jack wasted no time making his next move. He had learned to carry out important tasks himself.

He reached for his phone.

Dial tone.

*Ring, ring.*

"Security International, Patrice speaking. How may I . . . ?"

"Patrice, put me through to Foster."

"Yes, sir. Is everything okay?"

"No. I need Foster now."

"Yes, sir. Right away."

A minute passed. Jack held a tight fist to his chin.

"Foster," a voice said at headquarters in Tel Aviv.

"We've lost Nathan."

"What?"

"He disappeared at a parade."

"Where are you?"

"Bo-Kaap."

"In Cape Town?"

"Yes. We were planning to leave this afternoon."

"When did you last see him?"

"Five minutes ago. He slipped away from us in a crowd."

"Someone will notice him."

"I have a terrible feeling about this. The area is crawling with towel heads."

"I'm sorry?"

"Camel jockeys. Nothing but turbans as far as the eye can see."

"Ah."

"We had no business coming here. I had a strange feeling as soon as we arrived."

"Kids of billionaires don't go missing by accident. Someone wants something. Want me to alert the team?"

"Yes, right away. Draw what you need from the emergency fund. I deposited $5 million into the account last week."

The call ended.

Jack peered down Büitengracht as a marching band continued to play.

> *Morena boloko setjhaba sa heso*
> *(God we ask you to protect our nation)*
> *O fedise dintwa la matshwenyeho*
> *(Intervene and end all conflicts)*
> *O se boloke, O se boloke setjhaba sa heso*
> *(Protect us, protect our nation, our nation*
> *South Africa—South Africa)*

A south wind rustled palm trees in Table Bay. Twin seabirds hovered over fishing trawlers and scattered crumbs of molded rye.

"Ayyy." The old fisherman reached for his net. His freckled face was red and lean. Deep wrinkles on his neck told the story of a gritty existence he could not shake. He had no trusted friend, save an eternal sea that fed him and nurtured him since he was young. His weary eyes peered at a clock tower across the bay. Age wore on with the stubbornness of Father Time.

He lit a cigarette as schoolchildren sang a ballad in front of a posh hotel. The old man blew a puff of smoke and remembered his youth. Sun-beaten lips cracked open as he smiled. An ache in his chest made him feel older still.

A covey of seabirds glided over the *Jolly Roger* and a haunted mansion the old man recalled from his boyhood. He remembered his devoted father who taught him his trade, the mother who fed him with love each day.

The old man shut his eyes and prayed, as the setting sun slipped further away.

## Interlude in Tel Aviv

Reuben gazed at a portrait of his father whom he had recently buried. On his desk was a black and white photograph of his grandfather dressed in military garb.

It was no doubt a joyful occasion on 5 April 1920, when Gerald Reuben entered the world, and my, how that world did change that year. The first commercial radio broadcast aired in Pittsburgh. Prohibition began. Women were granted the right to vote with passage of the nineteenth amendment. The Bubonic Plague swept through India. Pancho Villa retired. Joan of Arc became a saint. France prohibited the sale of contraceptives. The New York Yankees acquired a promising young hitter named Babe Ruth from the Boston Red Sox. In Munich, a former army corporal laid out plans for his National Socialist Program—his name was Adolf Hitler. Polish troops occupied Kiev. The League of Nations was established. Bloody Sunday erupted at a soccer match in Dublin, and in Gerald Reuben's native Brooklyn, a loaf of bread cost twelve cents.

Sitting at his desk, Reuben reflected as much over the loss of his father's influence as for the gentleness of his spirit. It belied the fierceness of Gerald's character that was his alone during three decades of service as Director of Mossad. His words brought stability to a capable and eager lad, who desperately needed both to survive the intelligence community's unremitting pretense.

Civility was synonymous with the Reuben name. Gerald died on Yom Kippur, and with him passed an era, a time when life was simple and full of meaning. His formative years were marked by effects of the Great Depression and fortitude with which the greatest generation persevered. In Normandy, he'd fought so others did not have to. His reputation was molded by personal struggle that came first in the form of his beloved wife's death in childbirth.

Reuben's eyes fell on a photo of his dad, who was clad in army regalia. Gerald meant so much to so many: father, husband, leader, friend. He recalled the day his father passed and the dignified ceremony at his grave. Those who knew him knew the purity of Gerald Reuben's heart. He spoke with precision and led by example. He was Abel's link to the past and his family's heritage for which he felt a deep pride.

A briefcase lay open on the mahogany desk. Beside the desk stood a bookcase packed with his father's favorite reads: original collections of military treatises, complete works of Joyce and Melville, a row of Shakespeare and Graham Greene. Gerald's conviction and classical manners were gleaned as much from timeless works of fiction as from experiences in the heat of battle. His life was hewn from principled conduct that Abel naturally assumed as his own.

His phone buzzed.

"We've got another one," Mel said in a somber tone.

"Another what?"

"Another kidnapping."

"Where?"

"A wealthy couple reported their five-year-old son missing in Bo-Kaap."

"Bo-what?" the director said.

"Bo-Kaap, a Muslim enclave in Cape Town. It's small but significant."

"Time zone?"

"An hour ahead of London. It's 2:30 local time."

"Did you notify the team?"

"Yes."

"Are they Americans?"

"His father is a Jewish multibillionaire from Europe. Not sure about his mother."

"We should inform London."

"I just spoke to Foster. It's his boss's son who's missing."

Dellon Foster, corporate clean-up man, tried and true, there was nothing he had not seen. He was ex-CIA, if there was such a thing, and handled tedious problems discreetly. Men like Foster did not view the world as an average citizen stifled by naiveté. Rather, he saw society's grim underbelly for what it was—a cesspool of primates yet to evolve—and knew the law of the jungle written by the wisdom of ages, the clockwork that moves important people. Occult forces of money, religion, and military might, which make the world turn, hide behind a cloak of normalcy and masquerade evil that lies beneath.

"Let's convene in ten minutes," the director said.

"Copy that. I'll alert the team."

Reuben reached for a stack of memos. A reporter interrupted his attention on the flat screen television opposite his desk. She said, "According to Secretary of State Ellen Rodham, in the Trafficking of Persons report of March 2009, much remains to be accomplished on the human rights front, especially regarding the root causes of human trafficking. Current policies and procedures fail to limit trafficking of vulnerable populations. From young girls coerced into marriage after kidnapping, to ethnic minorities denied citizenship or birth registration, to migrants forced into manual labor, prevention efforts have not been effective and require us to investigate causes that contributed to an increase in human trafficking in recent years."

As he drew a memo from the never-ending pile, Reuben thought how odd it was that Mel had phoned him about a kidnapping as he reviewed reports of similar occurrences in Asia and Europe.

Philippines

Leah was promised a job as a waitress in Berlin, but was forced to work in a Nigerian brothel instead. She was sold by her trafficker to a man who operated his sex trade in a heavily guarded complex. Guards accompanied Leah whenever she left the premises with her trafficker. She was confined to a life of servitude in a textile mill and worked there for almost ten years before saving enough money to bribe a security guard and buy a ticket home after she escaped one night.

Cambodia

Ratha was born to a very poor family in Phnom Penh. When she was eleven years old, her mother sold her to a man in a neighboring province who blindfolded her and forced her onto a boat during the night. She was serially raped by drunk men from London who paid her captor $1,000 each. The following day,

Ratha was thrown overboard and swam to shore. The trafficker forced her back into the boat at gunpoint, and then took her to a brothel where she remained for two years until finally he let her go.

Romania

Cristina flew from Bucharest to Lisbon where she was promised a job serving drinks in a chic café. Upon arrival, she was taken to a town not far from Lisbon and forced into prostitution. Her traffickers demanded five hundred euros a day and she was beaten with a club if she did not pay. Her traffickers broke nearly all her teeth and forced her to do heroin and methadone. She escaped with another girl and together the girls found shelter in an Orthodox Church. Cristina relocated to Paris where she is currently living and studying to be a nun.

He exited his office, walked down a corridor, greeted agents who awaited him, and took his place at the head of the table in the briefing room. A glass door closed in the hall.

"What kind of sick bastard gets his jollies from a five-year-old?" he said.

"That's easy, Abel," Foster replied, "the radical Muslim kind."

Reuben sighed.

Foster continued. "Seventy-two virgins and political ascendancy in your native land—who wouldn't risk his neck for that?"

Mel said, "We uncovered a disturbing account from a memo written by a Jim Farley in January 1968. It details the unfortunate saga of a child named Charles Fernandez, which was flatly ignored by all major media of the day."

"No surprise there," Director Reuben said.

"Based on Farley's report and files obtained from New York's Surrogate's Court (Cause No. 44,122), the child's father, Joseph Fernandez, died of cancer on December 28, 1967. He was preceded in death by his wife, Sophia. While in Morocco, Mr. and Mrs. Fernandez reported their ten-year-old son, Charles, missing on November 21, 1951. At that time, Mr. Fernandez was an executive in the Morrison-Knudsen Company and charged with overseeing construction of a runway at Nouasseur Air Base near Casablanca.

"State Department files include news reports about the child's kidnapping and an ensuing investigation conducted by French authorities. CIA records of the kidnapping claim the case was opened by an in-country field officer who investigated a possible connection of local Moroccan nationalists to the kidnapping. The most notable fact from examination of available records is that no demand for ransom was ever made."

"That's strange."

"It is. Charles Fernandez, now twenty-six, currently resides in Cape Town. He's represented in matters of his father's estate by Abram Khan, a Pakistani expatriate who lives in Bo-Kaap. The will of Joseph Fernandez was probated by his sister, Hannah Fernandez Brauer, who stood to inherit all assets under the will if Charles, who was presumed dead, failed to make a claim on the estate. Mrs. Brauer hired a private investigator who visited Cape Town and discovered Charles Fernandez did in fact reside there, and was known affectionately as Taco Negro, I'm quoting here, 'for he lived among the blacks.'"

"Noted," the director said.

"You can't make this up."

"Anything else regarding Taco?"

"By all accounts, he's a practicing Muslim and attends daily prayers at Auwal Mosque in Bo-Kaap."

"What are the odds of that?"

"I have the investigator's report in hand."

"Go on."

"Further investigation revealed Mrs. Brauer suspected that Charles was indoctrinated by an Imam Faisel Rauf, a radical Muslim cleric exiled from Yemen more than a decade ago. Charles has since gone MIA after refusing any contact with Brauer."

"What happened to the money?"

"Court records show Mr. Fernandez inherited more than $700,000 from his father's estate. Examination of transfers from the account indicates the entire inheritance was wired to Arab Bank in Sana'a."

"Perhaps Rauf needed money for jihad."

"Maybe so. Two bank accounts in Cape Town bear his name. One is jointly held with a fellow Yemeni expatriate named Asram al-Munir."

"Looks like we have a suspect. Did you mobilize the informant?"

"Yes, he's there now." Mel leaned back in the chair and crossed her legs.

The director's interrogation continued. "What's the latest on Islam in the African subcontinent?"

"Robust and burgeoning," Foster answered. "The religion has grown rapidly in the sub-Saharan and has an ardent following in Cape Town."

Reuben pursed his lips and adjusted his tie. He said, "How reliable is intelligence from London?"

Mel queued Shiffman, a junior advisor. He said, "Spurious at best, and perhaps ill-informed. There are more Muslims in West Africa than there are Arabs in the world, but London and Washington seem not to care."

Reuben listened earnestly. "Any other hotspots?"

"Algeria, Angola, Benin . . . the list reads as an alphabetized collection of the world's most obscure places."

Reuben scowled. "Not to mention the rest of the continent's Islamic players who remain disengaged."

"We haven't a single ally in Europe," Foster said. "It's us against the world."

Mel scribbled on a pad.

"Where are the feminists when you need them?" Reuben asked.

"Sir?" Mel replied.

Foster said, "Resistance to oppression, freedom for all. Nowhere are women more oppressed than in the Muslim world, yet we haven't seen a single feminist rally or protest. Are feminists afraid of radical Islam?"

They waited for Mel's reply. She said, "We're afraid of being killed. But what would we be fighting for—the splendor of Darfur or the glory of Sana'a?"

"No," the director said. "You would fight for innocent women and girls, who live under constant oppression."

"Touché."

"Pas de touché. Why pander to the vermin?" Reuben asked. "Our greatness is that despite futility we continue to fight."

Mel didn't answer.

Foster said, "It's time Washington and London got serious about radical Islam."

Mel perked up. "What do you mean?"

Foster struck a serious tone. He said, "Bobby Kennedy, the Olympics in Munich, Tehran in '79, Marine barracks in Beirut, TWA Flight 847. The nation of Israel will not back down. With or without England and the United States, we will be a force for good in a fallen world. Terrorism is a threat to civilization itself. Freedom is always at risk."

His audience was quiet and still.

"Has America forgotten 9/11? They are no different than ancient Hebrew people who dispensed belief in God every time their sovereignty was renewed. Isn't freedom still sacred? Aren't some things worth fighting for? Do Americans believe in anything?"

"The US still includes the word God in its motto," Shiffman said.

Foster replied, "Perhaps they should add a word: 'In God We Do *Not* Trust.'"

A veteran advisor chuckled.

Mel said, "Let's debate religion another day. In the meantime, what are we going to do?"

Foster leaned forward. "Pan Am 103, the World Trade Center in '93, US embassies in Kenya and Tanzania in '98. This is clearly a religious war."

"Don't confuse us with facts," Reuben said.

Mel interjected, "We get it, sir, but what are you going to do?"

An awkward silence filled the room. The director's brow turned in. "Do? What can we do? Those with nothing to lose have only to gain."

"Are you in favor of racial profiling, Abel?"

Foster was not through. "Mel, all of the aforementioned attacks were carried out by radical Muslims. Have you ever wondered why the United States has a porous border or why Western Europe allows large-scale immigration? You don't see Jews immigrating in staggering numbers to Arab countries. Why do you think that is?"

Mel didn't answer.

"What would happen if Jewish people attempted to migrate in droves to the Middle East? What consequences would befall them if they tried?"

Mel fiddled on a notepad.

"Thousands of people would be killed. Want to know why? Because Arabs wouldn't stand for it. Attempts to dilute Arab populations would be construed as an invasion of their land."

"Are you opposed to immigration?" Mel asked.

"No. But it's high time the West dealt with the proverbial eight-hundred-pound gorilla in the room. Al-Qaeda and ISIL told us what they were going to do. Why are we surprised? They've stockpiled untold quantities of weapons and explosives, and would like nothing more than to acquire a nuclear bomb."

Mel was silent.

The director said, "We're fighting the worst kind of enemy: one that has no face, no centralized authority, no governing body, or even a headquarters. Radical Islam is an extreme religious order that is criminal in nature, criminal in background, criminal in intent, and operating throughout the world. Jihadists target Hindus, Christians, Jews, and in some cases, fellow Muslims. They've targeted women and children, and will stop at nothing in pursuit of their stated goal of subjugating the entire world to Sharia law."

"Can't argue with you, boss," Foster said.

"What do we know about this fellow, Mister Asram al-Munir?"

Shiffman said, "His name is derived from Arabic and means 'brilliant one who was cut off.'"

"Sounds like a terrorist," Reuben chided.

"So, you are in favor of racial profiling," said Mel.

Foster spoke with conviction. He said, "Singling out an Islamic extremist because of name or appearance isn't racial profiling. It's prudently targeting a likely suspect."

## 9

The taxi stopped at a traffic light.

"He'll turn up somewhere," Jack said. "Just wait, you'll see."

"You don't know that, Jack!"

"He's not the first kid to slip away in a crowd. Someone will notice him."

"Ah!" Carmen spun her neck away from him.

"You're upset. I understand."

"No, Jack, you don't!"

"Carmen, will you relax? Dellon is aware. We're still within the golden hour."

"My only son, missing in a foreign country."

"We'll find him." Jack reached for his wife's hand as she began to sob.

Carmen recoiled. "I turn my head for two seconds and look what happens."

Jack was silent.

"Poof! He disappears!"

The traffic light turned green. Carmen wiped a tear.

"He'll turn up," Jack said with conviction. "You'll see. Someone will notice him."

His wife's desperation echoed in his head. *Ja-cob!*

They arrived at the corner of Buitenkant and Albertus. The two-story building was nondescript. Posted in a window next to the entrance: Cape Town Central Police Station.

They entered the office in haste. Décor was all around: a collage of passports framed by an onyx border, photos of dignitaries whose faces were easy to recognize, an autographed rugby ball, a bust of Mandela. South African and Dutch flags hung on opposite walls in the informally outfitted space. Carmen glanced at a placard. There was the saying again, *Bona Spies.*

A clerk sat at her desk as a custodian vacuumed the floor. "Good day," the young woman said. She placed a stack of papers aside. "May I help you?"

An office door slammed shut down the hall.

Carmen smiled through her fear. "Hi, I'm Carmen and this is my husband, Jack. We need to report our son missing."

"I'm very sorry to hear this." The clerk reached for a pen.

"Can you help us? His name is Nathan. He's five years old, about this tall." She raised a hand chest high. "Please, you must help us find him right away." Carmen wiped a tear with the back of her hand and the clerk reached for a tissue.

"I understand. You must be terribly frightened." The clerk made for her phone. "Have a seat. Would you care for a cup of water?"

"No, thanks," Carmen said.

"What is your son's name?" the clerk asked.

"Nathan Daniel Goldwyn."

"When did you last see him?"

The clerk scribbled on her pad.

"About an hour ago."

"Where was he?"

"We were in Bo-Kaap for the parade."

"On Wale Street," Jack added.

"It had just started. There were people everywhere, and a marching band. He slipped away in a crowd."

"May I ask why you were there?"

"For the parade."

"Coon Carnival," said Jack.

"You mean Kaapse Klopse," the clerk said with a hint of indignation.

"Yes." Carmen moved to the edge of her chair. "There was a parade with a marching band led by a dwarf."

"And a man dressed as a pirate with a talking bird."

"You went to a parade with your son, and now he's missing?"

"That's right," said Carmen.

"I see." Puzzled, if not annoyed, the clerk doodled on a page.

Carmen squeezed a tissue and wiped another tear. "We were watching the parade when a dwarf dressed as a leprechaun passed by."

Jack nodded.

"Your son slipped away with a leprechaun?"

"Yes, maybe. We don't know. We followed the parade for a block or two."

"He may have been lured away by the pirate," Jack said. "We can't say for sure."

"It happened so fast."

The clerk leaned back in her chair. "This is very strange." Suspicion leaked from her face.

"Oh, please!" Carmen pleaded. "Can't you do something? Please, help us find our son!"

Tall and slim in her knee-length suit, the clerk rose from her desk. She said, "I understand your concern. You must be terribly frightened. Anyone would be. But this is going to take some time. As you know, the first hour is very important."

She turned and made for a hall.

Jack pursed his lips. Carmen's face oozed disgust. The smugness of a half-hearted clerk, how loathsome. Any woman should understand the desperation felt by a lady whose child was missing on foreign soil.

A moment later, the clerk reappeared. She spoke as if caught in a hypnotic trance. "The commissioner will see you right away."

The Goldwyns walked down a short hall to a corner office.

The clerk said, "Would you like some tea?"

"No, thanks," Carmen replied.

She scanned the desk that was packed with photos of the commissioner's family. An empty revolver holster and a stack of papers rested on the floor. In a bureau charged with maintaining peace, not a single gun was seen. And this was a haven for safety?

The commissioner entered the room.

"Hello," the gentleman said. His big, protruding eyes bounced off them.

Carmen gave an anxious smile. She looked for his weapon, but saw none.

"I understand your son is missing."

"Yes, he is."

Carmen raised a tissue to her face.

"Now, don't you worry. We'll move heaven and Earth to find him."

"Oh, please . . ."

The commissioner twirled a pen as he sat across from them at his desk. He said, "Tell me your son's name."

"Nathan Daniel Goldwyn," replied Carmen. She wiped a tear.

"There, there now. We've found hundreds of children for worried mums like you."

"He's just a helpless boy."

"Have you notified the consulate?"

"No, we haven't," Carmen answered.

"The consulate?" Jack said.

"May I ask why?" The commissioner reclined in his chair.

Tension streamed through Carmen's neck. She grew angrier because of the man's flippant tone.

"My only son . . ."

Carmen's emotion had gotten the best of her.

Jack interjected. "No reason, really. Can you help us?"

The commissioner said, "The first step is to notify appropriate personnel in the consulate. They are more accustomed to this sort of thing and have resources necessary to organize a search." His face held a stoic expression as he reached for a phone.

The clerk entered with a stack of mail.

"Who are you calling?" Carmen asked.

"Interpol."

Only a moment passed before he hung up the phone. He wasn't very determined.

"The line is busy," he explained.

Carmen reached for her husband's hand.

The commissioner folded his arms. "A few years back a couple reported their child missing at the same festival and we were able to locate him within a couple of hours. I've no reason to think we won't have the same good luck in finding Nathan. In the meantime, here's the latest correspondence we received on trafficking."

"Trafficking?" Carmen asked.

Jack said, "Is there anything you can do to help us?"

"Unfortunately, no. I would start with the American consulate. Ask them to contact Interpol if you haven't located Nathan by close of business today."

The commissioner stood and extended a hand across his desk.

"I suggest you employ all available resources right away."

Jack hailed a cab.

Carmen's lips quivered as she opened a pamphlet. With misty eyes, she read.

United States Consulate, Cape Town
Consul General Michaelyn da Silva
2 Reddam Avenue
Westlake, R.S.A. 7945

Advertisement: UN Commission on Human Trafficking

The Democratic Republic of the Congo

By age twelve, Kristof had been abducted thrice by soldiers in the Congolese Army and forced to carry supplies to locales in the nethermost parts of the war-torn nation. He was among some one hundred civilians abducted in the late '90s and subjected to hard manual labor involving manufacture of heavy artillery and transport of illicit substances, including heroin. Children in local primary schools were among those taken by force, lest their parents be murdered in front of them. If they got tired during travel, as was often the case, soldiers beat the children. No provisions of food were made available during travel, and they ate whatever they could find in villages they passed through.

Ghana

Amee was born to a destitute family in Accra. A neighbor offered her father ten thousand cedis to give her away. He consented and the girl was sent to a brothel in Bangkok known for servicing wealthy businessmen from the West. Her passport was confiscated. Traffickers forced her to engage in commercial sex acts and her refusal resulted in beatings until finally the despicable acts became routine. They made her peruse casinos to attract men, then seized her money for expenses related to "travel and accommodation."

The ring of kidnappers was exposed by a French journalist and prosecuted in a Ghanaian court. With assistance of Catholic Charities, Amee and the other girls returned to Accra and are trying to rebuild their lives.

Ethiopia–United Arab Emirates

At age ten, Dela left her home in East Africa and resolved to make a better life for herself and her mother who was recently widowed. She wanted desperately to earn money, but from her third day of work as a cleaning maid in a Dubai hotel the manager beat her daily. The beatings continued for three years until . . .

"Oh, my god." Carmen reached for her husband's hand.

"What does it say?"

His phone beeped once and displayed a call from an Israeli area code.

"You'd better take this," said Jack.

Carmen didn't budge.

"It's my sister."

The hours that followed were a blur. Carmen's mind spiraled out of control with fears she had never known.

Could Nathan really have disappeared? Was he taken for ransom by an arms dealer? Were radical Muslims going to kill him? Was he already sold into sex slavery? Carmen's face was flooded with worry. How would she cope with the loss of her only son? Could her marriage to Jack withstand such a trying event?

*Who could have taken Nathan?*

As her mind plunged into memories of her missing son, she craved the numbness imparted by pills on her nightstand. She dared not blame Jack. After all, Nathan was his son too.

She remembered her childhood home in Vienna and recalled her father's gentle touch when she was a girl, but most of all she thought of Nathan.

Carmen stood in a trance on a sidewalk next to Büitengracht. Before her lay stacks of tabloids splashed with tempting photos and shocking headlines: "Man Gives Birth to Penguin Twins," "Frenchman Caught Raping a Cat." Flyers advertised real estate for rent in Hout Bay: For Let, R18000. A newspaper blasted Zuma for an illicit affair. Only a few copies of the local rag remained.

Carmen sat on a concrete step in front of a hair salon. A few locals pranced by, not speaking. She peered right and left along Wale Street. There was no sign of her only son. She turned numb as her eyes crept over a pamphlet.

Her employer cast boiling water on her face and smote her after she collapsed onto the floor. She was denied medical attention and incurred wound infections necessitating amputation of her legs. She was required to have sex with another maid on video. If Dela refused, her captor placed a hot iron on her back and threatened to kill her and her mother too.

Carmen wept as the bell at Saint Mary's dinged six o'clock.

## 10

Rauf sat at his desk in the basement of Auwal Masjid. Concrete blocks soundproofed the office. Any connection to the civilized world ended at the front door of the historic building. From the bowels of the mosque there was no hint of the celebration that went merrily on through the streets of Bo-Kaap. He rubbed his eyes and stroked his beard. Evening prayer would soon begin.

Leyla sat across from him.

The anointed one's voice was soft, composed. He said, "We want women to play a role in society, but your appearance runs counter to Islamic law."

"No, it doesn't," she said.

"You must reveal your culture and intellect through a means other than dress."

"No, I don't."

Their tête-à-tête was out of place. Arguing about traditional Islamic dress during the Kaap Klopse parade? How absurd.

"You must understand. We want you to play a role in society, but a woman who insists on showing her body will not be tolerated by Islam. It is a violation of holy law."

Leyla did not back down. "That's a lie and you know it. Who are you to say what is unjust?"

"Who am I?" he asked. Never had he been so insulted. He stood across from her, a clinched fist planted on the desk.

Leyla's eyes turned small and cold. She said, "I sense your indignation. It is plainly evident on your face. Has Islam not warned against wrath?"

His stare might well have killed her.

"Where is your niqab?" he chided.

"What am I, a Byzantine?" Leyla asked with a smirk.

"How dare you insult Islam!"

"Sir, allow me to educate you." Her taut spine stiffened even more. "The niqab is a decorative piece of clothing that was adopted into Muslim culture during Arab conquest of the Middle East. It is not mandatory, and I, like millions of Muslim women, choose not to wear it."

"The Prophet's wives covered themselves around men they did not know. Why shouldn't you?"

"Candidly, sir, I am not married to Mohammed."

"But you are held to a higher standard."

"Nonsense. The niqab is a cultural tradition. It has nothing to do with Islam."

Rauf cowered. Sweat oozed from his pores. He said, "On the issue of hijab, religious scholars agree that if a woman revealing her face leads to temptation or other things, then it is forbidden."

"Why can't men control their sexual urges?" The anointed one recoiled. "Am I responsible for them?"

Rauf trembled in his soul. He said, "Even when permitting the revelation of a woman's face, we place restrictions on this privilege. A woman is not allowed to reveal her neck or hair. She is not allowed to appear with makeup or jewelry. Religious scholars have agreed on this too."

"A woman can, a woman cannot. Who are you to mandate feminine behavior?"

"You are entirely out of line."

"Sir, I have read the holy law just as you. Who are you to decide how I should behave? Why do you treat me as less capable simply because I am a woman? The Lord created me as equal to you in my duties, punishment, and reward. When you fast, I fast. When you pray, I pray too. When you steal, your hand is cut off, and so it is with me. This is the greatest evidence that I am no less of a person than you. I know how to present myself, and am no less able to maintain my honor than you."

Rauf seethed. He wiped his brow and sighed.

Leyla was not done. She said, "There is a difference in opinion among scholars in Islam on whether the niqab is an obligatory form of hijab. When I appear in society, I demand that my face, which constitutes my identity, be easily seen. Under no circumstances will I allow my identity to be obliterated."

"That is not—"

"From age six until high school, and later when we go to university, we are forced to memorize the Qur'an. Whoever dares to question or contest anything is called upon to ask Allah's forgiveness to avoid eternal punishment in hell. But you who frighten the innocent with hell have brought them hell on Earth. You have banned books on enlightenment and democracy. You have prevented the mind from operating, thinking, comparing, and choosing, even though it is the same mind our Creator gave us to choose between paradise and hell. Our Lord set man apart from animals by creating him in his likeness, giving him freedom to choose his path in life and consequences waiting in the world to come. Deeds are measured by intent, and as the Great Teacher taught us, good intentions steer our behavior."

Rauf stroked his beard.

Leyla's eyes narrowed. "Our little ones are brainwashed daily in Qur'an memorization schools, which purport to teach Arabic necessary for survival in modern society, but instead leave not a single teaching or doctrine open to interpretation, which is essential to understanding Islam and its holy mysteries. We've been patronized and duped into believing a lie, except for a few of us women who've been spared by God."

She turned and slammed the office door.

Kidnapped children arrived at Marhaba Muharram, located a few kilometers southeast of Cape Town, with fear melted on each face, their horror fueled by uncertainty over what another day might bring. Between desperate pleas for freedom, they cried out for food and water in a place where neither was found.

"Let me go! I'm hungry!" a boy cried.

"I'm thirsty!" another screamed.

"Me too! Get away from me! I want my mum!"

Orphans were locked in a three-by-four-meter room and given just enough bread and water to keep them alive. Malnourishment gave rise to scurvy. Blood oozed from youthful gums. Each child was a soldier in training. They fought like feral cats over crackers and molded bread. The basement was no different than Sana'a, where modern sanitation did not exist. Each child smelled of urine and excrement. Feces was caked on little fingers and toes. The stench of a rotting corpse wafted up from a stairwell: a diabetic child lay dead in the cell. The place reeked of roadkill, neglect.

Following an emotional cleanse spanning more than a week, the children were no different than animals roaming a desolate terrain. Day and night were always the same. They shivered amidst haunting cries in the basement's cool, damp air. Out of nowhere, a wood furnace came alive only to bake them. Sweat poured from the children's faces, bathing the grimy floor beneath their bare feet. It was impossible for them to sleep.

A week passed, and then real torture began.

Deprived of basic needs, each child was easily controlled, stripped naked, bound with a rope, gagged until he puked, and forced into solitary confinement in a tiny cell devoid of light. The door was locked, the room pitch black with solid concrete walls and no egress or source of heat. Constant obnoxious noise played through a speaker made sleep impossible in the poorly ventilated space. Thirst was relieved only by lapping contaminated water from an aluminum pan slid under a huge metal door. After several days without food or sleep, the children were beaten with a chain. Trapped inside a cage, each child was suited for any scheme. Pliable, defenseless. Life in Marhaba Muharram was a living hell.

Ali was charged with oversight of the whole enterprise. As a captor, he created a tragic bond and made a habit of opening a door and slamming it again—the echo reverberated inside his head. Each child was rendered an emotional cripple. The diagnosis? Stockholm syndrome *in situ*.

Throughout the torture, Ali expressed no emotion at all. Suppression of hostility was a way of life in his radical Muslim world, especially for a jihadist whose actions were devised by a conniving imam. History takes note of those who die in glory for what they believe. Adherents to the faith are forbidden from drawing attention to themselves with jewelry or makeup, but are permitted to blow themselves up and captivate the interest of the entire civilized world.

Redemption came after breakdown: light through a window, chants from the Qur'an, a hot plate of food, an oasis of water for little ones to drink, the welcome cleansing from a powerful hose. Hope sprang anew. Orphans who survived the first three days were given clothes, food, and their very own Qur'an. White smocks covered their tiny bodies as they followed Ali into the prayer room at Auwal Masjid. A thin line of smoke wafted up from ceremonial incense as little ones prostrated on lavish carpet in their first show of obedience to Allah. They sat before him with anxious eyes. You saw the children and thought of a campfire, kindergarten, little soldiers prepping for an epic battle. Torture had ended, for now. Alas, it could happen again at any time.

Imam Rauf stood before the children and held forth open hands, his doughy palms turned upward. He said, "If you want to see your parents again, you must always do what Allah says."

A painful silence came and went. The air was hot and still. Rauf raised a finger toward the back of the room. His turban was perfectly set. He said, "Let nothing trouble you, children. Allah shall take away your fears."

The children turned. There stood Ali, delicately balancing two baskets at opposite ends of a long bamboo pole held against his shoulders. A dust-stained turban rose from his head, a loose kurta covered his loins—he might have come from Istanbul. Skillful as a jester, he lifted the pole over his head, and then lowered it onto the floor.

"A moment of silence, children." Rauf folded his arms and grinned. No one stirred.

"Maestro, your flute!" the imam exclaimed.

Ali stood tall. His narrow lips offered a conniving smirk. A gourd flute appeared in his hand. Minutes passed as he blew and blew. Up popped twin cobras that swayed their heads, their necks wiggled back and forth. Ali swung the flute as the snakes' hoods rocked here and there. *Loo loo loo, loo loo loo.*

"Arrrr!" the little ones screamed.

A tussle ensued between two of the boys. Ali spotted them with sinister eyes. He tossed them a treat, which they refused.

"Picky eaters, eh?" Ali said. "Just be thankful you have something to eat."

He raised a hand to swat at them.

Rauf lifted his robe waist high, exposing himself, and then folded his arms as the children cried.

They had forgotten what home was like.


Carmen stood in the middle of Wale Street and panicked more as minutes passed. Fear pulsated in her ears. Her pleas had gone unanswered. By now the crowd had dissipated, and still there was no sign of Nathan.

"Jack, what are we going to do? What if we never see him again?"

No answer. Jack paced back and forth.

Hysteria reached its crescendo. With pressured speech, she approached anyone who would listen and pleaded, "Excuse me! Please! My son is missing. Have you seen him?" Her feet shuffled on the sidewalk. "Pardon me. Sir? Madam? His name is Nathan. He has blond hair and blue eyes . . ."

A stranger's dismay magnified her panic. She bounced from person to person in the dwindling crowd. "Have you seen him? He's five years old, about this tall." She held forth a hand to indicate his height. "Sir? Miss? Excuse me!" She stumbled forward. A sour taste oozed in her mouth. Desperation was etched on her face. She licked her lips and winced.

"Nathan! Nathan!"

Another couple passed.

"Crazy bitch," a man said.

"Not if he's really missing," his wife answered.

"Not our problem."

The woman peered back over her shoulder and mouthed, "I'm so sorry."

With that, Carmen's heart sank. She fell to her knees in the middle of the street. With her face in her hands, she began to sob.

Jack embraced her.

"Did you find him?" she asked. "Did you find my baby?"

"No, honey. Not yet."

He held her close as tears flowed down her cheeks. Her voice was raw from frantic screams.

"Let's go," he said. He rested his chin on her head, then reached for a phone.

"We can't go! We have to find him!" She sobbed uncontrollably.

He dialed Captain Lou.

"Hello?"

"Lou, Carmen is a wreck. She needs to rest."

Carmen gripped his arm and cried.

"Want me to send for you?"

"Yes, right away. She's not fit for a cab."

Established during apartheid in 1985, Khayelitsha Township remained as Cape Town's largest slum. Xhosa, its primary language, was spoken by most inhabitants, including Jonas and his brother, who lived in a dilapidated shack.

Jonas walked wearily past a communal water source and toilets en route to his home.

"Sell any Buddhas today?" a man said, his eyes bloodshot from crack cocaine.

Jonas walked on. Jeers were as common as pig dung in seedy alleys where the worst of mankind lived.

The man shouted, "Hey, boy. Gimme yo' money or I beat you right now."

"Do it," Jonas said. "Do it and I'll kill you."

He threw back a curtain in his shack and stepped inside. His brother, blind since birth, slept on a mat.

A radio played a news broadcast.

> Police are searching tonight for a wealthy tourist's son who went missing at Kaap Klopse in Bo-Kaap earlier today. The five-year-old boy was last seen as the parade marched down Wale Street amidst a crowd of revelers, and . . .

On the other side of town, darkness fell over Table Bay. Bars and restaurants grew feverish with holiday cheer.

On a sleek *Royal Flush* moored in front of a grand hotel, a somber mood prevailed. Mayor Frohm arrived to gather information about Nathan's disappearance.

A doctor exited the master stateroom. He said, "I've given her another pill. She will no doubt sleep the night through."

"Thank you."

"Any news about your son?"

"No," Jack said. "We're expecting a call from Pretoria at any time. Then we'll find and kill the son of a bitch who took our precious son."


To a casual observer, Mother City poses no threat to the modern world. Cape Town is a delectable lunch in Hout Bay, M4 at rush hour, busy roundabouts by Freedom Stadium, Lion's Head and Bascule Bar, a parliamentary proceeding, and languid afternoons on Clifton Beach. But to the discerning mind, Mother City is something more: a titillating amalgam of ethereal bliss and imminent peril, an intoxicating panorama with a distinctly evocative and exotic flair. Civil order rules the day. But at night, vice and exploitation reign in shantytowns and sex orgies, Mavericks Gentlemen Club, a human trafficking ring, and coveted bags of black tar heroin smuggled in with holy books. The *Jolly Roger* pirate ship, a corrupt imam and his sinister protégé, the ominous call to prayer—they too are Mother City.

## 11

"Your bird is funny!" Nathan said, "What's his name?"

Asram did not reply.

"His feathers are pretty! How do you make him talk?"

Asram whispered with head bowed and eyes half-closed, "What have I done?"

His nervous eyes scanned the flat. A fly buzzed passed his ear. Its wings tickled a bead of sweat on Asram's cheek. His face was plain as a beaten stone. He'd spent many a day lusting for a life he would never have—a family, wealth, political dominance in the land of his youth.

He recalled the last meeting he had with Rauf in the privacy of Auwal Masjid. The soothing voice returned to his head. "Look at you, all grown up," the anointed one had said. He'd run his fingers through Asram's hair as he grinned. With his sharp goatee and beady eyes, he looked like the devil himself. Terror that started when Asram was a boy lasted into adolescence and instilled in him as an adult a kind of noble dread. He knew what it meant to live in fear and how to instill in a vulnerable child a sense of purpose in the face of desperation. To obey was to save one's soul. It was written—thus sayeth the anointed imam.

"I want to see the clowns! Where are the clowns?"

"*Raaack!* Time to party! *Raaack!*" the parrot sang.

Nathan petted the colorful bird. "You said there would be clowns!"

Asram tried to focus. A jihadist mind is never at peace. *We have some planes. Just stay quiet and you will be okay.* He knew he could emerge triumphant in jihad.

A small open hand gripped the boy's neck as he played with the talking bird. Asram gagged Nathan with a rope so tightly he could not speak, and then bound his wrists and feet so firmly that he could not move.

Asram's face broke into a grin. "Ready to go to the mosque, Mr. Nathan?"

A group of children sat in a circle on the second floor of the mosque. They colored animal cutouts with crayons and paid no attention to the man in the pirate suit or the parrot on his shoulder until the bird sang, "*Raaack!* Time to party! *Raaack!*"

Imam Rauf appeared in a doorway. His silver hair glistened in light from a naked bulb overhead. The spontaneous party had reached full speed.

"What is this?" said the anointed one.

Asram snapped to attention.

"*Raaack!* Allahu Akbar!" the parrot cried.

He kneeled before Rauf and said, "I bring you this child to save him from hell's fiery gate and infidel pigs, both Christian and Jew."

Silence.

Asram peered at Rauf from the cold concrete floor.

"You what?" said the anointed one.

"I took him today from the infidels."

"Hi there, mister!" Nathan said with a grin. "Have you heard the talking bird?"

Rauf cast an angry stare at Asram. "Are you mad?" He looked at the boy. "Where did you find him?"

"At the parade on Wale Street. He was with his parents, the evil pigs."

Rauf shifted his feet.

"From the Minstrel. They must be terribly afraid."

The anointed one whirled his head. Anger seeped from his eyes.

Asram said, "You may teach him or trade him as you see fit. Perhaps he is right for . . ."

"What?"

"Imam, I know about the children."

"You what?" Rauf stammered over his words. "Who have you spoken to?"

"I know there are children here who—"

"That is not so!" Rauf said.

Asram rocked back and forth and prayed, *There is no god but Allah, and Mohammed is his prophet.*

"You fool! I told you!" Rauf exclaimed. He grinded his teeth. "Why don't you listen?"

"But, Imam Rauf, I know there are . . ."

*Whack!*

Asram reached for his chin. Nathan scurried down a hall and squatted to hide his face.

"Look what you've done!" A lone finger pointed at Asram's face. "You'll bring the authorities here!"

"But, sir, I—"

The anointed one struck him again. His face boiled with contempt. "Speak of this and you will pay with your life. Do you understand?"

"Yes, imam."

Asram rolled on the floor as a penitent bemoaning his most heinous sin.

"If you speak of this, I will have you killed."

Asram rose and faced Rauf, and then bowed again as an unquestioning slave obedient to his master until the bitter end. He said, "But, sir, I—"

"Enough! What's done is done. The boy is your responsibility. He must be gone by sunrise. Have I made myself clear?"


By nine-thirty the children were sound asleep.

Rauf sat at his desk. He contemplated the opportunity before him. More than anything, he yearned to restore Islam to its former glory. Still, he needed an operative to assist in his quest, a point man who would acquiesce no matter the cost. He considered consequences in the event something happened to Asram, who would do exactly as told no matter how risky the task. To be sure, no one would miss him. Rauf could not think of a reason to avoid using Asram as a catalyst to assist in his ruse. Already Asram had confided in the anointed one as a trusted spiritual advisor who counseled him in the wake of his parents' death. He had observed Asram's transformation from vulnerable youth to faithful warrior, whose spiritual angst yearned for a means of expression. Perhaps he had something to offer. But first, the boy Nathan had to be cleansed.

What better place to plot a global terror attack than sleepy Bo-Kaap? Its cobblestone streets and colorful facade were anything but a threat. No one would suspect a peaceful enclave as the new seat of radical Islam. He sat in his chair as his mind raced with delusions.

But what if his racket was made known?

He shut his eyes and envisioned heavenly treasures that awaited: a sprawling mansion and crystal sea, streets paved with solid gold, hordes of naked virgins who were eager to serve and please. He had plenty of culprits to blame for social injustice, most notably the secular West. Class warfare had been used without fail as a catalyst for social change. Rauf had often referred to social injustice from the minbar. No wonder aimless youth flocked to Auwal Masjid on Friday afternoons. They needed to escape the madness of secular life in an unruly world. *Seventy-two virgins at your beck and call? Who wouldn't kill himself for that?*

Human trafficking was rampant in the sub-Saharan. Those who orchestrated the crime were virtually immune to charges brought by those who prosecute such heinous acts. Despite primitive techniques and frequent miscues, kidnappers were seldom caught. Moreover, few authorities bothered to prosecute nebulous crimes. In the event of discovery, any policeman could be easily bought. If exposed, Rauf would face no significant recourse from law enforcement officials at home, nor from the politically correct postmodern West, and least of all from Washington, where prudence is held as a liability and a trait that is patently forbidden.

For many years, Rauf operated the Madrassah at Auwal Masjid under the guise of religious charity and funded the whole endeavor with contributions made to further the mission of Islam.

Following an aggressive social media campaign, benefactors sent donations from every corner of the globe. Even South Africa's Parliament had contributed to Rauf's altruistic cause. Millions of rand were available to cover expenses at the mosque. City officials learned of the Madrassah and many a needy child was sent there. Within a year they had outgrown the ramshackle old house where children had lived under supervision of Malay women who had never left the Western Cape. Elders voted to purchase the adjacent building, and thus was born the Madrassah at Auwal Masjid.

Rauf stood a pace off the rug. So what if the anointed one lined his pockets with a few million leftover rand? Every good deed merits a lasting reward. Rauf had a vision of what Auwal Masjid could be—the centerpiece of radical Islam—but he needed new blood to wage his holy war. For months, he had prayed fervently to Allah. He pleaded for divine revelation, yearned for a fresh command. What stellar feat could he attempt to produce a desired reward? How would his personal jihad proceed?

A moment later he dropped to his knees. He raised his hands as he rocked back and forth and sang, "*Allahu Akbar*" (God is great). Rauf prostrated before Allah. *Sujood* is the secret of Muslim prayer. Hope came alive on bended knee. Two very different worlds would collide and with a mighty force. Brilliant thoughts formed in his head. He prayed for strength to see them through. If victorious in jihad, his efforts would be met with tangible and eternal rewards. But what feat would warrant such precious gifts? What heroic act could he undertake?

With a pivotal weapon like Asram, his loftiest goal came within reach.

*Now this is the Law of the Jungle*
*as old and as true as the sky*
*And the Wolf that shall keep it may prosper*
*but the Wolf that shall break it must die*

*As the creeper that girdles the tree trunk*
*the Law runneth forward and back*
*For the strength of the Pack is the Wolf*
*and the strength of the Wolf is the Pack*

## 12

Suri's curves were exposed by her sparse sleepwear. She might have been a nymph, Venus of Urbino, a modern goddess of love that made one marvel at her feminine form. One saw her chest and thought of Titian, *Bella Donna*, an aristocrat's daughter. Soft bronze skin slid over rose-colored satin sheets. Passion radiated from a flawless face, though she wore no lipstick or mascara.

She rolled over in bed. Her dark brown hair was pulled back into a shoulder-length ponytail. A bare hand lifted the remote. She advanced the television to a new channel and an Arab journalist appeared on screen. He spoke with fervor reserved for harrowing news: "Why do young men and women turn to terror? Has the War on Terror made our world a more dangerous place? Is Modi's government leading India down a treacherous path? We'll discuss these issues and more with former Afghan president Hamid Karzai on *Al-Jazeera Investigates*."

Down the hall, Leyla tossed and turned. Her head raced with emotions from a hectic day. She recounted the arrival of emaciated children, hungry for food and love. One by one they sauntered through the basement of Auwal Masjid and clung to her after their arrival from Marhaba Muharram. She had often wondered where the children came from.

Suri knocked on her bedroom door. Leyla sat up in bed.

"You won't believe what happened."

"Tell me," Leyla replied.

"Remember the Europeans who needed an au pair for their son?"

"Yes, I remember." Leyla massaged her temples with both hands.

"He disappeared."

"Disappeared?"

"Vanished in Bo-Kaap."

Leyla didn't move. Her body froze on the double bed.

"It's terrible. His father phoned me."

"How awful!"

"Truly, it is," Suri said. "His mother is unable to function. It's been on my mind, so I can't sleep."

"Did you meet the boy?"

"Yes, Friday at Noon Gun. He's so cute. His father said he slipped away from them at the parade."

"Parade?"

"The Minstrel."

"You mean Coon Carnival?"

"Yes.

"That's odd."

Suri nodded. "Very odd. There was a massive turnout this year. You'd think someone would've noticed him."

"True."

"He was chasing after a leprechaun."

"Even more bizarre."

"It's all very strange."

"Kidnapping a helpless boy, who would do such a thing?" Leyla said.

"I know. It's a hideous crime, and a bold move, even for an experienced criminal. And to think, he hasn't been caught."

"Could a terrorist have taken him?"

"I thought about that too."

"Scary."

"It is," Suri said, "but what can we do? I'm still going out for a drink."

Tables in the hotel restaurant were fitly laid. Suri noted the romantic atmosphere of the bar and smiled at a sign posted in a window: EAT DRINK LIVE LOVE.

Only a bartender looked on from his corner spot in the spacious room. A white apron smeared with citrus juices covered his waist. His mind was keen on the task at hand. He straightened a row of whiskies and gins for what must have been the hundredth time that week.

A soft tune hummed overhead as floodlights over the bar turned dim.

> Uit die blou van onse hemel (From the blueness of our skies)
> Uit die diepte van ons see (From the depths of our seas)
> Oor ons ewige gebergtes (Over our everlasting mountains)
> Waar die kranse antwoord gee (Where the echoing crags resound)
> Sounds the call to come together, and united we shall stand
> Let us live and strive for freedom, in South Africa our land

"Welcome to Bascule," the bartender said. "May I know your drink of choice?" His voice rang with a tone in keeping with his playful mood.

Several minutes had passed since Suri entered the room. She had thought he would never ask.

"I'll have a cosmopolitan."

The bartender turned away from her, and as he did a voice behind her said, "Names of cocktails befit those who order them."

She spun her head to a handsome face.

The voice had come out of nowhere. He said, "It's Suri, is it not?"

There was nothing remarkable about him, except that he knew her name.

"This one's on me," he said.

Suri was not amused. She had no hint of interest in him, though she wasn't there to drink alone.

A moment later the bartender appeared. "Top-shelf Macallan?" he said.

"Sure thing, double shot. Bring us two," said the mysterious man.

"Right away, sir." The bartender bowed his head and turned away.

"Will you be dining alone?"

Suri's eyes darted at the mysterious man. "You tell me," she replied. She gave him a half wink and crossed her legs.

"Not if I can help it." The man sat in a chair across from her. "Tell me about Maersk."

Suri froze. She didn't know what to say.

"How long have you been with the company?"

"How do you—?"

"Just trying to make conversation, Miss. Don't be difficult."

"But how—?"

"One discovers things here and there. Never mind how. Answer the question."

"Maersk is great. I've been there just over a year."

"I see." His tone sharpened. "Are you Muslim?" he asked.

"Excuse me?"

"Where were you born?"

"Who are you?"

"Answer the question, please."

"I will not."

The bartender set matching tumblers in front of them. "Would you care for an appetizer or bowl of pretzels?" he asked.

"No, thank you," Suri replied.

"Calamari, please," said the mysterious man. He adjusted his necktie.

"Coming right up."

"May I have the check?" Suri said.

The bartender nodded.

"You were born in Netanya."

Suri didn't move.

"When did you immigrate here?" He leaned forward slightly. "And why?"

"I'm sorry, but you are completely out of line."

"A few months back, no?" He moved closer.

"You're beginning to scare me. I'm going to leave."

"Not so fast." The man planted a hand on her purse.

"That's my handbag. Give it back!"

"In a while, after we chat."

"Who are you?"

"Where are you parents?"

"My parents are in Tel Aviv."

"I know they are."

"Then why did you ask?"

"One picks up things, you know. When may I see you again?"

"I must go now. May I have my purse?"

"What are your parents like?"

"Give me my handbag now or I'll scream." Her eyes scanned the room. The bartender was no longer there.

"Your late husband, was he kind to you?" She wanted to slap his jaw. "Do you miss him?"

"Give me my purse or I'll report you."

"Do it," he said.

Suri folded her arms. For a few moments, neither spoke.

"I'd rather not report you, but I will if I must."

"I've been arrested before."

"I'm not surprised."

"Your calamari, sir," the bartender said. He set the plate down and left them again.

The mysterious man laid a thousand rand on the table. He said, "Meet me in the foyer if you want your purse."

In an odd way, it always seemed easier to obey. Suri followed him into the foyer. A pianist played softly. The mysterious man rested a hand on her shoulder and whispered in her ear.

"Don't think I'm going to sleep with you," Suri said.

"Don't flatter yourself," replied the mysterious man. He led her to a lift and pressed a button. "I just want to talk," he said.

"Right. And I just want my purse."

The lift door opened and Suri entered.

"Relax. You'll get your purse."

Suri's eyes darted right and left.

He said, "I'll see you soon."

She reached for the handbag and he obliged. The next move was hers to make.

As the lift closed, there it was sticking out from her purse. A key card in a tiny envelope was marked with a handsome logo: Cape Grace Hotel – Suite 801.

## Interlude in Tel Aviv

Décor was lacking in the briefing room. A window spanned the height of a wall and afforded a grand view of the ancient land. Father Abraham would be proud. Tel Aviv stood as a thriving metropolis built over remnants of an abandoned port long forgotten by modern man. The old, native, and liberated race flourished once again, though it bore no resemblance to its forebears who fought and died in their beloved Gush Dan. Twin flat-screen televisions hung on the south wall. Atop a credenza were a bouquet of yellow roses, a water jug with paper cones, and a digital projector with its matching screen. A map of the world replete with topography and color schemes indicating Israeli presence in hostile domains adorned another wall. This was no place for show and tell, but rather a place for discussion and planning, a venue where intelligent men and women mulled over their homeland's worst fears in private.

Committee participants had been chosen by the prime minister, who had not yet arrived for the briefing. Senior advisors sat at a conference table made of gopher wood. Each official was composed, subdued. Restraint is a trusted friend in the face of uncertainty.

Foster arrived in the briefing room before anyone else. Stolid and focused, he replayed the facts again in his head. It was a tale meant for primetime: a wealthy couple reported their only son missing in Bo-Kaap, a sleepy Muslim hamlet in Cape Town. The boy's father was Jewish, a multibillionaire descendent of Lord Rothschild, no less. His mother was a secular European and erstwhile Roman Catholic. There were no leads, according to local police, but Foster knew better. The boy, Nathan, hadn't simply disappeared. Someone had taken him.

But why?

No ransom had been solicited.

Who was behind it all? Had Islamic radicals hatched a plot more ambitious than ever before? Could a Muslim kidnapping ring have turned even bolder and graduated to the global stage?

Reuben waited for the phone to ring. More than a few times he imagined hearing those encouraging words, "Good news, sir. We've found the boy safe at last." But such notice never came.

It was Monday, and the mass of papers on the director's desk indicated the rigor of a job that seemingly had no end. Reuben reached for a memo.

December 21, 1991
United States Embassy
Nairobi, Kenya

US State Department liaison 86-012 visited Joint UNHCR/ UNICEF refugee encampment for Sudanese children in Lodwar, Kenya on December 1, 1991. Identity of 346 children registered at the camp is attached hereto. Our liaison interviewed a number of children regarding the status of refugee camps in Sudan. Reports indicate approximately 500 child refugees remained in a camp on the south side of Juba, Sudan, near the Cathedral of St. Theresa. Reports of the number of children in other refugee camps around Juba were not clear.

Nine boys reported they were kidnapped and held in a compound near a mosque in northwest Juba for two months. The kidnapping took place just after Ramadan. The children reported no abuse. They were released together at the entrance to the refugee camp on the east side of Juba. Identity of the children and our liaison's interview notes are attached hereto. Reports indicate an attempt to set up a Muslim indoctrination program at the camp in Juba.

CBD

The sound of footsteps intensified. An assistant escorted Prime Minister Reznik to the conference room. They cleared a line of offices and the door sprang open.

Seated in the briefing room were Reuben, Foster, Mel, and a half-dozen agents from the intelligence team. Reuben stood at the head of the table.

"Ladies and gentlemen, the prime minister," he said.

The men and women stood, but did not speak.

"As you were," Reznik said. His severely receded hair was combed to one side.

Reuben said, "Okay, folks. Time is short. Shiffman, let's start with you."

An owlish man in his late twenties leaned forward and set his reading glasses aside. He said, "A pair of suicide bombers killed thirty-one people and injured dozens more during an attack on worshippers at Al-Moayad Mosque in Sana'a. Both Sunni and Shiite were among victims in the attacks carried out during sunset prayers. The first jihadist detonated a bomb attached to a belt of explosives. The second ignited a car bomb that exploded outside the mosque where bystanders attempted to rescue victims of the first attack. Al-Moayad Mosque is located near Houthi rebel headquarters in the Yemeni capital, but neither they nor ISIL have claimed responsibility."

"Does it ever end?" an advisor asked.

"Not without a relentless show of force," Foster said with a heated tone. "It's the only solution no one has tried."

His folded hands rested on the conference table.

Reuben agreed. He said, "Some animals simply cannot be tamed."

"Does that mean we have to kill them?" Mel asked.

A big-picture guy, Reznik saw the forest in every tree. He said, "Civilization requires that we get this right. There is no room for error."

Mel blinked and rubbed her neck.

"Mankind has a long history of diplomatic failure," the prime minister declared.

Foster said, "This is a chronic problem. Since Adam and Eve, humanity has been cursed by nature. Remember what Darwin taught us. Man is an animal whose socialization depends not on convenience or habit, but on necessity. His cooperation in society develops as a means of survival. Our enemy has a barbaric worldview. Jihadists draw strength from deception and mayhem. For them, as beasts in the wild, survival depends on victory in eternal conflict. It's a way of life. The strong win the struggle and live. The weak are condemned, not to defeat or subjugation, but to death and oblivion."

Mel's spine stiffened against her chair. "Not all Muslims are predators, Dellon."

He said, "That isn't the issue. That isn't the issue at all. Capitulation has failed us. Negotiations bite us in the ass every time. One cannot compromise with a throat cutter who has only his life to lose. He will beat you at his murderous game every time because he has less at stake than you do. He has only his life to lose, and his murderous kind must be exterminated. For all he knows, in his delusional mind, seventy-two virgins really do await him in paradise after he blows himself up."

The prime minister cleared his throat and said, "Poverty has been on the rise throughout the region for more than two decades. Hence the increasing number of suicide bombings, which are sadly and unacceptably too close to home. Since 2000, there has been more than a fivefold increase in the number of people killed by terrorists. Last year more than 30,000 people died in terrorist attacks, with more than 80 percent of them occurring in Iraq, Afghanistan, Pakistan, Nigeria, and Syria. Countries reporting record numbers of deaths due to terrorism reached an all-time high in 2013."

Reznik paused and glanced at his timepiece.

Foster said, "Negotiate if you wish, but doing so means not only defeat but also death: death of freedom, death of democracy and self-determination, death of countless innocent men, women, and children, Sunni and Shiite, Muslim and non-Muslim, by bomb after bomb after bomb."

Mel asked, "Are you prepared to justify death in the name of justice?"

The prime minister turned to face her. He said, "This is no time for apologetics or legalese. Those who desire to live in peace and defend themselves in the War on Terror have no need for justification. Use of lethal force is a matter of self-preservation, nothing more, nothing less. Sometimes we must sacrifice life to save it, and when facing a culture of death, we must fight with strategy, motives, and weaponry that enable us to kill terrorists before they kill us."

Mel uncrossed her legs, rested an elbow on the table, and said, "Will you accept loss of innocent life as inevitable?"

"Yes, because to do otherwise is to usher in an even greater loss of life."

No one stirred in the conference room.

Foster spoke again. "Multiculturalism and political correctness have raised their ugly heads and dictated a defeatist mandate to us far too many times. There is no cause for speculation about who is behind it all. We know who the enemy is. They have made themselves known in the boldest of ways. We have untold causes for action in the form of murder of innocent life by a self-proclaimed perpetrator who celebrates a culture of death. But we also have the ability and means of burying this enemy with bullets and bombs and missiles of our own."

Reuben said, "There are no real consequences for terrorists these days, especially in the United States."

"I'd be punished more for raping a cat than carrying out an act of terror," an assistant said.

"You rape pussycats, Eliot?" Shiffman whispered.

"You get the point," his sidekick said.

"I get the point all right, sick bastard."

"Al Qaeda, ISIL, these throat cutters are thick as thieves," Foster said.

"It's true," the prime minister said.

"Jihadists are made from the same despicable mold. It's time we faced the dragon head-on."

Reuben asked, "Has anyone read the latest report on human trafficking from the UN Security Council?"

"We have," Mel said. She lifted a remote and the report appeared on a video screen.

"Very well," the prime minister said, "Will you show us page 92?"

The projector advanced to the following slide. In the next instant, a voice read:

Kazakhstan

Lisa was promised a visa through the US seasonal worker program. The processing fee was steep, but the thought of working in America was worth the price. Lisa arrived in Kansas City ready to work, but was seized by traffickers along with other girls who applied to the program. She was forced to clean rooms in some of the best hotels in Chicago. When Lisa refused to work, the traffickers threatened to cancel her immigration status.

In March 2008, four Uzbeki nationals were arrested on charges of forced labor in several states. They posted bail and fled the country within two days.

France

April ran away from home when she was fourteen years old and moved in with an older man who sexually and physically abused her and convinced her to become a prostitute. After a few weeks, she contracted numerous sexually transmitted diseases and became addicted to cocaine. The police arrested April when she was sixteen on charges of prostitution. No effort was made to find her pimp and she was granted probation for fifteen months.

Tajikistan

Dara left her village in Kazakhstan for a better life in Astana. She was abducted by a trafficker and sold to a local pimp. After years of forced prostitution, Dara escaped and was found by police. She was in the third trimester of her pregnancy when she arrived at a shelter for battered women. Dara is being trained as a cosmetologist at the shelter and will leave once she finds employment and a place to live.

"How's that for justification?" the prime minister asked, his eyebrows raised.

Silence rushed over the room.

Reuben was a principled man. "Think of the legacy left by Isser Harel, who founded this organization in 1951. We detained former Nazi Adolf Eichmann from Argentina, and brought him to Israel to stand trial for war crimes. We've taken down Arab guerrilla leaders responsible for the massacre of Israeli athletes at the Munich Olympic Games in 1972. We've assassinated terrorists and rescued hostages taken on airliners, in tunnels, and brought others to safety after they were held captive inside mosques in distant lands.

"I could go on, but I must now ask you to consider what kind of legacy this generation of Mossad will leave. Are we up to the challenge we face? How will we protect this land while staying true to the reputation and tradition of the finest intelligence bureau the world has ever known?"

Reuben sat high in his chair.

It seemed Mossad was ready for war.

# 13

Suri entered without making a sound. She eased the door behind her closed and stepped into a fateful silence. Soft light from a bedside lamp illuminated the hotel suite. Never had she felt so alone. She entered the bedroom and scanned the luxurious space.

Where was the mysterious man? Was she really alone? An imminent victim of a secret predator's dastardly scheme?

Her eyes sprinted back and forth in the room. She edged forward a pace. On the desk was a collection of items that belonged to a man of purpose: a datebook, fountain pen, a pad on which notes were written. A few words leaped off the page: encryption, Foster, al-Munir, Dorp Street, egress in event of attack.

Suri sat on a chair.

"I've been waiting," a voice said. Still, he wasn't seen.

She turned. "Sorry, I'm on a break from my job."

The mysterious man entered the room. He approached the desk and sat across from her. "Early is on time, on time is late."

"I didn't know I was on the clock."

He thumbed a yellow notepad and reached for a pen.

"You're allergic to dates and almonds, is that so?"

"How did you know?"

"Never mind."

"Excuse me. I said how did you—"

"I understand your marksmanship leaves little to be desired."

"I can hold my own."

"You finished first in your last competition."

"That's true. May I ask—"

"Your ex was SAS, no?"

"Who are you?"

"Let's just say I'm an operative for a man of action who knows how to get things done."

"What do you mean?"

"In business and private life, he brings events to pass by force of will. The world is easy to navigate when one knows who's in control."

"Sounds intriguing."

"He's the most capable man I know. Plays by the rules and still gets around, all while maintaining a low profile."

"Does anyone know who he is?"

"No. By comparison to the über-rich who often flaunt their wealth, he's essentially unseen. A multibillionaire with a clean conscience has no one to appease."

"Why does he meddle in international affairs?"

"It's what intelligent people do. Some for notoriety, others simply because they can."

"What motivates him?"

"Sense of duty. He has money, power, and endless prestige. He's reached the pinnacle of success and has nothing left to do, except rid the world of imminent evil."

"Are you referring to jihad?"

"Label evil as you please, Miss Cohen."

"Does he act alone?"

"For now, yes. But he's not opposed to cooperation with like-minded folk who have courage to lead a vital mission."

She repositioned her hips on the chair.

A gentle breeze blew in from the patio.

"Look, you invited me here. What do you want?"

To this he did not immediately respond. Instead, he paced back and forth in the room. He would pose the questions, and she would answer them.

He sat on a chair across from her. "How is your Afrikaans?"

"*Vertel jy vir* my (You tell me)," she said in perfect pitch.

"Impressive. Is that your native tongue?"

"No, Hebrew is. I also speak English, Arabic, and Farsi."

"We know," the man replied. "We've studied your past."

"I'm sorry?"

"Translate this sentence." The mysterious man spoke with a metered pace, as if to assert his power.

"Who is we?"

The conversation was already off-key. He pointed at a sentence on the notepad: Liberty above all.

"Translation, please," he said.

Anxiety lodged in her voice as though she were an invisible bystander observing a confidential exchange. "*Liberty bo alle.*"

"Remember that," he said.

Suri nodded.

He directed her attention to an English phrase: "For God and country."

"*Vir God en land,*" she said without delay.

"You're right for the cause. I'd expect no less from a prime minister's daughter."

"Excuse me?"

"Your old man sends regards."

"I'm afraid you are mistaken. My father died a month before I was born."

"Don't be fooled. World leaders have skeletons too."

"I'm not willing to participate in your game."

"Israel needs you. Your father needs you. The homeland is at risk."

"I told you. My father—"

"Is the most powerful man in the Middle East."

"Prove it."

The mysterious man pulled a file from his briefcase. Dark, bold letters read, CONFIDENTIAL: Paternity test. He referred to a photo and said, "You have his chin and nose."

An illicit affair and neglected daughter notwithstanding, Reznik had been elected in a narrow victory after a hard-fought campaign that unfolded amidst controversy surrounding his involvement with a multinational private security firm comprised of expatriated members of American and British counterintelligence teams. A month had not yet passed since his election and already his will was tested.

"Reflect on the news as much as you please, but remember, we have work to do."

Suri didn't move.

"Washington and London have their agendas, but nothing as immediate or essential to survival as is the case in Tel Aviv. Israeli sovereignty is always at stake in the nuclear age. Your father has a lot to bear. Perhaps you'll meet when the mission is done."

Her mind was paralyzed, not with fear or rage, but hope at the prospect of learning the truth by connecting with a father she never knew.

"But, I—"

He tossed a smartphone, which she caught awkwardly.

"You will receive daily instructions by encrypted text. We'll monitor your location in real time. A software program offering continuous surveillance has been added to your phone. Don't fret, it's for your safety. We have no interest in your private life."

She thought he'd said this before.

"Leaders of rogue nations have articulated *ad nauseum* their hatred for the Jewish state. Self-preservation is our undisputed chief objective. Never mind freedom or pleasure. Mere existence matters most. That's what the agency has always said."

"Sir, I was a linguistics major at UCT. I think maybe you should—"

"Linguists are a commodity in intelligence circles these days. Foster will debrief you nightly. You will provide updates as information becomes available throughout your day."

Suri went silent.

Intelligence? Foster? Debrief? Updates throughout her day? It was all so different from a drab routine.

He rose, paced the room, and said, "Espionage, like war, is a practical undertaking. It proceeds with discretion, and rightly so. Heed your emotion if you're given to dissent."

His lecture had started to interest her.

"Bo-Kaap was a little-known enclave. Its native Malays were too beautiful and peaceful to trigger suspicion of an ignoble scheme, but Dorp Street is now Ground Zero."

A wall clock ticked passed quarter of ten.

"Don't fret if I go MIA. It's part of the job. No news is good news, the saying goes. One is seldom noticed on intelligence tours, unless he makes a dreadful mistake."

The summer sun took its customary place in the horizon and the mysterious man leaned close to her.

He said, "Miss Cohen, tell me what you know about Auwal Masjid."

*The mosque?* she thought. He had used her legal surname.

Suri's heart sank.

This couldn't be good.

It was a mid-day service like any other. Rows of sandals lengthened at the entrance of Auwal Masjid. The prayer room was humid as hell.

One of the elders read a passage from the Qur'an. Silent prayer lifted troubled souls. Broken spirits on the brink of death came alive. Steady eyes of a muezzin cased over Bo-Kaap from the balcony of an olive-green minaret. A moment later, the call to prayer began. The muezzin's lips quivered as penitents thrust headfirst onto the carpet. Men froze as obedient statues in a collective bow before Rauf. The call to prayer beseeched all men to shun distraction in a fallen world. If only priests and rabbis could see, how much better the world would be.

The prayer room was warm, its air heavy and moist.

Rauf stood motionless at the minbar. He said, "Let us reflect on the concept of submission and its application to our lives."

Every face was calm and still.

"If peace is your utmost desire, you must yield to the message of holy Islam and surrender your will to tenets you know are right. My friends, we hasten to be in the light, for in light we see all things clearly. No man should be afraid of death, for death is a part of life. Without death there can be no life, and without life there can be no death.

"Mysteries implicit in life and death form a cycle from which no man can escape. Our bodies return to dust and enrich the earth from which we came. Leaves die and return from trees unto the earth to nourish and renew it as rain. Beloved, without death there can be no better life. You see, peace is the inevitable consequence of submission to the will of Allah. Devote yourselves to a life of obedience at any cost. Be loyal to Islam for the sake of Allah and nothing else."

An urgent message was offered by a most learned imam, its desired effect summoned by a forceful tone.

The anointed one gripped both sides of the minbar and declared, "In a square in Nazareth, just below the Basilica of the Annunciation, which the enemy has unduly claimed, a Qur'anic verse on a billboard warns: 'Whosoever seeks a religion other than Islam, it will never be accepted of him, and in the life hereafter he will be one of the losers.'"

Violent tendencies boiled in young men whose lives had been filled with hurt.

The anointed one spoke with authority long missing at Auwal Masjid. His sermon suggested a life of meaning through submission to a higher cause. He implored lost men to a better way—the way of holy Islam. Words he spoke were infallible in the minds of those who heard them.

The service drew to a close. Men prostrated in silence before Allah. Protection was granted to those who faced Mecca on bended knee. A gesture here, a whisper there, fervent prayer was better than sleep.

Sacred inscriptions on pale sheetrock called to mind extraordinary thoughts, not of gracious genies, but the precious blood of martyrdom.

Dorp Street was empty, save the old fisherman who napped in his lean-to.

Not a whisper was heard as orphans dried their feet in tiny stalls and prostrated before Allah. The only sound was that of flowing water as it lapped the floor in a stall.

Nathan donned a turban and matching smock, then descended a staircase leading to the back of the worship hall.

Inside the minaret, Ali flipped an audio switch and queued the muezzin who stood ready to belt the call to prayer from a balcony as he faced east.

*Ya Ilahi ta qayamat ye chaman taaza rahe*
*Har shajar, har nakhl iss ka phoolta, phalta rahe*
*(O, Allah, may this garden be flourished till doom's day*
*May every tree and every branch of this garden flourish and blossom)*

Mealtime followed evening prayer.

Leyla knelt beside the newest orphan. "Hi, there! What's your name?"

"Na-than," the boy replied.

"Are you okay?"

"I want my mum." His speech was muffled and slow.

Leyla faced her little ones. "Children, we have a new friend with us tonight. His name is Nathan."

"Hi, Nathan," the little ones said in unison.

The boy didn't speak.

Leyla said, "Remember, the prophet Mohammed told us we must obey Allah and his Blessed Messenger at all times. But after that, who else did he tell us to listen to and be close to?"

"Your mother!" the children screamed.

"Well done. Let's make Nathan feel welcome by asking him to sing with us."

> *Who should I give my love to?*
> *My respect and my honor to?*
> *Who should I pay good mind to*
> *after Allah and Rasullullah?*
>
> *Then comes your mother*
> *Who next? Your mother*
> *Who next? Your mother*
> *And then your father*

Nathan began to cry.

## 14

Asram heard a knock on his apartment door. For a few moments, time stopped. He stared through a peephole. To his surprise, it was Rauf.

"Imam, come in!"

Asram marveled at the presence of Rauf in his modest home. With a state of mind approaching nirvana, he gazed at his idol in a spirit of reverence, if not veneration.

Rauf sat across from him at the kitchen table. He said, "Maybe the boy is right for madrassah."

His words lifted Asram's spirit as a mid-day prayer. It was as though he was born to kidnap the helpless boy. Asram's face beamed with malevolent pride. At last, fate had smiled on him.

"My son, you have carried out a most noble act. We believe you are destined for greatness."

"I pray so, Imam."

"Now, come with me. I have something important for you to do."

Carmen had not fully recovered. Against her doctor's advice, she took to the streets on Tuesday with armed escorts who searched for Nathan along with her. After dinner, she insisted on a return to Bo-Kaap.

STARNER JONES

As Carmen turned the corner of Wale and Büitengracht, Suri settled a bill with her stylist and exited a salon. A human trafficking notice was posted in a store window.


India

Neha was born into poverty in Bihar, the poorest state in India. His mother was desperate to keep him and his three brothers from starving, so she accepted a fifteen-dollar advance from a local trafficker in exchange for one of the boys. Neha was sent to a carpet factory located a hundred kilometers away. The loom owner forced him to work nineteen hours a day, allowing him only enough time to eat and relieve himself. If he made any mistake in the intricate design of rugs made in the factory, he was beaten until he bled.

Neha and another boy packed enough food to sustain them and rolled themselves in one of the rugs that was packed into a box and shipped to the United States. They were discovered at a port in Miami and sent to a hospital where they were treated for malnutrition and pneumonia.

"Mrs. Goldwyn?"

Carmen spun her neck.

"It's Suri. Do you remember me?" Her dark brown hair was long and wavy.

"Yes."

"I was terribly saddened to hear of Nathan's disappearance."

Carmen held a stack of security briefings. "We're going to find him."

158

"May I ask what you are reading?"

"Accounts of missing children."

"Is there anything I can do?"

"Help me find my son."

"Have the police offered any leads?"

Carmen sighed. "No, they've not been helpful at all. We reported Nathan's disappearance to the police commissioner. He made a trite remark about worried moms like me and asked if we had notified the Consulate."

"Children go missing too often. It's becoming more common, I'm afraid. Have you heard of the Lost Boys of the Sudan?"

"No. Who are they?"

They moved to a table at a nearby café.

Suri said, "Since the 1980s, Sudan has been ravaged by civil war, which has already claimed more than half a million lives and spawned countless numbers of refugees. Among them are some twenty thousand children, mostly boys under eighteen. They were separated from their families for more than two decades. The Lost Boys of the Sudan trekked across an unforgiving wilderness in search of food and safety. Many died journeying between Juba and Addis Abba. Those who survived are in humanitarian relief camps in Kenya, South Sudan, and Uganda."

Carmen cradled her forehead with both hands. A cup of espresso remained untouched. She began to weep. "What a sick world," she cried through a river of tears. "How did this happen?"

"As Plato said, 'Wise men pay attention to their vocation and avocation, and allow fools to rule them.'"

Carmen reached for a tissue.

"Two million children are trafficked every year, and not one politician cares. Trafficking is the norm in many African cultures and originated in traditional forms of migration when young boys ventured into manhood amidst social chaos prevalent in the region. Tales of geographic mobility abound in tent cities and shantytowns, where imams relay stories of triumph and perseverance to young men who lack direction in their lives. Some children were sold to shepherds who forced them to see after cattle during nighttime drives.

"Prior to intervention, kidnapped children were often not returned home. But since 1992, UNICEF has intervened and returned more than a thousand boys to their families. About fifteen thousand remain in refugee camps."

"How do you know so much?"

"My mother is married to Israel's Ambassador to the UN. He says incompetent world leaders are responsible for the rise of terror, and my uncle who is a member of the Knesset agrees."

"I see."

"Perhaps I've overhead too many of his conversations with members of the Human Rights Council.

"At the height of the civil war conditions turned even worse. Fearing their captors, many boys left their families and villages for Juba and Khartoum in hopes of finding work or entering school. Few had any notion of what lay ahead. Upon arrival in cities, most of the boys resorted to panhandling or petty crime to pay for food. They sacrificed everything to swindlers or bandits they faced along the way. Many fell victim to disease or starvation. Others were so weakened by hunger and fatigue that they fell on the roadside and became prey for lions."

"Why would anyone take my Nathan?" Carmen asked. "Do the people who took him want money?"

Suri reached for Carmen's hand. "My uncle says this has been studied at length. There is no systematic link between terrorism and poverty."

Carmen wiped a tear as her head hung low. "I just want my Nathan back."

"We all want that for you, and for Nathan."

Suri peeked at a bodyguard then turned to Carmen. She said, "If there is any hope of finding Nathan, we must locate him ourselves."

"Okay, but how?"

"Let's chat more."

"We're having a midnight vigil at Saint Mary's Cathedral."

"I'll meet you in front of the church after the service."

Carmen heard a child's familiar voice. She detected his soothing accent several meters away. There he was again, the boy with his box of icons and local shells. He held a hand-carved statue of the Blessed Virgin overhead.

"That boy really knows his way around," Carmen said. "We saw him scaling the waterfront the day we arrived."

Suri eyed the boy. She said, "That's Jonas. Sadly, he grew up too fast. He was left to support himself and a handicapped brother after his mother died."

"Where is his father?"

"He never knew him."

"Where does he live?"

"In a shantytown called Khayelitsha. Conditions there are worse than deplorable."

"He's persistent, that's for sure."

"There's nothing he won't do for a few hundred rand, and he'll spend every cent on his brother and a tombstone for his late grandfather, who raised him after his parents died."

"Do you suppose Jonas could help us find Nathan?"

"It's worth a try." Suri rested a hand on Carmen's shoulder. "Even a stopped clock is right twice a day."


Rauf marched up the stairs. He had always relished time in front of the children.

Two dozen boys sat in the prayer room.

"Maestro, your flute!" Rauf exclaimed.

Ali stood tall and sneered. He held a gourd flute to his lips and blew an ominous tune. Moments later, cobras popped up from their cage. With fangs exposed, they wiggled their necks in a fierce reptilian rage. Ali swung the flute back and forth as he danced beside the minbar.

*Loo loo loo, loo loo loo.*

"Are you ready for your first mission, little ones?" Rauf said with a narrow grin.

"Yes, imam!" the children shouted.

One by one they passed the minbar, as Asram dispensed bags of black tar heroin into their satchels.


Jack and Carmen dressed for the vigil aboard the *Royal Flush*.

"I'm not thrilled about going to a house of worship just because my son has been kidnapped," Jack said.

"What's the matter? Don't you believe in God?"

"Believe what?"

"Do you believe in anything?" Carmen asked.

"I believe what I see, nothing else."

"Why are you so hostile to religion?"

"I'm not hostile to religion. I'm hostile to falsehood."

Carmen didn't know what to say.

Jack said, "Face it, dear. There is no such thing as heaven or hell. But you and billions of others have accepted the teaching that there really is a little red devil with a little red cape who holds a pitchfork in the depths of hell. We are told that hell is a place of eternal pain and torment, yet the central nervous system stops processing neuronal impulses at death and is thus incapable of sensing pain of any kind."

"Where did that come from?"

"The bound book, no less. Look it up, it's in there."

Carmen didn't speak.

"Religion seethes with fantasy and magical beliefs. Jihadists believe seventy-two virgins will greet them in paradise the moment they detonate themselves. That kind of falsehood contributes to the rise of terror."

Carmen looked at her hands that once held tiny Nathan. Calmly, quietly, she began to pray.


No seats were unfilled at Saint Mary's Cathedral.

Jack and Carmen arrived after the service began and sat on a pew in the back of chapel. Suri followed close behind as the choir sang a libretto by Chanticleer.

*Those lives were mine to love and cherish*
*To guard and guide along life's way*
*Oh God forbid that one should perish*
*That one alas should go astray*

Father de Silva greeted congregants as they exited the nave. He was a slender man in his late sixties and had aged well.

"Your sermon was lovely," Carmen said.

"Thank you, dear. You're very kind." The priest smiled and held forth open hands as he spoke. "I pray daily for your son's safe return."

"Thank you, Father." Carmen shook his hand and peeked at Jack.

The priest looked at Jack and said, "*Illigitimi non carborundum.*"

"I'm sorry?"

"It's my favorite Latin phrase," said Father de Silva.

"What does it mean?"

He leaned next to them. The priest's eyes peeped right and left. "Don't let the bastards get you down."


Jonas paced back and forth in front of the church.

"Postcard for your kinsmen? Precious jewel for your lovely bride?"

"How's business?" Suri asked. Carmen and Jack lingered a step behind.

He lifted the box for her to inspect. "See for yourself."

"May I ask where you are from?" Carmen said.

"Cape Town. Mother City is all I know."

"Where are your parents?" Carmen asked.

The boy darted his eyes at her, not moving his head. He said, "I never knew my father and my mom died giving birth to my brother."

"What about your grandparents?" Jack asked the street urchin.

"They perished in Rhodesia, sah. Want to buy a cross for your lovely bride?"

Carmen's eyes alit with hope. "I like this one," she said as she petted a burgundy crucifix.

"Three hundred rand," the boy said.

"What's your name, son?" asked Jack.

"Jonas." He cradled the box next to his side. "See anything else you like?"

"Jonas, I have a question for you," Suri replied.

"No answer is free."

"I understand. We need your help finding someone."

"Who?"

"Nathan, he's slightly younger than you. He went missing in Bo-Kaap earlier this week."

"Fine. I'll help you." The boy held forth an open hand. "How much are you willing to pay?"

"Have you ever been to the madrassah at Auwal Masjid?"

"Ten rand per question, a thousand more if I find him."

"Fair enough." Carmen reached for her purse.

"I've never been an orphan at the masjid. Thank God, I do not trust in Allah."

"Jonas, how would you like to make a few thousand rand?" Carmen asked.

"Now you're talking, ma'am. Thugs and whores rule the alleys in Khayelitsha Township where I live. I have to get paid some other way."

"Who do you live with?"

"My brother."

This was life in the heterotopia he called home. An innocent childhood had been robbed of its sweetness by a heartless world and perpetual squalor in the township where he lived, a place simultaneously mental and physical, incapable of being defined.

"Is this your only source of income?" Suri asked.

"Afraid so," the boy said. "I used to be a runner in drug deals and a go-between for pimps and thieves, but now I work the streets in a more wholesome way."

"I see."

"No risk in peddling, miss, but if get caught trespassing, I'll be arrested or worse."

"Name your price," Suri replied.

"I'll do whatever you ask for five hundred rand."

"Deal."

"Pay me now."

"Why?"

Jack went for his wallet.

"My brother is sick. He needs medicine to get well."

The boy smiled as he collected the money.

"Thank you, sah. Now where did you last see your son?"

## 15

Suri exited the hotel with the mysterious man. He escorted her to a limousine where a chauffeur nodded and opened a rear door.

"Where are you taking me?" she asked.

The mysterious man didn't answer. He ducked his head inside, then reappeared suddenly. "All clear," he said without emotion. He held forth an open hand. "After you."

They sat opposite one another in the back of the limo. As its wheels began to turn, so did Suri's mind. She recounted events of the day as a logician traces the course of a costly gem in transit. Her destination was still unconfirmed.

The mysterious man adjusted his collar. He poured three fingers of bourbon into a tumbler and said, "Should I drink alone?"

"If you insist."

He reached for a bottle.

"Miss Cohen, are you surprised that some of the greatest heroes and heroines from centuries past fell into their roles unexpectedly?"

The question was delivered with utmost appeal.

"No."

"Most interesting lives entail an unanticipated turn of fate."

"Profound. But why are you telling me this?"

"Men and women aren't political animals, as some elites proclaim. Rather, we are prisoners of a frail nature doomed by the worst decisions we make."

Suri sipped her bourbon slowly. Already she was more at ease.

"At the heart of the human narrative is our awareness that no amount of encyclopedic knowledge creates our destiny or makes it less mutable. Herodotus put it best when he wrote of a nameless Persian soldier who predicted his army's defeat and remarked, 'The bitterest pain to human beings is to know much and control nothing.'"

Suri's thoughts went to a simpler time, to the memory of playing alone in her adopted father's office while he was away. As a girl, she had dreamed of swooping in to save the day as a famed heroine of yore. She fixated on the prospect of becoming something more than a high-ranking financier her family wanted her to be. Because of her gender, she had almost dispensed with lofty dreams. The potential for grand accomplishment had all but escaped her mind until a heart-to-heart with her mother inspired her to press on.

Determined women invariably met resistance for asserting themselves throughout the Middle East. But instead of vexation, she drew strength in the face of adversity. Discrimination would not distract from any goal at hand. By eighteen, she had entered her sophomore year of college and qualified for Israel's Olympic Swim Team. At twenty, she won first place in Europe's largest triathlon. By twenty-three, she had earned two master's degrees, one in engineering and another in Arabic. Still, her potential was not recognized by anyone of note. Amidst a culture of prejudice and subterfuge she aspired to do something noble.

"Go on," she said.

The mysterious man savored his bourbon.

He said, "You're about to know a lot, and control a lot too—more than you ever thought you would."

Suri imagined the eccentric man was right.

The limousine raced eastward along M2. They passed a primary school, an empty church, and Heideveld Mosque, located due south of a busy interchange.

"Where are you taking me?" Suri asked. "No more games. I want to know."

"A facility close to Pretoria, the headquarters of SAS."

Blood pumped harder and faster through her neck and chest. It was there that her ex-husband had died during a rigorous training exercise.

"Any questions?"

"Just one," she answered.

"Go ahead."

"Why me?"

The mysterious man responded candidly. "The answer is simple. Liberated women with Western-leaning sympathies don't grow on trees. You've been tapped as an asset who deserves a chance to shine."


The flight to Pretoria was not idle time.

Suri read the *SAS Manual on Tactical Espionage* as the mysterious man updated Foster, responded to emails, and requested backup in the form of a dozen Special Ops who were to arrive at a secret location near Bo-Kaap in less than a week. By then Suri's tactical training would be complete, provided she achieved each benchmark as her mentor had planned.

A perfect score on the college entrance exam was evidence of her ability to perform most any intellectual task. Her history as a gold medal recipient in Olympic swim competitions made no one question her physical might.

They deboarded the aircraft in Pretoria and made for a chopper that awaited them in the same airfield. As the bird levitated over a busy tarmac, Suri adjusted her headset and her eyes darted at the mysterious man.

"Am I your first recruit?" she asked.

"Yes. As we said in surgical residency: see one, do one, teach one."

Their Hummer roared into the rural outskirts of Gauteng Province. Minutes later a commando dressed in combat fatigues saluted them at the entrance to SAS Headquarters. A sign in front of the guard shack read: Reconnaissance Commando School, Est. 1976, We Fear Naught But God. Known locally as the Recces, South Africa's Special Forces Brigade is the nation's primary Special Ops unit comprised of counterinsurgent elites who specialize in reconnaissance capabilities and novel parachute techniques.

The mysterious man made the agency's selective nature clear to Suri. He said, "Less than 10 percent of recruits receive induction into the prestigious club. If successful, one enters the ranks of a heralded group of freedom-loving warriors who are highly secretive and expertly trained."

Suri didn't balk.

"An athlete of your caliber should do fine, unless you're hiding a weakness we haven't seen."

They entered the barracks. A set of fatigues and a maroon beret with its distinct laurel blade emblem lay on a cot.

He said, "I'll give you a few minutes to change and meet you outside."

Suddenly, she felt quite alone. Now that her big break had come, what would she make of it? Her background as an endurance swimmer had surely prepared her for the rigor of any physical test. Still, she had no idea what to expect.

Dressed in her new fatigues and maroon beret, she exited the barracks and wiped a bead of sweat from her brow.

The mysterious man did not delay.

"Your first course is the mental fitness test. We'll begin right away."


Back in Cape Town, Jonas savored interactions with a crowd. In a crowd was opportunity.

After a dry run at Farmer's Market on Wednesday morning, he scaled Longmarket Street with eyes peeled, then scampered in front of a café and clothing store. A motor vehicle crash in a roundabout drew stares from rubberneckers as an ambulance crew attended an injured child. Minutes before, a taxicab had slammed into the rear of a cargo van. An assembly of onlookers was small. Disinterest grew as people turned away. A medic applied a splint to an injured girl not quite preschool age.

Jonas edged closer. His instinct sharpened as he approached the scene. He squatted beside the van, his pupils fixated on two children who sat on a sidewalk a few meters away. They were boys, about his age, dressed in Muslim garb. But they were not like other Muslim children he had seen. They were fair skinned, Europeans, he presumed. He peered at one of the boys who looked back at him, but the boy was not there. His face held an empty gaze. Was he in shock? The crash had been a minor one. Hardly a dent was made.

A policeman questioned the driver. Their exchange was too animated. Something was amiss.

"These children are severely malnourished," the medic said.

"That's impossible," replied Ali. "They eat three meals every day."

"All of them are badly bruised, looks like this one has scurvy."

"We were jerked about in the wreck."

A black sedan stopped next to the cargo van. The police commissioner and a man dressed in a dark business suit approached. The commissioner called the head officer away. They shook hands and spoke to Ali before an envelope was exchanged.


Suri passed the mental fitness test without a hitch. Next came arms training.

Six-dozen targets were set at distances ranging from thirty to three hundred meters.

Low clouds drifted west as heat blazed from the brightest sun. The mysterious man handed a carbine to his trainee.

He said, "The arms course typically lasts two days. You may forego the second day with a score of thirty-eight to forty during your session this afternoon. I'll give you a few minutes to warm up. You need to stay hydrated in the heat. Would you care for something to drink?"

"No," she answered stoically.

He turned and made for the barracks.

She employed the carbine shoulder high. "A warm-up isn't needed."

*Ka-pop! Ka-pop!*

The mysterious man took another step and froze. Cautiously, with a hint of nervous expectation, he turned to observe a most impressive site.

*Ka-pop! Ka-pop! Ka-pop!*

In the easy way she maneuvered the rifle, she might have been a seasoned military vet. The weapon was her bitch. She exhibited perfect technique.

*Ka-pop! Ka-pop!*

Suri alternated targets of variable lengths, hitting the bull's eye dead center a half-dozen times.

"Not bad, soldier. Can you do it at night with thirty kilos of gear strapped to your back?"

"I don't see why not."

"Follow me," he said.

She set the carbine aside.

"You shoot as skillfully as we were told."

"I was the first female president of Valley Gun Club in Cape Town last year, and led a tour of hunters on week-long safaris in Namibia on holidays."

He smirked. "Yes, I heard."


They made tracks to the barracks where a hearty lunch of gemsbok and potatoes awaited.

The mysterious man sat across from his trainee.

He stirred a glass of fresh tea and said, "A nation's security is often at risk due to a knowledge deficit on the part of policymakers. Look no further than a government's reliance on Special Ops as a panacea for policy failures. The divide between politicians who make the rules and those who play by them is vast and widening. In many cases our objectives are at direct odds with theirs.

"When executed properly, laws pertaining to interrogation of enemy combatants benefit the cause of freedom immensely.

But when politics gets in the way of prudent intelligence, consequences are unfortunately lethal. Coupling budgetary restraints with a naïve worldview is undeniably dangerous. What's needed is balance between practical austerity and compassionate diplomacy.

"Leaders of the finest intelligence communities in the world maintain constant contact with each other. During the '80s, Mossad and CIA gained a reputation for superior training in a never-ending quest to preserve Western ideals. After the enemy's successful execution of the September 11 terror attacks, there was a concentration of power and influence at the highest level of Mossad. Cooperation with forces that keep the world safe became stronger, more transparent, and more mutually beneficial than ever before. In the wake of attacks on the World Trade Center, the wealthiest families in the world felt threatened by the rise of terror. They too underwent a consolidation of power and influence. Consequently, those put in charge of select families turned to Mossad for protection and delineation of a survival plan that uses methodologies developed in anticipation of evolving peril.

"In cooperation with SAS, Mossad provides greater security with fewer personnel comprised of hardened professionals and veteran hit men whose expertise is never in doubt. Through unconventional espionage techniques we accomplish more with less, in contrast to governments that are plagued by paralyzing bureaucratic rules. Our plan is simple, and has been adopted by the world's richest bloodline, whose headquarters were relocated to Reunion Island two hundred kilometers east of Madagascar. As the saying goes, it's lonely at the top, but the view is worth isolation."

Suri took a bite of meat.

The mysterious man stayed on point. He said, "We recruit men and women who are in some way detached from the world, yet able to thrive therein. In today's intelligence community, there is a critical need for professional types who have affinity for hostile and politically unstable regions. We bring about lasting change in those locales through use of direct, time-sensitive, low-visibility missions that employ indigenous forces, whose regional knowledge informs our own and increases the chance for success.

"Typical special operators are emotionally mature and highly trained. Most are twenty-eight to thirty-five years old, married with a family, and have at least eight years of active duty experience in general purpose forces. Your dossier is unique. We like that about you."

Suri nodded.

"Your cultural and linguistic training, physical and mental toughness, and dual master's degrees set you apart from all but our most coveted assets. You'll meet them in time."

"Has your next mission been finalized?"

"No. We haven't identified a firm civilian or military target yet, but all signs point to one that is highly sensitive. If instinct serves me right, we're looking at special recon, hostage recovery, and counterterrorism missions all rolled into one operation. Thus, we expect a mission with considerable risk.

"The challenge is to limit potential hostage casualties and soften their impact on civilian life. Furthermore, a breach of security at any number of locales would upset world markets in a matter of minutes. Our goal is to temper reactions and restore peace and routine commercial activity as soon as possible.

"If successful, the mission will deliver a lethal blow to the enemy, upset global terror networks, and be readily visible to billions of people across the globe."

Jack and Carmen returned to the *Royal Flush*. Foster met them inside.

They needed time apart. Both acknowledged that.

"I'm going to lay down," Carmen said. "Let me know if the authorities call."

She wiped a tear and trudged up the stairs.

A minute passed. Neither man spoke.

Jack held his face in one hand then turned to his trusted advisor.

Foster said, "No one of your stature can rely on government in a situation like this."

The multibillionaire agreed.

He needed a plan.

## 16

Carmen fumed with anger.

"I'm not overreacting, Jack!" She shoved a brochure in his face. "Read this!"

Jack sighed as his eyes swung back and forth over a page.

Laos

Tse left his tiny village in southern Laos to find work in a nearby town. He had no formal education and supported his mother and grandmother after his father died. A trafficker promised Tse he could earn $170 a month stitching garments at a factory in Thailand. He trusted the man because he was a fellow Lao, but never made it to the garment factory. Instead, the trafficker took him at night and pushed him into a van bound for the coast of Thailand. When Tse stepped out of the van, he was met by a watchful gunman who led him to a fishing trawler. For two years, he heaved nets of fish during the day without rest. He ate and slept on a crowded deck with dozens of children whose language was different from his own. He was beaten regularly.

Tse watched his traffickers beat a fellow child laborer until she died. After two years of forced servitude, he escaped in a boat and ran through the jungle until he reached the home of a witchdoctor who took him in and gave him money for a taxi ride to the Lao Embassy in Bangkok. From there he returned to his family where he lives today.


Jonas perched on a windowsill outside the second story of Auwal Masjid. His wide, expectant eyes peered into a vacant room that had once been a library. He inhaled deeply, then flung himself through an open window. Silent as an insect, he descended a staircase. Halfway down, his eyes beheld a horrific scene.

Three-dozen children dressed in white robes stood with their backs against a wall. A solid black mask, semiautomatic rifle, and bowie knife rested on the floor in front of each child.

Rauf stood at the minbar. He said, "At last, dear children, your Day of Triumph has come. Today you are warriors for Allah, and no longer bound by manmade law!"

Masked gunmen strapped bombs to the children who shouted, "Allahu Akbar!"

Rauf marched back and forth. "Are you ready for jihad, little ones?"

The children responded in unison, their clinched fists thrust in the air. "Allahu Akbar!"

"It is the will of Allah for you to wage jihad against all infidels, be they Christian or Jew!"

The children shouted louder. "Allahu Akbar! We are martyrs for Islam!"

"Ah, yes, my little ones. This is your Day of Triumph! The time for jihad has come!"

Twin pigeons squawked next to Jonas.

Nathan peered up at him. "Look!" he said, a lone finger raised at the boy. "He's watching us!"

Jonas spotted Nathan. One of the birds squawked again.

Rauf threw a nervous stare at Jonas. He turned to scurry away and as he did a young, gaunt man drew a knife and held the blade against his neck. It was Asram.

"No, Asram!" Rauf exclaimed. "Put your weapon down!"

Again, the children screamed. "Allahu Akbar! We are martyrs for Allah!"

Asram dropped the knife.

Jonas leaped onto a rooftop. His breaths became heavier as the prospect of his capture seemed inevitable.

Rauf made for his office. A laptop uploaded the day's encrypted email. An urgent message from Riyadh captivated his attention. Had the Saudi prince agreed to meet with him? His nervous eyes soaked up every word: Château de Chillon, Lake Geneva, 7 January, 9:00 a.m.

He fell to his knees.

Could it be? Had decades of unwavering devotion to jihad at last gained the Crown's attention? Had the Afghan opium cartel become too powerful and too lucrative for Saudis to ignore?

He needed to plan and scheme. With less than a day to prepare for the most important hour of his life, Rauf had no choice but to leave someone else in charge. He had just enough time to tidy up the week's opium orders, arrange delivery, book a flight, meet with Ali, and pack before his red-eye flight left Cape Town.

He entered a password to decode an encrypted email, and was elated to read, "Order: Qur'an, 10,000 copies."

He thought, *Ten crates at a million dollars a pop.* Fate had anointed him. His nervous eyes scanned the screen again.

Ali rapped on the office door.

"You wanted to see me, Imam?"

"Have a seat," said Rauf. He folded the laptop shut.

Ali sat on a metal chair across from him. His big belly shown under a long flowing robe.

"I'll be away for a couple of days and am leaving you in charge. It's a great responsibility, but I believe you are ready."

"I appreciate your confidence in me, Imam. All will be kept in order. May I ask where you are going?"

"To a meeting in Europe. Nothing to fret about. Keep an eye on the Goldwyn boy. He's of great value to us."

Leyla heard every word as she kneeled in a nook down the hall and waited for Ali to pass.

She rapped once on the office door and entered the room.

"Who's there?" Rauf demanded.

"I know all about your sick game," she said, pointing a finger at him. "Your evil scheme is by no means justified by any religious act."

"What game?" the anointed one pleaded.

"Turn yourself in or I'll go to the authorities myself."

Rauf popped up from his chair. He said, "Do it and you'll surely die."


Rauf exited Auwal Masjid with a piece of luggage on wheels. He stepped onto the sidewalk next to Dorp Street and spotted a woman he'd never seen before.

She approached him without delay, whether Muslim or not he couldn't tell. Her mood was determined and sure.

"Pardon me," she said, "I'm looking for my roommate, Leyla. Is she here?"

"She's busy in class. May I help you?"

Her phone buzzed. Suri peeped at the only word on the screen: BLOCKED. She swiped to answer the call.

"Hello?"

"What are you doing?"

"I'm sorry. Who is this?"

"Who are you working for?"

She raised a hand and covered an ear. "I think you have the wrong number."

"Miss Cohen?"

"Yes. Who is this?"

"Watch your back."

The voice had no emotion.

"Excuse me? Who is—?"

Dial tone.

As she stared at the screen, the phone buzzed and a message appeared: Stay away from Auwal Masjid.

It was then Suri realized she had entered a clandestine league. As a child, she had eavesdropped on many a call inside her family's home. But now she had dispensed with make-believe.

A moment later Rauf was gone.


"What did you see?" Suri asked.

"A ceremony," Jonas answered, gasping for air. "It was creepy. There was a snake charmer with a bamboo flute and dancing cobras. I saw children being trained by a terrorist who put contraband into their backpacks."

"What else?" Carmen said.

"A sermon about jihad. The imam blessed the children, then I left."

"How come?"

"The imam was onto me."

"Was Nathan there?" Suri asked.

"Yes, I saw him."

"Is he safe?"

"I think so, for now. But I fear they are planning something big." Jonas wiped his brow. "Auwal Masjid isn't a haven for children. It's a terrorist breeding ground where children are turned into suicide bombers in preparation for jihad."

Carmen wept and looked at Jack. "Oh, my son, please tell me this isn't happening!"

## 17

It was a grand occasion. Attendees had come from across the globe. A continuous stream of private jets taxied into terminals at Cape Town International. Names on the guest roster were synonymous with the world's uber-rich. A caravan of limos awaited those who arrived in time for dinner the night before. Posted outside the sleek high-rise on Castle Street: Sotheby's Diamond Auction, Wednesday, 5 January, 0900, Invitation Only, Interpreters will be provided.

Bloody Marys were poured during a scrumptious brunch. Tablecloths were neatly pressed. Employees donned tuxedos and attended the needs of every patron.

The auctioneer said, "Good afternoon, ladies and gentlemen, and welcome to Sotheby's.

"The Archduke Joseph Diamond, a seventy-six-point-zero two-carat cushion-shaped diamond, of perfect D color and internally flawless clarity, possesses a charm like no other. Its impressive size and superb quality, combined with its Golconda origin, makes it one of the world's most famous and desirable stones. It was named after its first recorded owner, Archduke Joseph August of Austria."

A crowd of four hundred fell silent.

"Little is known about the exact history of the diamond, but it is believed that Archduke Joseph August passed the diamond to his son, Archduke Joseph Francis. Records show it was deposited into a vault at the Hungarian General Credit Bank on 1 March 1933 in the presence of a state counselor. Three years later, it was sold to an anonymous buyer who deposited it into a safe during the Second World War. The diamond reappeared in 1961 at auction in London, and subsequently in November 1993, at Sotheby's Geneva where it sold for $6,480,000. Sale of the Archduke Joseph Diamond presents a unique opportunity for established collectors."

Hands were raised throughout the floor as bidding became intense.

Located on the ground floor of the building was a nursery and day care for children and grandchildren of Sotheby's guests. Boys and girls played croquet on artificial turf. Others held hands and danced around idle playmates, as another group of children laughed and played on a swing set while their babysitters looked on.

A caterer's van stopped in front of the building.

"ID, please?" a security officer said as he adjusted his belt.

The driver handed over his license.

"Thank you," the officer said. He recorded the driver's name and age. "I'll note your tag number as you park. Good day."

The driver nodded back at him and the van edged forward.

"Okay! It's lunchtime! Everyone inside!" a woman inside the day care cried.

"Yay!" The children sang as they raced into a spacious room.

The caterer's van came to a stop at the front door of the day care. Each side of the vehicle held a collage of familiar logos.

A middle-aged, pale-skinned Arab man exited the passenger side and made for the rear of the over-sized van. His head was covered with a baseball cap, sporty sunglasses shielded his eyes. The van backed toward the building's entrance, beeping a half-dozen times before coming to a halt. The man at the rear spun his head right and left, then opened the doors of the van.

All clear. He gave a signal to his partner and shouted, "Allahu Akbar!"

The men covered their faces with masks and prepared to enter the high-rise.

One of the sitters opened the front door, and as she did, two tranquilizer darts met her in the neck.

"Nobody move!" the driver said with a thick Middle Eastern accent.

The children gasped.

A woman said, "Boys and girls! Come this way!"

Bewilderment filled the room. A frightened girl fell to her knees. The children gasped and cried, too afraid to resist the men.

"Let's go!" the driver screamed.

"No, please!" the sitter pleaded. "In the name of God, I beg you!"

"Allahu Akbar! We are martyrs for Allah!"

"They're only helpless children! Please, take me!"

"Now!"

Gasping and crying, the little ones filed into the back of the van.

Both sitters were left behind. Where was the building's security team?

As the last child was shoved into the cargo van, the driver spun his head.

The van proceeded through downtown and accelerated east on M4 before exiting onto a two-lane road. It went south for a kilometer then made a sharp left turn onto another road abutted by a hayfield. After turning into the field, the van stopped at two hundred meters. The men moved quickly around four corners of the vehicle to unclamp latching mechanisms before climbing into the loading bay and closing the door behind them.

The deafening sound of a heavy cargo chopper was upon them instantly. With military precision, the rectangular cargo bay of the van was engaged by the aircraft and lifted away from the chassis. The bird ascended a thousand meters and headed west toward the sea.

## Interlude in Tel Aviv

By 9:00 a.m. Thursday, the usual crowd had assembled at headquarters.

Seated in the conference room were Reuben, the prime minister, Mel, and a half-dozen support staff.

"How did we get to this point?" Reuben asked.

"Good question," Mel replied.

"Are diplomatic efforts really that futile?"

"Seems that way."

"Anyone with half a brain would assess this situation and arrive at the same glaring question."

"And that is?"

"What is the origin of the conflict that swept across the Arab world during the last few years?"

"By conflict you mean—"

"The answer is the Arab Spring."

"But its origin is anyone's guess. Inflation? Religious persecution? Ethnic conflict?"

"No, it's not anyone's guess," the prime minister intoned.

"Enlighten us," Reuben said.

"Most scholars agree, the Arab Spring, or as some have called it, the Arab Awakening, set the entire region on a predictably dangerous course."

Mel said, "We've all heard the term Arab Spring, but what was its impetus? How did the movement give rise to global terrorist threats we face today?"

The prime minister assumed a momentous tone. He said, "In most Middle Eastern nations, political leaders rise to power in a vacuum. In 2010, a series of violent demonstrations and protests coalesced into a political and economic movement that would have been considered a revolution at any other point in history. However, conditions for such a revolution were made ripe by the very authorities that refused to label it as such."

"By authorities, you mean the United States?" Mel asked.

"Yes, I mean the United States, whose foreign policy left a power vacuum which created the spark that led to the Arab Spring. Turmoil spanned multiple countries, each of which had its own inherent causes and contributing factors."

"Why did Arabs rebel? Was it not because of increasing poverty, rising food prices, and human rights violations, not to mention unacceptably high unemployment?"

The prime minister did not stall.

"The Arab Spring resulted from the failure of the War on Terror that was waged chiefly by the United States and its European allies. It occurred because of a failed attempt by those same governments to import American and Western European democracy and self-government into a region antagonistic to both. For time immemorial, revolutions have occurred when great masses of people perceived themselves as unable to live happy and peaceful lives due to economic hardship and political oppression. Events took place that changed the nature of society and political landscapes that determine an individual's chance of living a happy life.

"Consider Tunisia, where revolution occurred because of the self-immolation of a street vendor named Mohamad Bouazizi, who was arrested and beaten by police for the crime of failing to register his vegetable cart. Bouazizi attempted to reconcile with local officials who refused to meet with him. This innocent, peace-loving man, Bouazizi, set himself on fire, an act that exemplified people's rejection of the status quo. While he was dying in hospital, anti-government demonstrations sprung up throughout Tunisia and were the direct result of his actions. Bouazizi died on 4 January 2011. Ten days later, Tunisian president Ben Ali fled the country. Bouazizi's self-immolation and subsequent death gave rise to a wave of protests that sparked uprisings throughout the Arab world. Riots and demonstrations erupted in Algeria, Jordan, Kuwait, Morocco, and Oman. Seven years later, Syria is still in a civil war.

"It all started with a humble, yet heroic street peddler. Within three years of Bouazizi's death, Mubarak was ousted from power in Egypt, Qaddafi was driven out of Libya, and Ali Abdullah Saleh gave up the fight in Yemen. The reason for each leader's demise was simple. In the case of Mubarak, it was because of an increasing income gap and the widely publicized fact that half of Egyptians live on less than two dollars a day."

The prime minister was not done. He faced the group and said, "Ladies and gentlemen, the lessons of the Arab Spring are clear. The first is imposition of individual freedom is not practical in a region dominated by escalating unemployment, political corruption, and lack of freedom. The second is that America's political leadership fails to appreciate the critical role a dictator plays in the pursuit of peace in the Middle East. The longer an autocrat stays in power, the shorter time it takes for him to be removed. Saddam Hussein, Hosni Mubarak, Muammar Qaddafi, Bashar al-Assad—all were stabilizing forces in their respective countries. To remove any of them from power was to create a vacuum that would be promptly filled by militant jihadists such as ISIL, a group that may as well have been formed, albeit inadvertently, by the United States."

Mel asked, "Is it wise for us to blame the United States for the Arab Spring? Is America not our strongest ally?"

"Of course, the United States is obviously our strongest ally, but its degree of involvement in the Middle East shifts with each change in administration."

"Where do al Qaeda and groups like the Muslim Brotherhood fit into ISIL's agenda?" Shiffman asked.

"The Muslim Brotherhood has grassroots support in Egypt. Similar religious groups in the region garnered widespread attention throughout the Arab Spring. Strained diplomatic relations between the West and predominately Muslim nations magnified the importance of Islam in the Arab world. This is especially true since the fall of the Soviet Union, which kept Islam in check.

"Imagine a county ruled by a dictator. There is no constitution or free press, no right to vote or civil discourse, only a ruling theocrat or monarch with absolute power. Then, almost overnight, the populace is given a constitution, freedom of assembly and press, and a national election during which a new leader is chosen. How should people, who for centuries have lived under entirely different political circumstances, be expected to conduct themselves? It's no surprise that regimes propped up by Western influences don't last in the Middle East. By necessity, lasting democratic reforms occur only following significant loss of life in war."

Mel said, "What does the enemy perceive as the chief function of Islam?"

Reznik paused. His mind simmered his answer a bit longer than the one before. He folded his hands on the conference table and said, "Jihadists believe Islam should guide the creation of society and that governments not based on Sharia Law are apostate and, thus, legitimate targets of jihad. Their expressed goal is an Islamic vanguard. ISIL is a jihadist terror group formed in the spring of 2013 as a spawn of al Qaeda. Its expressed purpose is to create an Islamic religious state based on Sharia Law in Iraq and Syria."

"Is the State of Israel prepared to enter the ranks of nation builders?" an advisor asked.

"Historically, Israel has opposed regime change in neighboring states. Unknown dictators may be more dangerous than those we know. In some instances, we have strongly opposed such changes. For example, we were displeased with Mubarak's removal in Egypt, which had become our strongest ally in the region and Israel's primary supplier of energy. He, more than any world leader, knew the importance of peace with Israel."

"Now we're in a hellhole," an advisor said.

"Okay," Reuben said. "Let's dig our way out."

STARNER JONES

## 18

The meeting was held on Friday at Château de Chillon, a medieval island castle on Lake Geneva just south of Veytaux. Located at the eastern end of the lake, on a sliver of earth between Montreux and Villeneuve, the architectural jewel affords a breathtaking view of never-ending pines and cedars in the Rhone's Alpine valley. One gazes at the castle and calls to mind Victor Hugo, Lord Byron, a romantic poem, shiny chalices on an ancient dinner table, a Roman outpost, striking chateaus in a quaint hillside village framed by snowcapped tips of Dents du Midi.

Three men sat in a spacious room overlooking Lake Geneva: the leader of the Palestine Liberation Organization, the minister of petroleum from the world's most valuable private company, Saudi Aramco, and his sidekick, who was a strategic representative of the same.

Rauf was last to arrive.

"Did you know Lake Geneva forms the shape of a crescent?" the PLO leader said.

"No, I didn't," the Saudi oil minister replied.

"It is the will of Allah that we should meet."

"Indeed," the minister said. He sat in a Victorian chair.

"The beauty of this splendid lake has long been celebrated, but it is only from the easternmost end between Vevey and Villeneuve that it assumes an Alpine character. Southward, the mountains of

192

Savoy and Valais are rugged and somber, while those of the northern shore unfold in vine-covered slopes, villages, and sprawling castles. All are striking, but none as magnificent as this."

The minister agreed. He said, "It is a fitting venue for this occasion. How should we proceed?"

"With a mutual goal in mind," the leader replied.

"And what is that?"

The PLO leader stood. He faced the lake with clasped hands tucked behind his waist. Piercing rays of sunlight glistened over the lake. He said, "For misguided Sunnis, armed struggle is a way of life. Diplomacy is little more than a flippant head nod to pragmatism and, in the case of the Palestine Liberation Organization, a necessary gesture made to pacify a compromising UN."

The minister interrupted him. "Civility and cooler heads be damned. Jihad and ego matter most."

"Some would agree."

"You are not sold on jihad?"

The leader of the PLO faced the minister. "No more than you."

"Explain," the minister implored.

"Founded in 1964, as the sole legitimate organization with liberation of Palestine its only goal, the PLO is aptly named. Its stated objective is plainly written, its claim of cooperation never rescinded. But how many celebrated treaties have been flatly ignored? How many peace accords foiled by those with something to lose? How many deals have been retracted? How many covenants broken? How many attempts at mediation and geographic realignment rendered inert? How many innocent lives have been sacrificed? And yet the organization, whose ethos is personified in a never-ending and murderous jihad, carries on as the West exchanges a myopic view of the Middle East for total blindness and diplomatic decay.

Since 1974, the PLO and its observer status have seemed out of place for a gang of Muslim men held as a terrorist organization by the United States and Israel until the Madrid Conference in 1991."

"For good reason, don't you think?"

"No. Remember the inaugural summit in Cairo in 1964? What happened there?"

"I haven't the slightest idea," the minister said.

"The devolution of Palestinian advocacy."

"What does any of this have to do with oil?"

"It was an activity that morphed into the next phase of perpetual jihad unrecognized by all, except the Arab League."

"Saudi Aramco is the Kingdom's economic engine and the largest private oil company in the world currently valued at $10 trillion. My company has only one concern."

Rauf had been waiting to speak. "And what, may I ask, is that?"

"Crude oil," the minister said stoically. "Our sole aim is to serve the Kingdom and maximize profit from the sale of crude oil drawn from our reserves."

"What if we could help you accomplish just that?" the leader asked.

"How?" At least the minister had not yet left.

"With cessation of commerce through the Strait of Hormuz."

"Anyone who breaches security in the Strait would create a global oil crisis in a matter of hours."

"Precisely. And in so doing assume an upper hand in Middle East negotiations."

"Control of production and distribution of oil is the decisive factor in defining who rules whom in the Middle East. We are entirely comfortable with opinions major world powers have of our company."

"What about justice for my people?" asked the leader.

"I'm sorry?" the minister replied.

"How long will Zionists be allowed to occupy our land?"

"I'm a businessman, not a scholar or diplomat. My only concern is the bottom line."

"My people's future is in your hands."

"What do you mean?"

"After the Oslo Accords, negotiation and diplomacy became official policy. Ancient history mandates that because of two peoples' claims to a disputed land, the nation of Israel cannot be simultaneously occupied in peace. The Balfour Declaration, a Mandate for Palestine, and actions based on them, are null and void. Claims of historical or religious ties of Jews with Palestine are incompatible with history and the concept of statehood. Judaism is a religion, not an independent nationality or secular creed. Nor do Jews constitute a single people living in a nation with an identity of its own. They are merely citizens of the state in which they reside. Nothing more, nothing less. Palestinians are Arabs. We possess legal right to a homeland, our homeland, and have the right to determine our destiny in accordance with a collective wish. This is all we ask. The PLO has always, above all, labeled Palestinian people as Arabs. This was a natural consequence of the PLO beginning as an offshoot of the Arab League. It also has a tactical element to ensure the backing of Arab states. In recent years, Arab identity has remained a natural impetus of the Palestinian State. It is a reference to the Arab State envisioned in the UN Partition Plan."

"What does any of this have to do with me?"

The leader paced back and forth. He said, "Sir, I've come to offer you the prospect of an enormous return in exchange for a simple favor."

"You have my undivided attention."

"We've established that any breach of security in the Strait would create an imminent global crisis."

"That is true. Iran has tried numerous times and failed miserably."

"Only because it had no cooperation from people who matter."

"Right again. The risk of war and subsequent sanctions are unacceptably high."

"What if there were a guarantee, an assurance of peaceful resolution in such a crisis?"

"You mean no chance of war?"

"Yes."

"How could this be?"

"It's a presidential election year in the United States. The US is war weary. Billion-dollar campaigns are in full swing. Any candidate who hints of a brewing conflict will be met with certain defeat."

"Are you suggesting that my company ignore a security breach in exchange for a proximate spike in the price of crude oil drawn from reserves in the Middle East?"

"I am indeed," the leader said. "Now do you understand? My people's future is in your hands. I hope we can reach a deal. Your company would reap untold profits from sale of crude oil in a crisis that would afford me an upper hand in negotiations with Jerusalem."

"I see."

"Time is ripe for another fatwa," the leader said, "and now we have a suitable target."

## 19

A week had passed since Nathan had disappeared.

Helicopters swarmed over Bo-Kaap. A hostile mob festered on Dorp Street.

In the stillness of the worship hall, Asram kneeled on a rug. His prayer was simple and clear. He faced the minbar and rocked back and forth as his voice intoned, "Subhana rabbiyal adheem" (Glory be to my Lord Almighty).

Ali approached from behind him. "We have to escape," he said with unbridled alarm.

Asram interrupted his prayer. "What? Abandon Auwal Masjid?"

"We have no choice. The crowd is growing restless. They could overtake us any time."

"What about the children? Where will we take them?"

"Wait here," said Ali.

Asram grew tense as moments passed. As a child, Islamic dogma repelled his fears and protected him from doubt. But now he was older, and his soul yearned for truth. Orthodoxy weighed heavily on his mind. When he was young, Islam kept him in line and nourished his soul. When he was old, it would give him peace reserved for obedient imams.

"I need you," he cried aloud. "Imam? Tuan Guru? Blessed Prophet, I need you."

Rauf was divinely inspired to speak on behalf of Allah. His opinions had influenced Asram's every word and deed. Sunni doctrine was irrevocable truth, the only kind that mattered, and rightly wielded by learned imams to govern decadent people who had not been tamed by personal epiphany or moral guilt. But the anointed one was not there.

Asram sat on a chair, legs crossed, and fingered his thin goatee. Thunderous sounds from a chopper grew louder as it hovered close to the masjid. His smartphone alit with an urgent message. A fatwa had just been released.

Ali dashed up the stairs. Spotlights crisscrossed windows on the second floor. Outside the mosque, television crews camped at the corner of Dorp and Büitengracht. A reporter loitered at the front entrance of Auwal Masjid.

Panting for air, Ali stepped into the spotlight.

The young woman faced a television camera and offered a summary of the week's events. She said, "Day four of the standoff in Bo-Kaap where authorities say a special needs child, the son of billionaires Jack and Carmen Goldwyn, disappeared last Sunday. Throngs of protesters have shown constant support for a mandatory raid of mosques in the area in attempt to locate the boy. With me now is Ali, a worshipper at Auwal Masjid. Sir, what is your response to happenings in Bo-Kaap this week?"

Ali wasted no time. His answer was firm and plain. "Invasion of the holy space is an affront to Islam. This would never be tolerated by the West. We have no information about the missing boy and are as mystified about his disappearance as those who are looking for him."

The reporter pressed him more. "Can you tell us the condition of children who are housed in the Madrassah at Auwal Masjid?"

The next moment Rauf appeared. He approached the reporter and grabbed her microphone.

He said, "The Madrassah at Auwal Masjid is not just a madrassah that doubles as an orphanage, but rather fertile ground for intellectual and spiritual growth for children of all races whose parents are not around to see after them. You see, my friends, we Muslims take care to raise our children in preparation for life in a free, civilized, and democratic society."

"Terrorist!" a protester yelled. "Islam is a farce!"

"Jihad will not be tolerated!" another screamed.

Moments later the raucous crowd drew near Rauf. Hundreds of protesters raised clinched fists as they shouted in unison. "Is-lam sucks! Is-lam sucks!"

They paced back and forth and cried, "Raid the mosque! Raid the mosque!"

Ali's spirit shrunk with dread. He had no buffer zone to separate him from the maddening crowd. His phone buzzed as a fatwa appeared on screen: "Time is ripe for Zionists to surrender land which is rightly ours and has been since antiquity. Death to infidels, be they Christian or Jew."

On the tenth floor of a high-rise, Leyla reclined on her bed. She advanced the channel to local news and turned a page of her favorite magazine. As she scanned the page, a news anchor reported the day's events.

"Violence broke out today in Cape Town as Malay Muslims called for an end to persecution they claim has rocked their otherwise peaceful enclave in recent days. Conservatives called for a raid of the oldest mosque in the country, located on Dorp Street, after billionaires Jack and Carmen Goldwyn reported their son missing while visiting Bo-Kaap on 2 January. Five-year-old Nathan Goldwyn remains missing at this hour."

Leyla heard a knock on the door. She cringed and dropped her phone. In an instant, a masked intruder was inside her apartment.

An automatic rifle nudged her chest as the man's terrifying voice said, "Greetings, Miss Leyla. Why don't you come with me?"

Carmen gripped the silver cross that hung from her neck as she waited with Jack in the foyer of the mayor's office.

A receptionist said, "The mayor will see you now."

South African politicians are as coy as any other. The mayor was predictably brief. His scant grey hair was not simply the result of age. Something else was to blame. Embezzlement of public funds? An extramarital affair? The latest in a flurry of public scandals?

Mayor Frohm was a tall, thin man. One saw him and thought he might live another year or two at most. He said, "I'm terribly sorry about your son. I wish there was something I could do."

"We believe there is," Carmen said.

The mayor didn't answer.

"You can start by granting police the authority to search the Madrassah at Auwal Masjid for evidence of stockpiled weapons and contraband."

Frohm nodded and darted his eyes at Jack. He said, "You know that isn't possible. To do so would risk escalation of a tenuous situation and create more danger for everyone involved."

"More danger?" Carmen said in disbelief.

"It's a matter of public safety, you see."

"Public safety?"

"I must refuse your request in the name of—"

"Political correctness," said Jack. "It's modernity's primary concern."

"No, in the name of religious freedom."

"Whose freedom?" Carmen asked.

"Malays are entitled to practice what they believe."

"My son is missing in your city and all you offer is concession to Islam?" said Carmen.

Jack said, "Let's go, dear. I suspected this would be a waste of time." He reached for his wife's hand as they turned to leave.

In a corner of the mayor's office, white linen sheets partly covered bold letters stamped on a large wooden crate: HOLY BOOKS—HANDLE WITH CARE.

News of a homespun kidnapping ring penetrated airwaves. Copy desks buzzed with unease. Danger was all around. It lurked in shifty shadows, narrow alleys, seedy streets, ragged prayer rugs, and crowded mosques. Local television stations aired continuous coverage of the week's events. A boisterous mob descended on Bo-Kaap.

By sunset Friday, a full-scale riot ensued and halted commerce in the Mother City, whose citizens were paralyzed by constant alarm. A reporter and cameraman marched up Dorp Street as furious crowds gathered on opposite sidewalks. Hundreds of Sunni men barked as wild dogs hungry for fresh meat. Elder members of the mosque stood in silence and held a simple cardboard sign that read, PALESTINE IS OUR HOME.

Asram paced back and forth in front of the masjid. He adjusted his turban and shouted in synchrony with the crowd: "Allahu Akbar! No peace for Israel!"

A group of whites across the street shouted, "To hell with terror!"

A Dutch reporter held a microphone as a camera rolled. She said, "There is growing concern in Cape Town about a possible kidnapping ring reportedly headquartered in the building behind me, Auwal Masjid, the nation's oldest mosque, located on Dorp Street. Authorities say it was here, on these streets, that a boy, Nathan Goldwyn, son of a prominent Jewish multibillionaire on holiday with his family, went missing during the Cape Minstrel in Bo-Kaap earlier this week. Young Nathan was last seen by his parents on Wale Street. As of now—"

The woman was overcome by a wave of sound that emanated from across the street. A thousand protesters representing a myriad of races and creeds shouted, "Raid the mosque! Raid the mosque! Raid the mosque!" She turned to the camera, her hands struggling to steady the microphone.

Protesters jammed the entrance to Auwal Masjid. By eleven o'clock, the few dozen Malay men who guarded it were no match for an army of freedom lovers who had come to set Nathan and other children free from the yoke of radical Islam.

The crowd stormed Dorp Street with axes and sticks and forced their way into the mosque through street-level windows and the main entrance that faced east. Upon entry into the masjid, Carmen and Suri found an empty prayer room.

"Nathan!" Carmen screamed.

Suri yelled as loud as she could. "Hello! Is anyone here?"

Not a single child was seen.

Carmen panted, shoved a protester aside, and raced to the second floor.

"Nathan!" a fireman screamed. "Children!" His voice echoed upstairs.

Suri kicked down the door of the basement office. She spotted a wooden crate in the corner and lifted a handle. As she did, an unmistakable odor of freshly spilled heroin penetrated her nares. She jerked her head away and gasped.

Within minutes, every room of the mosque had been searched. No trace of a child was found.

"Boys? Girls?" Suri exclaimed.

No reply was heard.

The ravenous crowd searched every room in the mosque.

Where did the children go? When did they leave? By what route had they exited?

Carmen slipped on a rug and fell.

"Are you okay?" Suri asked.

"Yes, I'm fine, only a scratch." She reached for a rail by a staircase, and as she did a plank on the floor gave way.

"My foot, it's jammed!"

Suri stood close by. One heave at the slender hallway rug dislodged her foot and, more importantly, revealed a pivotal clue—a handle on a trapdoor.

Could it be? A hidden passage in the basement of Auwal Masjid? Where could it possibly lead?

Suri leaned forward on her knees. Her hand drew open the door.

"Is that . . . ?" Carmen asked.

"A tunnel. Yes, I'm afraid so."

"Anything else?"

"A handwritten note."

"What does it say?" Carmen asked. She peered over Suri's head.

In bold letters, it read: DEATH TO INFIDELS.


Midnight on Dorp Street was bright as day. Camera lights beamed over sidewalks and storefronts as reporters hastened to deliver the chilling news.

Good evening. We are in Bo-Kaap, where hundreds of people have just raided South Africa's oldest mosque, Auwal Masjid at 43 Dorp Street.

Critics of radical Islam have long suspected foul play inside madrassahs and orphanages throughout the Muslim world. Nathan Goldwyn, son of billionaire Jack Goldwyn, disappeared earlier this week. The boy's mother claimed to have evidence that madrassahs inside mosques all over the world double as holding areas for victims of human trafficking and breeding grounds for future terrorists.

Sources familiar with the matter say Carmen Goldwyn will call for United Nations involvement during a press conference outside Parliament tomorrow. Authorities have called for confirmation of Mrs. Goldwyn's assertion. Her request for police involvement was not granted, though law enforcement in riot gear are present here tonight.

A muezzin sang the call to prayer from a mosque on Chiappini Street. More than a hackneyed tune heard only now and then, it resonated as a memory one could not shake. It wafted through streets of Bo-Kaap and a lone window facing east.

Rear doors of a cargo van sprang open. Two-dozen children filed out of a manhole and crammed into the back of the van. Heavy doors slammed shut.

Ali's knuckles turned white as he held the steering wheel. He sped under a traffic light as it turned red.

"Watch your speed!" Rauf said. "We're almost there!"

The van rounded a corner and proceeded north toward the port where a fishing trawler and a half-dozen freighters were unloaded.

A reporter updated viewers from Auwal Masjid. She said, "The headless body of Cape Town resident Charles Fernandez, known by locals as 'Taco Negro', was found earlier today just steps away from the cannon at Noon Gun. The heinous act was recorded on video released minutes ago. The man's body was identified with a tattoo of his nickname on the right forearm. His murder is believed to have taken place last week."

Protesters formed a circle around Carmen in the worship hall. A reporter pushed a microphone in front of her and said, "Why did you say the Madrassah at Auwal Masjid was a cover for a global Muslim kidnapping ring headquartered in Cape Town?"

"Because it is," Carmen answered. "There is no madrassah or orphanage at Auwal Masjid. It's a terrorist breeding ground where children of all ages and creeds are turned into suicide bombers."

"But, ma'am, your son Nathan is not here. It seems the raid failed to confirm your assertion."

"My son has been taken away along with dozens of children who were kidnapped and held inside the mosque. The time has come for the civilized world to face the dragon of radical Islam head-on, and we are leading the fight."

The reporter asked, "Why did you report that children here were victims of abuse?"

"Because it's true."

"How can you make such an accusation without a shred of evidence to support your case?"

STARNER JONES

"We have plenty of evidence. We have first-hand intelligence from someone who infiltrated the mosque. I stand by the claim."

"What do you have to say about your claim that Nathan was taken by a kidnapper connected to the mosque? Why did you report a connection between the mosque and radical Islamic terrorists in Yemen?"

"My husband and I have close ties to someone intimately familiar with happenings at Auwal Masjid. Imam Rauf is the mastermind of a global opium cartel and jihadist kidnapping ring that has operated inside his mosque for decades. He has a vast network that spans more than seventy-five countries on six continents. Our source has uncovered his connection to ISIL and al Qaeda operatives in Syria, Iraq, Afghanistan, and Yemen. He is a menace and a scourge to humanity and will be eliminated."

"Why have authorities not acted on this information?"

"Ask your friends at Interpol."

"But ma'am—"

Carmen faced the bright lights and camera head-on. "We will stop at nothing to find our son."

## 20

Graveyard shifts at Container Terminal were busier than daytime. Volume surged as an industrial whistle blew the stroke of midnight.

A thunderstorm blew in from the west.

Rauf yanked open the guard shack door and pointed a rifle at the security chief.

"Come with me," he said with a portentous air.

The man raised his hands and stood.

Thick drops of rain popped on a metal roof.

"I want the fishing trawler."

"But—"

"I want it now."

"Sir, I—"

"Now!" He stabbed the man's neck with the gun barrel.

The security chief reached for a key.

"Fuel is very low."

They hurried onto the trawler as the storm became more severe. Rauf peered at the fuel gauge. The chief's assertion was confirmed.

"Let's go!"

A veteran ship captain appeared. "What the hell is going on?"

Rauf raised the gun. The captain turned slowly. Rauf kicked the door shut as the man started to leave.

"Not so fast. You're coming with me." He poked the rifle barrel in the captain's back and the two men deboarded the boat.

The fishing trawler skirted away from the port with Nathan and other children on board, along with Leyla, Ali, and the security chief who steered it.

"Faster!" Ali shouted.

He stared angrily at the chief, smacking a rifle against his head.

"I told you, it's low on fuel!" he pleaded. "We're going as fast as the engine allows."


Back at port, Rauf stood next to the ship captain.

He said, "Do as I say and you won't get hurt. Understand?"

Jihad had been the anointed one's lifelong dream. The Madrassah was wildly successful. Until now, no one knew. Untold public funds were used to support an expressly Muslim cause, and still no one complained.

Rauf's mind burned with contempt. His hatred for Christians and Jews boiled to the point of rage. He would sacrifice everything for a promise of eternal peace in the world to come. Contentment had eluded him in the earthly realm, hence his commitment to a life of service in the name Allah.

Asram looked on as Rauf pressed the gun into the captain's chest.

"What do you want from me? Just say it. I'll do anything you ask."

"Is the *Maersk Mandela* your ship?"

"Yes."

"Lucky you. Care to show me around?"

A few kilometers northwest of Cape Town, Robben Island rose in an eternal sea. Its history was as varied as those who had lived there. You saw it under a night sky and imagined a whaling station, a leper colony, maritime peril spawned by mutiny on the *Meermin* slave ship.

Children of all ages sat quietly as they listened to Ali. He said, "To understand the human experience, you must first understand the dynamic nature of Islam. Only then can you understand why we refuse to assimilate into non-Islamic cultures. Rather than conform, Islam must conquer those who oppose it. Only then will you see your parents again."

The little ones gave a collective gasp.

"Do not fear what you do not know, children. Let the holy Prophet reveal eternal truths to you." He held a colored poster for them to view. "First, Allah created, from his glorious light, the light of Muhammad (May Peace Be Upon Him). Then, Allah created all other creatures from this perfect and wonderful light of Muhammad.

"Allah then divided Mohammed's light into four parts. From the first part, He created the Supreme Throne. From the second part, He made the writing pen. From the second part and third part He created denizens of souls called the *lauhe mahfooz*. He then divided the fourth part into four separate parts. The first was used to create angels bearing the throne, the second part was fashioned into His wondrous throne, and with the third part He created angels known as *farishta*."

Nathan was confused. He said, "Mister, with all this splitting, is anything left?"

Leyla whispered in the boy's ear then escorted him away.

Ali said, "Once again, He divided the fourth part into four other parts—the first went to creation of the heavens, the second part was used to create the Earth, and from the third part He created heaven and hell. Again, he divided the fourth part into another four parts—the first was used to create radiant eyes of believers, the second was used to create light for souls, the third part was used to create the light of *Kalema* (La Ilah Illa Allah Muhammad-ar-Rasul Allah). And with the last part Allah created the rest of the Earth. *Subahanallah!*"

The children were clothed with matching smocks. Comportment emanated from their faces as they sang.

*Ya Ilahi ta qayamat ye chaman taaza rahe*
*Har shajar, har nakhl iss ka phoolta, phalta rahe*
*(O, Allah, may this garden be flourished 'til doomsday*
*May every tree and every branch of this garden flourish and blossom)*

Ali stood before the children. "All right, little ones. Time for your evening med."

They formed a line and waited.

Nathan sobbed. "I want to go home!"

Ali's massive hand grabbed the boy's neck and squeezed.

"Ouch! You're hurting me!"

He stabbed the boy's arm and injected a colorless juice.

Rauf wielded an AK-47 as the Maersk freighter was pumped full of fuel.

A dark sky lurked over Cape Town. Dim light from a quarter moon glowed on a glossy surface of the enormous ship.

A clock in the galley turned 9:00 p.m. It was time to pray again.

Asram prostrated on a scrawny rug. Its frayed ends called to mind his childhood cut short by a Zionist bomb. He rocked back on his knees and adjusted his turban. Led to radical Islam by a fatal combination of desperation and hurt, his jihad had begun many years ago, but the present mission was not as he envisioned.

The ugly patchwork of his life would never change. He heard the bomb explode again in his head. His mind was cursed by perpetual gunfire that echoed down a fiery street. His mother's wounded face was forever etched in his mind. Frantic cracks of a bazooka ricocheted off thatch huts where his fellow Muslims lived. Bullets penetrated the mosque where his father prayed. A young woman screamed over her injured baby on a dusty street. Her cry was like childbirth without the ensuing and redemptive joy a mother feels after labor has ceased.

He bore hysterical madness of heartfelt grief and pain of losing his parents for no reason at all. Life had become almost unbearable to him. Asram recalled an admonition the anointed one had taught, the edict that was in strict accordance with holy Islam. *Assalatu khayrum minan naum* (Prayer is better than sleep).

There is something enticing about radical Islam: the promise of spiritual purity, of fame, and an endless supply of virgins are too appealing for desperate men to resist. Islam preys on idle minds and offers irresistible possibilities to reach one's full potential through participation in a never-ending holy war. Jihad is satisfaction of every primal need: food, clothing, shelter, and, above all, perpetual war. Hopeless men need only vow to live and die as militants, and in return receive unlimited access to rewards offered by grateful and charitable imams. Devotion to the cause ensures entry into a global society whose leaders take orders from none other than Allah.

Asram had once been poised to serve Islam at any cost and recruit other desperate men to wage jihad on the liberated, secular

West. Submission had been antecedent to victory. Thus saith the Qur'an, "Islam is the only divine and holy remedy."

But something about the present mission gave him pause.

The freighter idled near Robben Island.

"Take me to shore in one of your skiffs," Rauf demanded. He aimed the rifle barrel at the man's chin.

The captain obliged. "Anything you say, holy man."

Rauf stormed into the kramat and pointed the gun at Leyla. Ali bound her hands and feet to a chair, and then covered her mouth with a slab of tape. She looked with horror as Ali slammed Nathan onto the floor. He gagged the boy with a rope so tight he couldn't speak.

Whack!

Rauf socked him square in the face with the back of his hand. Blood spurted from the boy's nose.

Leyla squirmed wildly on a chair.

Asram observed from across the room.

Rauf approached him in an uncontrollable rage. The anointed one stood over his protégé and declared, "Ali is coming with me. I'm appointing you lead warrior in jihad."

Gallantry rushed in his head. Asram knew this was his lucky break, the opportunity he had long awaited. He set his eyes on Nathan. The vulnerable boy was a fitting sacrificial lamb. His Jewish father might well have fired the missile on his family's village in Sana'a.

Asram stood next to a window. A cool breeze kissed his face. He peered toward the heavens in an evening sky. Freedom seemed a lifetime away.

But something prevented him from harming the boy. The small, tender voice in his head said no. His chest was heavy with sadness he could not shake. A clear conscience held him back. His head was filled with madness unfit for a wayward youth who had only his life to lose.

Asram had once found peace by heeding the words of the anointed one, but now he was trapped on a highjacked ship, and forced to execute a despicable terrorist scheme.

He caressed his thin goatee. "Why am I here? What have I done, and why is Rauf so mean?"

Jonas ripped back the curtain in his tent. His brother lay on a threadbare couch.

"What's up, bro?"

"Not a thing." His older brother lifted the bad leg with both hands.

"How's your pain?"

"About the same."

Jonas tossed a bottle of pills.

He said, "Bo-Kaap is on fire tonight."

"Yes, it was on the evening news. Did you just come from there?"

"No. I watched from a few blocks away."

"Do you know who kidnapped the boy?"

"No, but I saw him in the mosque on Dorp Street."

"You went to Auwal Masjid?"

"Yes, someone paid me to check it out."

"Bro, I told you. When are you going to learn? White people use us as pawns, especially Jews."

"His parents are very nice."

"Don't be fooled. They paid for you as a slave. I fear you've been suckered in."

"Let it go, okay? I pray he's still alive."

"Me too, but he may already be dead."

"I hope they find who took the boy and give them what they deserve."

A hush came over the tent, then Jonas said, "Remember those things that cannot be hidden, as grandpa used to say."

His brother repositioned the useless leg.

"Tell me."

"The sun, the moon—"

He paused and stared at the dirt.

"Wasn't there something else?"

Jonas lifted his head. "The truth."


Asram sat on a cot. He stared abjectly at a wall less than a meter away.

Rauf entered without warning.

"What's the matter with you?"

No answer.

"Are you not ready for jihad?"

"No, Imam."

"What?"

"I want to leave."

Whack!

Rauf walloped him on the back of his head.

Asram fell to the floor. He cringed in pain.

"Don't you ever say that to me!"

Rauf spat in his face.

Asram crawled to a corner. He brandished a rifle and panted.

"Touch me again and I'll kill you."

"Is that so?"

"Try me, fucking bastard."

"Where did you get that weapon?"

"Fuck you."

Rauf's eyes boiled with fury he had never known.

"Fuck you!"

He pushed the rifle into Rauf's forehead.

"Faisel Rauf, I ought to kill you!"

Rauf made a move for the gun.

"Kill you!"

Asram pulled the trigger and Rauf lost part of an ear. The anointed one cried out as a stream of blood spurted onto the floor.

Asram hobbled up a stairwell. His head spun right and left.

Desperate to flee, he smashed a glass cover with an elbow, pressed a button on a metal encasement, and lifted the handle. A moment later an emergency skiff deployed.

He slid down the hatch in a fit of sheer panic.

His lonely heart beat faster. He knew not what the next hour would bring.

## 21

As morning broke over the Western Cape, Robben Island sprang to life.

A turquoise-domed kramat commemorating Moturu, Prince of Madura, one of the region's first imams, stood on the north end of the island.

Nathan awoke before Ali and the rest of the children. He sensed a chance to run, tiptoed to the rear of the kramat, and exited through a doorway. A stiff wind stopped him on the beach, where African penguins frolicked with geese and leopard tortoises as hundreds of rabbits hopped on the sandy shore facing Table Bay.

He peered longingly at the mainland rising from the sea. Desperation overcame him as he jumped and waved. "Mommy, Daddy, over here!"

A mushy object washed up next to his feet. The boy looked down, and as he did, blood drained from his face at the sight of Leyla's severed head on the beach.

Suri sat at a table with Jack and Carmen on the *Royal Flush*. The mayor, the provincial minister for community safety, and Captain Lou stood by.

"We've searched every mosque and public shelter in Cape Town," the mayor said.

The provincial minister left no stone unturned. He said, "Are you sure? What about the old schoolhouse southeast of town?"

"Marhaba Muharram?" Suri asked.

"What's that?" Carmen said.

"An abandoned madrassah close to Rylands High School where Leyla graduated. She was forbidden from visiting Marhaba Muharram by Rauf."

"Wonder why?" Carmen said.

"The building should be condemned," the mayor chided. Too often his comments seemed out of place.

"Do you know how to get there?" said Jack.

Suri threw a wary glance at the dubious mayor. "Yes, I do. It's on the same block as International Peace College at the corner of Duinestraat and Johnston Road. The building is easily seen from Flat Road near Rondebosch."

"I've passed the locale hundreds of times while driving to and from my office," the provincial minister said.

Jack looked at the mayor glumly. "Clearly, it's worth a look."

A half hour later, members of Cape Town's swat team manned every entrance into Marhaba Muharram—Habibia Mosque as it was locally known. The building had an unforgettable façade with minarets sprouting up like giant turnips, the largest painted white.

Jack and Carmen arrived with an entourage.

"Oh, god! What's that smell?" Carmen said.

Frohm was obviously concerned. He had presumed the area's largest mosque was clean. Befuddled, he stammered over an excuse and said, "Sanitation has always been lacking on this side of town. We've replaced many a septic line, but the four odor remains."

Jack stepped into a hallway and the stench became stronger. A pool of urine was mixed with blood.

"Better alert the medical examiner."

The provincial minister reached for his phone.

Dirty needles and empty bags of heroin were scattered on the floor. Mildew thrived on sheetrock walls.

"Why is it so hot in here?" Jack said.

"I wondered the same. Maybe a heater was left on."

The swat team fanned out through the mosque, searching for clues in every room.

Carmen said, "Honey, do you hear that?"

The sound was episodic and faint.

"Yes, I do."

Ambient light from a remote window turned dim. Carmen yelped. She crept behind Jack down a flight of stairs. Suri followed. With each step, the sound became more intense.

Suri raised a flashlight over Jack's shoulder as they went deep into Marhaba Muharram.

The sound was like none Carmen had ever heard. "That awful noise, where is it coming from?"

Jack reached for a doorknob. A sliver of light showed at his feet.

"Careful," Suri implored.

He ripped open the door and a zoo of vermin shrieked. A mouse ran up Carmen's leg as rats clamored in aggressive retreat.

A trio of cobras recoiled and fanned their hoods as Carmen screamed.

Two members of the swat team appeared. "Ma'am, are you okay?"

Jack said, "Escort her outside, please. It's time for us to leave."

Carmen was assisted as she walked up the stairs.

The swat chief stood by an entrance with Mayor Frohm and Jack. As he wiped his brow with a cotton rag, he said, "We found a closet stuffed with corpses on the second floor and several empty wooden crates that smell like opium."

Jack stared at the mayor, who rolled his eyes obstinately and excused himself for the rest of the afternoon.

"In addition, we've seized more than eighty semiautomatic machine guns and a hundred thousand rounds of ammo."

"Whoa."

"Impressive, don't you think?"

"Indeed. Anything else?"

The swat chief replied, "The crates were labeled as holy books, but I haven't seen the first Qur'an."


Captain Lou opened a rear door of the black sedan. "Any luck?"

Jack said, "Nothing you wouldn't expect from certifiable psychopaths."

"Is there any place else you'd like to go?"

"What about the funny-looking shack on Robben Island? We passed it coming into port."

Suri perked up. "Oh, yes, the Morturu Kramat. I saw it once with Leyla during a tour of the prison where Mandela was held."

"Should we take the ferry after lunch?" Carmen asked.

"No, we're going now," said Jack.

Captain Lou was ready for action. "Wanna take the chopper?"

"Yes. Should be a five-minute flight."


The chopper sprayed a plume of sand as it landed on the rocky beach.

Jack and Carmen ran to the front of the kramat.

A speaker by the door played a horrific sound.

"Allahu Akbar! Allahu Akbar! . . ."

Jack stepped inside and beheld a child's head on a stick atop the martyr's grave. He tried to shield Carmen from the hideous sight, but was too late. Carmen shrieked.

With their precious son still missing, they had no place to turn and no place else to look.

Carmen's knees buckled as she wept. Tears of rage ran down Jack's cheeks as Suri embraced them.

Jack said, "This is a declaration of war. I'm going to Tel Aviv."


The old fisherman snoozed in his lean-to as shadows shifted on a sidewalk next to Burg Street. A rotten smell emanated from fish skeletons piled in a bucket next to his bare feet. He awoke to the pain of ants biting his blistered toes.

"Ay, be off. Will ya, mates?" He kicked one foot with the other to scatter the insects as he yawned under an afternoon sun.

It was four o'clock and his morning catch had been scanty. He had delivered only two kilos of Galjoen to the market in Table Bay and used his earnings to purchase a carton of milk and a loaf of bread. After a mid-day snack, he slept for an hour until insects brought his mind back to life.

He traipsed along Adderley Street and made his way east to Ocean Road. The old man watched as a giant metal container swung over a freighter. He recalled his father's stories from decades working as a crane operator in Tanker Basin. Having nothing but time, he walked along Marine Drive and passed Blastrite Harbour, using a cane to assist each step. From there he could not help looking back at the lively port as his mind flashed an image of his father as he arrived home weary from labor.

By dusk he had reached Lagoon Beach and sat peacefully on the sand. In the distance, automobiles hummed over a bridge on M1. Aromas from Wang Thai Restaurant intensified discomfort from hunger he had felt all day. The old man peaked over his shoulder at a row of bronze statues lining one side of the restaurant and yearned for a meal. Tourists on the patio feasted on roasted duck topped with red wine, ginger, and honey sauce. He sighed and reflected on his unfortunate lot in life.

Evening tide slid over the beach. Suddenly, he felt alone. Fleeting light from a January sun flickered over seashells, and his eyes were drawn to an orange raft a hundred meters from shore. He stood and peered at a man floating in the Bay.

"Hello!" the old fisherman called. "Are you okay?"

Hopeful eyes widened as he stood tall on the sand.

At once he was no longer alone. His eyes lit with purpose. A weary heart beat stronger than the minute before. No longer could he watch from shore. Eager to help, he untied a lifeboat from a pylon on the dock and reached for a paddle. A summer moon glowed in the sky, illuminating an empty beach.

"Hello!" The old man paddled fiercely. "I'm coming for you!"

The surf weakened as night fell over Mother City.

"Oh God, give me strength."

He paddled as quickly as he could.

As the fisherman approached the raft, he heard the man's breaths and a gurgling noise.

"Don't die on me," the old man implored. "Don't you dare!"

Asram looked up at him. In a weak voice, he pleaded, "Help me."

The old man smiled as a tear trickled down his cheek.

"You're going to hospital, my son."

Son. There was the sobering term again. It had followed him to the brink of death.

Son . . . my son. The word summoned emotions he couldn't escape. But this time he was grateful, instead of repulsed. There was hope for survival at the hands of a decrepit vagrant, no less.

"Where to?"

"Somerset Hospital in Green Point."

"On Portswood Road?"

"Yes."

"How will we get there?"

"Faith," said the fisherman. "How else?"

"Good thinking, old man."

"Hey. Watch it, boy."

"What do you mean?"

"I'm not your old man."

Asram struggled to speak. "It's a term of endearment."

"I don't need your pity."

"It's not pity."

"Ay, this is no time to argue, my son."

It seemed Asram couldn't get away—from tender words and caring men, from life, hope, and, most of all, random acts of love.


Within two days the *Maersk Mandela* had entered the Gulf of Oman. On Sunday at dusk, the freighter passed north of Muscat, and at 0600 the following day, the first light flickered through low clouds as the freighter dropped anchor in the Strait of Hormuz. By noon local time, fears of a geopolitical conflict impacted global oil markets, causing Brent crude to soar 30 percent.

Phones rang incessantly at International Maritime Headquarters in London. The Secretary General fielded calls from world leaders and corporate executives with interests in the region, and deflected the most important ones to Reznik's staff.

## Interlude in Tel Aviv

Reuben skimmed a memo at his desk.

Mel tapped on the door. She walked briskly into his office.

"Good morning, sir. We have an update from London."

"Do tell."

She sat in a leather chair across from him.

"The prime minister wants no part of the action."

"No surprise. Any news from DC?"

"Washington is mired in a presidential campaign. Candidates are too skittish to comment publicly."

"Or too afraid," Reuben smirked. "Have we anyone else to suspect of the kidnappings?"

"No one," Mel said.

"Where is Foster when we need him?"

"He didn't return my call."

"That's not like him."

"PLO escalated its message overnight, saying your accusation was an assault on Islam, and moreover this would never happen in the West."

"For once, they're right. We don't kidnap helpless children."

A landline buzzed. Reuben engaged the audio.

"Yes?"

"Sir, a Mr. Goldwyn is here with Dellon Foster."

Reuben's eyes darted at Mel.

"Speak of the devil and look who appears."

"We'll meet them in the conference room," the director said.

"He says the United States president is expected to arrive at headquarters before traveling to Moscow. The meeting was arranged by Prime Minister Reznik earlier today."

Reuben had long considered impromptu meetings as a way of life, but an unexpected meeting between the United States president and a multibillionaire whose son had been kidnapped surprised even him.

Foster entered the conference room with Jack.

"Good morning, Dellon."

"Morning, Abel. It's been a while."

The men shook hands.

"It has indeed."

"Any news?"

"None," Foster said. "I'd like you to meet someone." He turned. "Abel Reuben, Jack Goldwyn."

"Pleased to meet you, Jack."

"Likewise," Goldwyn said.

"How can I help?"

Foster said, "We've come to ask a favor of you."

"Anything for you, Del."

"We'd like you to record a meeting with the United States president."

"Here?"

"Yes."

"You mean today?"

"Yes, right away. We're expecting him anytime."

"That shouldn't be a problem."

"Jack has a proposition for him."

Reuben looked at the billionaire.

"I see."

"Hello, Jack," said the president of the United States. "Nice to see you, although I wish it were under different circumstances."

Jack waved a hand. "I'd like to ask a favor of you."

"I'll do my best," the president said. "What might you need?"

"Are you really this naïve?"

"Pardon me?"

Jack Goldwyn stood toe to toe with the United States president, his face no more than hand's width away.

He said, "There is no cause for speculation anymore. Radical Islam, in the form of ISIL, is behind all of this, as well as a global opium cartel that has been used to fund terrorist activity by al Qaeda and ISIL for more than half a century. The organizations are sophisticated in form and operation, and their joint motive is clear."

"Sure, it is. They want peace."

"Peace?" Jack said with an air of disbelief. "You think terrorists kill innocent people in the name of peace?"

"We'll be going now," Foster said, starting to rise.

The prime minister entered the room.

Jack Goldwyn was not done. His face turned blood red as he faced the president and said, "You, sir, are an imbecile."

"Now wait just a minute," the president replied.

"What the hell is going on?" Reznik intoned.

The president replied, "The situation is under control."

"Jack Goldwyn," the prime minister said, "How long has it been?"

Jack did not respond.

"You haven't changed a bit."

"I take that as a compliment coming from you."

"I see. Still think the world revolves around you?"

Jack grew more furious. He turned to the president. "Under control? Dozens of tankers holding untold volumes of crude oil pass through the Strait of Hormuz every day. It's the world's most pivotal location for international trade."

"I understand."

"Clearly, you don't, so let me explain. Sealing off the Strait of Hormuz will wreak havoc in oil markets. The Strait is a two-way thoroughfare connecting the Persian Gulf with the open sea. To the north lies the Islamic Republic of Iran; to the south, the UAE.

"Observers in Dhahran and Doha study radar data collected with military drones designed to track movement of vessels as they enter the Strait. Close attention is paid to the Traffic Separation Scheme, a two-kilometer buffer zone dividing incoming and outgoing traffic."

The president was stolid and terse. "Mr. Goldwyn, I understand."

"Really? You understand? I just spoke with an official in Dubai who keeps a record of the course and speed of each ship. What have you done today?"

Silence.

"The official said the *Maersk Mandela* broke every nautical rule when it entered the Strait, and completely ignored the security checkpoint."

"My god, how did they get away with that?" the prime minister said.

"Ask the Saudis," Jack said. "This morning in Dhahran, a watchman Skyped with cameras positioned on buoys and estimated the number of barrels of oil that left the Strait each hour. By sundown, one-fifth of the world's petroleum supply will pass anchorage points near the tip of Musandam, an enclave of Oman."

The president's eyes glassed over.

Jack slammed his fist on Reuben's desk, and then turned away. He peered at Foster.

"Fucking politicians! They don't know a goddamn thing."

The president tried to appease him. He said, "Both sides must agree to concessions if peace is to be achieved."

"Peace through sacrifice of an entire homeland?" Jack said. "Have you lost your mind?"

Reznik said, "Israel will not sacrifice land we rightly call our own."

The president countered, "The Middle East has always been mired in gridlock."

"This is what I get for contributing a million dollars to your campaign?" Goldwyn asked.

"I'm sorry, Mr. Goldwyn," said the president. "By the way, what was the favor you wished to ask of me?"

Foster said, "Let it go, Jack. Don't waste your breath."

The president turned. "Surely, you understand."

"I understand," Jack said. "I understand exactly. This is an election year."

"And the stakes are just too high. Whatever it is, I cannot grant your wish. To do so would jeopardize my reelection bid. I wish you the best."

"Pundits will have a field day with this," Jack said.

"With what?" the president asked.

"This entire conversation has been recorded."

The president was outraged.

"Fuck the pundits! Who are they? Self-labeled experts given to ceaseless inquiry, and yet forever in the know?"

"What a shill you are. I should've known—"

"I've had enough of your game, Mr. Goldwyn."

The president tried to leave. He shoved Foster aside and made for the door.

Jack blocked the exit.

He said, "I should've known better than to expect a noble deed from you during a reelection campaign."

"How would that look to the rest of the world, to Saudis, Iranians, and other Arab nations who've been devoted allies of the United States?"

Foster whirled his head. "Devoted allies?"

Jack said, "You think Iran and Saudi Arabia are devoted allies?"

Reznik weighed in, "Both nations are known sponsors of terror."

Foster said, "Islam once lay dormant in the Western Cape. Now radical extremists are on a meteoric rise. You want to know why?"

Silence.

Jack awaited the president's reply.

"Because of your naïve foreign policy, that's why," Jack implored.

Foster said, "South Africa boasts more than four hundred mosques. You think they built themselves?"

Again, the president was mute.

The billionaire struck a serious tone. "Expansions of radical Islam can be directly traced to funds sent from the largest mosques in Riyadh and Tehran. By 2030, the world's Muslim population will exceed two billion, with many becoming radicalized. Israel lives under a constant threat of extermination, and you have the nerve to question Israeli sovereignty?"

The president said, "Challenges to land ownership in present-day Israel are as old as the land itself. It's anyone's guess who the land really belongs to."

Reznik was beyond dismayed. He said, "That isn't true. It isn't true at all. Countless historical documents and archeological finds attest to our claim that the territory occupied by present-day Israel does in fact belong to descendants of ancient Hebrew people."

The president did not respond.

Jack's knuckles turned white. He stepped close enough for the president to feel his breath and said, "Millions of Muslim youth lack direction in a desperate world. Martyrs become immortal because of dedication to a greater cause. What would happen if the son of a bitch who kidnapped my son were caught?"

Every man was still.

"Religious tolerance is a useful tool for corrupt elitists like you, and those who serve their own interests in the political realm. The mere perception of racism is as heinous as child rape for government types. Anyone who breaches the sacred ground is sacrificed on the altar of public shame, and humiliated for committing an unforgivable crime. The lesson of the day is simple: Political correctness serves terrorists well."

## 22

The Goldwyns hunkered down at King David Hotel in Jerusalem the following day.

Suri met Jack and Carmen for lunch just before noon.

Foster's phone buzzed as a cryptic message appeared. It was Ari. He typed a code to decipher the words: What do you want me to do?

Foster drew a deep breath and exhaled slowly.

"Who's there?" Jack said.

"An asset you should meet."

"Who?"

"A disgruntled operative tired of bullshit at Mossad."

"You know him?"

"Know him?" Foster chuckled. "I recruited and trained him."

"Who is he?"

"Code name is Ari Bloom."

"Is he worth a damn?"

"Best I've ever seen."

"Pedigree?"

"His father left soon after Ari was born."

"What about his mother?"

"Retired, lives in Haifa, the nervous and overbearing type. She was very demanding when Ari was a boy."

"Siblings?"

"A brother, three years his junior."

"What became of him?"

"A hungry and half-witted lawyer. Lives in Berlin."

"Sisters?"

"None."

"What do you make of him?"

Foster was effusive in his praise.

"More than suitable, a prototype. He has a photographic memory and is fluent in seven languages."

"Vices?"

"He has a penchant for expensive scotch and busty dames who talk too much."

"Arrests?"

"None."

"Sounds promising. Can you bring him here?"

"Yes, sir." Foster stood. "He's arriving in a limo now."


A few minutes passed as they awaited Foster's return.

He entered the suite with the asset in tow.

"Jack Goldwyn, Ari Bloom."

"Hello, sir," Ari said.

Jack stood and greeted him.

"Thank you for coming."

They shook hands.

"I'm here to serve." Ari nodded at Carmen and Suri.

Foster said, "We have a genuine crisis on our hands, a perfect storm with an ignominious president in the White House, and a feckless prime minister to boot."

"Best I can tell, all politicians are the same," Jack chided.

Foster did not object. He said, "They know almost nothing about the Strait's geopolitical importance."

"Who controls it?" asked Jack.

They sat in a half circle.

"We all do," Ari replied.

Jack rolled his eyes in disbelief.

Foster agreed. "To some extent he's right. Vessels pass through territorial waters of Iran and Oman under transit passage provisions of the United Nations Convention on the Law of the Sea. Not all countries have ratified the convention, however. Most, including the United States, accept customary navigation practices affirmed by the Convention."

"Who keeps watch over the Strait?" Carmen asked.

Ari said, "Unfortunately, no one. Oman has a radar site known as the Link Quality Indicator to monitor the separation zone. It's positioned on a small island at the peak of Musandam Peninsula."

"God help us," Jack said.

"Does any of this address religious origins of the conflict?" asked Suri.

"We can't stop jihadists from killing themselves," Foster answered.

Ari said, "Not until heaven runs out of virgins."

Foster continued, "Disruption of maritime activity in the Strait would produce a catastrophic turn in the world's oil market. Moreover, Iran has said repeatedly that it would seal off the Strait if attacked by Israel or the US. Not to be outdone, a US commander has warned that such an action by Iran would be considered an act of war, and the US would not permit Iran to hold captive a third of the world's oil supply. While opinions vary on the matter, most petroleum strategists agree that Iran could impede traffic in the Strait for at least a month, and any attempt to reopen it would escalate the conflict. Since Iran would negotiate from a position of power in all future diplomatic negotiations, one can reasonably expect the nation to welcome any crisis in the region."

Jack's opinion was fitting. He said, "The survival of the free world hinges on our ability to promote maritime peace and commerce in the Strait of Hormuz."

A light flickered on the telescreen.

"Is that a fatwa?" Carmen asked.

All eyes turned to the television. Uncertainty cased over the room.

Rauf appeared on screen. He sat behind a desk and wore a plain white robe.

He moistened his lips and said, "Bismillah. In the name of Allah, May Mohammed Be Blessed and Peace Be Ever Upon Him. Greetings, infidels. We have your precious children. They are in safekeeping now. Our request is simple. To avoid death of your children and the wrath of Allah, renounce Israeli statehood by sundown Friday and declare Jerusalem the capital of Palestine. You have until five o'clock local time to grant our request."

His visage froze on the screen.

Soon his fateful words were heard all over the world, forever etched in the minds of ordinary folk and ruling elite, fervent believers, and infidels of every race and creed.

A moment later the screen turned black.

Reuben's phone buzzed at headquarters.

"Hello?"

"Reuben, this is Jack. Where's Reznik?"

"In my office."

"Let me guess. Sitting on his ass?"

No reply.

"Will the West ever get serious in its fight against radical jihadists who murder in the name of Islam? Just once I'd like to see world leaders find the courage to stand together and say, 'Enough.' As long as common sense takes a backseat to political correctness, we'll continue to lose the War on Terror."

Reuben agreed.

Jack ended the call.

A minute later Reznik's phone rang.

"Hello."

"I ask that you grant their request," Jack said.

"How did you get my number?"

"I have ways. Do we have a deal or not?"

"That is totally beyond the realm of possibility," the prime minister replied.

"If I had contributed to your campaign it would've happened already."

Reznik didn't argue the claim.

"It would give us time to plan."

"Jack, I understand Nathan's kidnapping is upsetting and you seek his recovery at any cost, but your proposal is untenable and I cannot grant the request. Countless Israeli soldiers have died to preserve freedom of our Jewish state, let alone innocent women and children who lost their lives in jihadist attacks on numerous markets and shops. Our nation has the most advanced reconnaissance capabilities the world has ever known. Your son is not alone. Dozens of Israeli children are on the ship with him. Their families are equally distraught as you are, and rightly. But we cannot sacrifice Israeli sovereignty to appease any terrorist group."

"Why not grant them a temporary peace accord?"

"They've done nothing to warrant a peace accord. Countless soldiers have died for the cause of a free Jewish state. David Ben-Gurion worked tirelessly to hold this people together, and I will do no less."

Jack shook his head as Carmen entered the room.

Their precious Nathan was as good as dead.


Protesters gathered outside Mossad Headquarters.

The meeting with Reznik quickly adjourned.

Reuben replayed the words again in his mind. *Help us, please. Nathan is our only son. We've nowhere else to turn.*

Reporters surrounded the prime minister as he exited the building. Microphones were thrusted in front of him. Flashes from cameras spotlighted his head. Questions came in rapid fire.

"Mr. Prime Minister . . ."

"What are your thoughts on . . . ?"

"Do you expect further terrorist activity in the event of an Israeli military response?"

"Sir, what was the mood of your conversation with President . . . ?"

Reznik said, "Every diplomatic decision made by the Jewish state has an inherent concession that we'd rather not make."

"What is your next move in the wake of al Qaeda's most recent threat?"

"Will Israel act alone if the UK and US decide not to cooperate with your plan?"

Experienced as he was in front of the camera, the prime minister winced as flashes blurred his sight.

"I cannot comment now," he asserted as his entourage motioned him along. He shoved a microphone aside. A rear door of his limousine flung open.

A reporter from Al-Jazeera asked, "Sir, isn't it true that Israel is as much a state sponsor of terrorism as any other nation in the Middle East, as stated by UN Secretary General Ban Ki-moon?"

Reznik harnessed the reporter with one hand and with the other apprehended her microphone.

He said, "Excuse me? The state of Israel does not participate in terrorist activity of any kind. If the UN and Mr. Ki-moon want to focus on real genocide, they need look no further than Hamas and ISIL, which are the face of radical Islam and intent on carrying out acts of barbarism that threaten humanity itself."

"But, sir, will you—"

"For too long, Western civilization has ignored the problem. Those who kidnap innocent children find support in radical Islam. Political correctness makes it virtually impossible to hold terrorists accountable for the taking of innocent life, so we eliminate without apology those who murder Israeli citizens.

"In Gaza, bloodthirsty Hamas fires rockets at Israelis from homes, schools, and mosques. Hamas uses Palestinian babies as human shields, and utilizes its own children as slave labor to build terror tunnels in a constant genocidal war against our people. ISIL beheads and crucifies children in its never-ending war against peace-loving Christians, Yazidis, and anyone who stands in the way of their caliphate."

"But sir, what do you say to . . . ?"

Gunfire rang out from a hill close by.

The prime minister ducked his head and turned.

"Take cover!" a man shouted.

Reporters knelt on the ground. Most of them scattered and ran.

Bodyguards drew weapons. A Jewish reporter stood tall. Her voice was heard above the commotion. "There he is, the man with the gun!"

Shots from a rifle rang out again. Bullets deflected off the motorcade. Rubber screeched on asphalt as a limousine carried Reznik away.

A flurry of gunfire fanned out across the road.

The shooter caught a fatal bullet to the head.

Jack saw the assassination attempt on live television. He reached for his phone and dialed Foster.

"Yes, sir."

"I've had enough."

"Unreal."

"You'd think the president would wake up after this."

"Don't hold your breath."

"Meet me in the saloon," Jack said.

"On my way."

Jack's mug held a look of resolve. He marched into the extravagant saloon with Captain Lou.

Foster entered.

"It's go time, Dellon."

"Agreed."

"This isn't a one-man job. We need manpower. Any thoughts?"

Espionage is an animal unlike any other. It bridges a gap between counterintelligence and common men, placing participants at risk of discovery and the dreaded gallows. Occasionally, discipline reaches the ranks of the super-rich, but seldom a multibillionaire and his charming wife whose special needs son went missing at a parade in an enchanting locale.

Foster said, "Desperate times call for decisive action. I'd like you to consider Special Ops."

The billionaire didn't speak.

"While SEAL teams are known publicly for direct operations such as the bin Laden strike, indirect shaping activities are equally important to long-term security interests and save many innocent lives through elimination of would-be terror strikes. Officials at Mossad, MI-6, and CIA have long debated the decision to combine strategic assets and counterinsurgent personnel. My position has always been that it makes sense to do so, if those imbued with decision-making capability have the same commitment to cooperation as those they call on for execution of a masterful plan. Working in tandem, intelligence communities amplify their effectiveness by leveraging infrastructure and exploiting strategic actions germinated from knowledge collected on various geographic and political fronts.

"On any given day, Mossad and the CIA operate in more than seventy-five countries and hundreds of cities from Boston to Bangkok. Most operatives carry out noncombat operations that are considered low risk. Due to the nature and diversity of threats facing Western nations, Special Ops forces are now in greater demand than any other time. With imminent drawdown in United States military expenditure, Special Ops will see a sharp increase in operational demand. Current forces produced at sites in the United States number about sixty-five thousand. A modest increase is to be expected by the end of the decade, but not enough to reach a satisfactory level to ensure domestic security. Only ten thousand or so can be deployed at a given time.

"These figures are woefully deficient. Strict requirements for entry into elite programs along with uncompromising emphasis on retaining top-tier fighters limit the likelihood of acceptable expansion. In fact, maximum growth rate is no more than 3 to 5 percent per annum. Thus, one can appreciate the luxury or, dare I say, necessity for those who can afford to train their own team of security personnel."

Jack leaned forward.

Foster said, "Given their ability to execute critical reconnaissance activity, Special Ops is the best choice one can make in an increasingly unstable world. Due to fiscal restraints and the nature of global politics, our team will assume a more significant role in years to come. We can preempt military conflict, amplify effectiveness of conventional forces, establish relationships with indigenous leaders of both legitimate and rogue states, provide precise targeting of known enemies, and offer high-resolution awareness that maximizes likelihood of operational success. All this we accomplish while leaving a tiny footprint and avoiding collateral damage and death. Are you with me so far?"

"I am," said the billionaire.

"Co-opting a trustworthy asset will enable you to protect your family and intervene in world affairs in a manner you previously considered impossible with traditional forces alone. Such a move represents the evolution of classical espionage as it combines with a global team of like-minded mercenaries whose operational focus addresses security problems once managed by conventional military personnel."

At once Jack saw years that lay ahead. Life had prepared him to lead a noble cause. With Foster as his guide, Jack Goldwyn could play an integral part in restoring freedom to oppressed masses. He could elicit positive change for countless people he wouldn't otherwise reach.

His focus returned to Foster.

He said, "You should first understand what Special Ops entails and the kind of problems we solve. Proficiency comes at a cost that escalates if assets are mishandled by those in charge. There is no substitute for a strong ground force. Assets prepare operating environments in the most advantageous manner possible. They are not, however, a replacement for conventional capabilities, and there are some missions Special Ops cannot perform. For example, they cannot fight pitched battles with heavy forces, execute naval power, or deploy nuclear weapons—at least not now. They aren't a replacement for a conventional large-scale military. When used appropriately, however, Special Ops are extraordinarily valuable, even irreplaceable, in advancing security interest."

"How long does Special Ops training last?"

"That depends on a candidate's preexisting level of skill. If everything goes smoothly, an exceptional candidate may complete training in a matter of weeks."

"Tell me about your selection process."

"We receive thousands of applications each week. Twenty-five candidates enter the course, and we choose no more than three. I've rejected entire classes before."

"What does training entail?"

"First, a candidate's background is thoroughly vetted. If cleared, he or she undergoes a series of psychological and physical tests. Next comes an intelligence briefing and subjective assessment of a candidate's self-control, analytical maturity, and fitness for a given mission. Those who demonstrate any hint of instability are removed immediately.

"The physical test includes one hundred continuous push-ups and sit-ups in under five minutes, a three-kilometer run in full gear in less than twelve minutes, and a sixty-foot rope climb over a treacherous rocky ravine. A candidate must scale a half-dozen three-meter walls and run ten kilometers in four hours or less. If successful, the candidate is inducted as an operative, and then enters Parachute School."

"Do you have any assets in mind?"

"I do."

Jack's head nudged forward. "Is there something you haven't told me?"

Foster drew a deep breath and exhaled slowly.

"Dellon, I want to know."

"They've been training at Headquarters in Gauteng."

"Who? Training for what?"

"You're in for the fight of your life, Jack. Not to worry, though. We'll stop at nothing and execute a mature strategy as planned."

"I want my son back. Do whatever it takes."

Foster nodded. He was nothing if not composed.

He said, "Preparations for a top-secret mission are underway. You've made the right decision, Jack. Special Ops is integral to a strategy that protects your family and assets for years to come."

"I'm counting on you, Dellon."

By now their connection was firm.

Foster leaned back on a leather chair, and rested his chin on a fist. He said, "There is a light in the eyes of select GIs as they ascend the ranks and are honed into efficient killing machines. Those who survive the gristmill emerge forever changed."

Jack's eyebrows lifted.

"Youthful exuberance and romantic loyalty are buried along the way. By thirty years of age, the dream of changing the world has died. Corrupt political symptoms seem impenetrable, patriotism for the weak and naïve. Optimism, which once beamed from wide, expectant eyes, is but a distant memory snuffed out by training and life itself."

"What are you trying to say?"

"I've spoken at length with Ari. He has friends who will answer his call."

"Mercenaries?"

"Indeed. Real-life heroes. Intelligent, multilingual, hard-bodied killing machines who stand ready for any task. Men who live perpetually off the grid, who know the meaning of commitment. They care not who pays the tab. They know the system and how to beat it."

"It's the kind of focus required to execute a vital task."

"Precisely."

"Who are they?"

"Ex-Mossad, Gurkhas, SAS, and CIA. Due to a level of cynicism common men don't understand, they're a step ahead of rival teams, including most veterans of Special Ops. Most demand payment upfront. A million dollars of gold or a beachside villa is the going rate. Take your pick."

"Do you know what a million dollars of gold weighs?"

"About twenty-five kilograms."

"A chore to lug around."

"Yep. With money their only goal and armed conflict their only concern, the agreement is simple: they fight, and someone pays. In the minds of seasoned mercenaries, vengeance is a quality to be praised, not subdued. For those borne of valor and conquest, emotional angst is a virtue, never a vice. Ascetics who deny physical and emotional pain are welcome in a world where death is a business, a specialty perfected in time."

A kilometer south of the Waterfront, Nazareth House stood on a spacious plot in Vredehoek with a smattering of hedges, an array of flowers, and mature hardwood trees. The stone building located at the center of the property was as solid as the faith of selfless heroes who ministered to the poor and needy, and its grounds were impeccably maintained by more than two-dozen nuns who lived there. When one thinks of convalescent homes, the mind raises images alien to those brought about by Sister Abby, who was approaching eighty years and had led the Order of the Sisters for more than a decade.

Her expansive manor was not like other convalescent homes. Commitment to a lifetime of service of the impoverished and desperate is not for everyone. But called as they were to a life of humility, the women found ample joy in a life well lived, and were known throughout the Cape for taking in those who had no place else to live. Piety, it seemed, implied no limit in matters of compassion or benevolence. The Order had extended its tradition of service from that of its foundress, Victoire Larmenier, Mother St. Basil, and no longer screened indigent subjects by age. More than a hundred souls were permanent residents of Nazareth Home.

Vulnerability ceased upon one's arrival to the property. The worst maladies were familiar to the Sisters who did their best to ensure dignity for the blind, deaf, lame, and those stricken with terminal disease.

The old fisherman sat in a quiet room with Asram. He said, "You see, my son, someone does care."

Soft light from a burning candle provided the only light in the room.

Asram turned over on the bed and closed his eyes.

"Want something to drink? Doctor says you must . . ."

They heard a knock on the door.

"Come in," said the old man.

The door creaked open.

"Hello!" Sister Abby sang. "Welcome to Nazareth House. It's so nice of you to come."

Asram lay still. He saw the Sister's silhouette on a wall, and was determined not to speak.

She sat next to him on the bed. A pale hand adjusted her headgear.

"I brought a candle for you." Her faced beamed a luminous smile.

"Ay," the fisherman said. "See, my boy?"

At last, the candle gave out.

An assistant raised a window. Brilliant afternoon light shown in.

Sister Abby held Asram's hand. "No more darkness. From this day, only light."

Asram turned on his back. A skimpy arm blocked his face from view.

"There, there." She patted his shoulder. Tension in his chest began to ease. "All is well."

The whole world seemed to brighten. The best of humanity sat beside him. Hope sprouted in his soul. He rubbed his eyes and said, "Thank you, Sister."

Her rosy cheeks glowed with compassion. "You're welcome, son. It's going to be okay."

Life had taught him only fear and a perpetual state of worry for no reason he could recall. To what had he attributed his angst? A deadly bomb, an act of Zionist aggression?

But why a tumultuous aftermath? Why a bombing at all?

Apprehension left him, if only in Vredehoek. Perhaps he should stay there, live there, work there. Experience taught him to fear what he didn't know.

"I dreamed I was dead," Asram confessed.

"Is that so?" the fisherman asked in disbelief.

"Your dream is only a dream," Sister Abby said. Her spirit was undaunted by any mention of death. "And as such it isn't real." She smiled sweetly and squeezed his hand. "But life is real, and now you have a home. And a family too, if you so wish."

Rebellion had left him. He had drifted through life for too many years and had not the strength to call her bluff. A heart that once felt only hate now had room for something more. How or why he didn't know or care. Perhaps it was a stroke of luck.

Asram peered deeply into her eyes, and fought back tears as she concluded with more tender words befitting a message he needed to hear.

Sister Abby rose without a sound. Her feet hardly touched the floor as she floated to the heavy wooden door held open by the fisherman.

Exiting the room, she said with cheer, "God bless you, son."

A cathedral bell tolled four o'clock.

## 23

An international media blitz ensued.

Continuous coverage of an imminent global oil crisis blanketed cable and network news. Rations were announced first in major cities along the eastern seaboard of the United States and spread west in a matter of hours. News sources around the globe beamed ominous headlines: "OPEC Influence Resurges in Wake of Gulf Oil Crisis" —*BBC*; "Oil Soars on Cessation of Commerce in Strait of Hormuz, Ripple Effects Feared on Wall Street" —*Reuters*; "Markets Reel on Petroleum Crisis Spawned by Terrorist Activity in Territorial Waters of Iran and Oman" —*Le Monde*; "Dow Crumbles as Oil Shortage Extends Beyond Middle East and Asia" —*El Mundo*.

Senate confirmation hearings of a recently nominated Supreme Court justice were cancelled, as were all major professional and college sporting events and domestic air travel until further notice. In Riyadh, the first of three disturbing videos depicted a horrific scene in which children, assisted by masked ISIL gunmen, strapped bombs to their chests in preparation for jihad. Children ages five to seven years marched as little soldiers and shouted, "Allahu Akbar! We are martyrs for Islam!" A moment later, another masked gunman appeared. He said, "Hand over the land that is rightly ours and has been since ancient times."

In Manhattan's Financial District, panic escalated to chaos as the Dow Jones Industrial Average plummeted 5 percent after the opening bell and triggered an automatic two-hour shutdown. Police and swat teams in riot gear stood behind a barricade on the steps of the New York Stock Exchange and prepared for an onslaught of protesters and malefactors who shouted obscenities and threatened civil unrest. Hundreds of arrests ensued.

Minutes after the closing bell on Wall Street, a reporter held a microphone at the base of the steps and struggled to keep her position. Amid cries for oil rationing, she faced a camera and yelled, "Declines of 30 percent result in a close of the market for the remainder of the trading day. Such was the case earlier today, as market watchers witnessed the sharpest fall in stock prices since the global financial crisis of 2008. Due to the market's lofty heights at the time of that pullback, drops fell short of even the 10 percent shutdown threshold. This was not the case in the wake of the ongoing crisis in the Strait of Hormuz. 2008's meltdown was sustained over a few months, but today's decline was more precipitous and thus more impactful and severe."

The *Royal Flush* had been transformed into a battleship, and Jack Goldwyn its determined war admiral. He rallied troops in the saloon with the yacht moored in Tel Aviv.

"Ladies and gentlemen, we're on our own."

A radio buzzed with chatter between officials at International Maritime who continuously monitored the Strait. A computer streamed video from London and lit up as an irregularity in nautical commerce triggered caution signals noted by observers both near and far. Diesel engines in the freighter turned cold. No distress signal was heard. Territorial authorities in Tehran acted first.

Jack listened as an official provided an update.

A sober voice said, "Iranian naval forces have been put on alert in anticipation of an imminent threat."

"Any news from Reznik?" Carmen asked.

"None," Jack said.

"Are you surprised?"

"No. At least he knows where I stand."

With that all eyes turned to the video screen.

A reporter held a microphone as a breaking news banner scrolled across the bottom.

"Volume, please," Jack said.

Today in London, a Shi'a Muslim cleric based in Sana'a sent an encrypted email, which has been decoded to reveal the location of more than eighty children who were kidnapped from corporate daycares and high-profile sporting events during the last few weeks.

BBC has confirmed details of the cleric's announcement that the children are in a Maersk cargo ship, which was hijacked in Cape Town. Sources close to the company say the vessel, which contained perishable goods including food and botanical products, was commandeered during a raid carried out while the ship was docked at a Maersk warehouse adjacent to Victoria & Alfred Waterfront.

It is not known what motivated kidnappers to commit these horrific acts.

Foster powered off the television. He rested an elbow on the table and said, "We've been over this before."

"My god, is this really happening?" Carmen said.

Foster spoke with precision. "Forty percent of the world's petroleum traverses the Strait, making it an ideal target for those interested in disrupting international trade, and a crucial location for military strategists."

Jack said, "Do we have contacts with significant interests in the region?"

"None but the civilized world. The existence of human life as we know it depends on the viability and peaceful transport of oil exported from the Persian Gulf."

Jack paced back and forth. "Let's hear more about the Strait. What is its width?"

"Thirty-three kilometers at its narrowest point off the coast of Musandam. Vessels are required to pass through territorial waters controlled by Iran and Oman under provisions outlined at the UN's Convention on the Law of the Sea. To reduce the risk of collision, ships follow a Traffic Separation Scheme with inbound ships using one lane and outbound ships utilizing another. Ship lanes are separated by a median three kilometers wide."

Jack listened intently.

"According to the US Energy Information Administration, fourteen tankers carry seventeen million barrels of crude oil through the Strait every day, with more than eighty-five percent bound for Southeast Asia. This accounts for thirty-five percent of the world's seaborne oil shipments and twenty percent of oil traded worldwide. The report stated more than eighty-five percent of these crude oil exports went to Asian markets, with Japan, India, South Korea, and China the largest destinations."

"So Western markets wouldn't be heavily influenced?"

"How could they not? The price of gasoline in the US doubled overnight. Speculation alone caused immediate panic. Any related industry will be similarly affected."

"Damn."

"It gets worse. In 2007, a report from the Center for Strategic and International Studies said seventeen million barrels of oil passing through the Strait accounted for roughly 40 percent of internationally traded oil, enough to cause a global economic depression if commerce is interrupted."

"Can you predict the political fallout that will occur if we don't act right away?"

Foster's tone sharpened. "PLO will say we orchestrated the whole thing to step up the price of oil."

"Would anyone believe them?"

"Who knows? There will be riots and protests in every capital throughout the Middle East, with chaos spreading to Europe. Meanwhile, OPEC is plotting against you as we speak."

A sense of dread filled the room.

Deployment of military assets had been a procedure routinely utilized in cooperation with the United States, but now relations were strained.

Jack leaned back in his chair. "Total mayhem."

"Not to mention a geopolitical crisis that will quickly present itself."

"Explain."

Foster obliged. "Protecting free access to Hormuz is among the most important duties of the US Navy. Since the first Arab oil embargo in 1976, the US has spent $8 trillion protecting oil cargoes in the Persian Gulf. This even though only 10 percent of oil passing through the Strait reaches the United States."

"ISIL wants something bad. What could it be?"

"To kill and terrorize."

"That's all?"

Foster said, "The Strait has not been immune to conflict. In 1988, a daylong battle dubbed Operation Praying Mantis was launched in retaliation for mining of the USS *Samuel Roberts*, and pitted the US Navy against Iranian forces in or near the Strait. US forces sank a frigate, a gunboat, and a half-dozen armed speedboats during the attack. Three months later, an Iran Air Airbus passenger jet was shot down over the Strait by the USS Vincennes. That attack left 290 dead and was labeled a case of mistaken identity."

Jack turned on the television.

A news anchor in London offered a brief history of conflicts in the Strait.

"Millennium Challenge 2002 was a major US military exercise that simulated an Iranian attempt to close the Strait. In 2007, the USS *Newport News*, a nuclear submarine, struck a Japanese crude tanker south of the Strait. Remarkably, no injuries or oil leaks were reported. In December the following year, the Strait of Hormuz played host to another naval dispute between US warships and Iranian speedboats after officials from the US accused Iran of harassing its naval vessels. Iran dismissed the allegations, which contradicted Washington's interpretation of the event, in which US Navy officials said they were close to firing on encroaching Iranian speedboats."

The hours seemed shorter as they passed.

Foster did not waste time. He said, "Jack, meet Professor Harritt, the world's nano-thermite expert on sabbatical from Cambridge."

"Nano-what?" Jack said.

252

Educated as he was, the well-read multibillionaire was not easily stumped, but the foreign term perplexed even him.

"The most powerful explosive in the world," the aged professor said with a heavy British accent. Gaunt shoulders jerked as tiny spectacles slid down his nose.

"Bar none?"

"Bar none. It runs through steel like crap through a goose."

He boasted of his discovery with evident zeal.

"I see."

The professor offered an ineffectual grin. He said, "To understand nano-thermite, you must first understand what ordinary thermite is and what it consists of."

Foster said, "Is that necessary? As long as it blows shit up."

Jack raised a hand. "Professor, continue."

Harritt nodded. "Thermite is an amalgam of a metal and the oxide of another metal in granular or powder form. Most blends employ use of aluminum and iron oxide. When ignited, the reaction yields molten iron and aluminum oxide, with melted iron that reaches temperatures in excess of 2000°C. Generated heat is enough to cut through structural steel, which melts at 1400°."

"Sounds useful. Is it possible to—"

The professor's shoulders jerked again. Though a stranger to megayachts, he was in his element when he discussed explosives. He said, "There is a variant of thermite known as thermate, a combination of thermite and sulfur. It's more efficient at cutting through steel, and is believed by some to have been used in the demolition of World Trade Center Building 7."

Jack stared into his eyes. "Are you suggesting 9/11 was an inside job?"

"My good man, some conversations are better had over a tall glass of Maker's Mark. I have an opinion on the matter, but no requisite bourbon to assist in stating my case." He paused, incapable of concealing his suspicion. "Alas, I digress. Let's see now, where were we?" He stammered a moment, and then continued in rapid fire. "Ah, yes, the explosive. Although conventional thermite has the capability to cut through structural steel, it is technically an incendiary and not an explosive. The point is, nano-thermite, also known as super-thermite, is simply put, an ultra-fine-grained variant of thermite that can be made into an explosive by adding gas-liberating chemicals.

"This material releases energy much faster than conventional energetic materials and has numerous potential military applications, such as rocket propellants, aircraft fuel, and as an explosive for use in acts of war. They are likely to become the next generation's explosive materials of choice, as they enable flexibility in energy density and power release through control of particle size, distribution, stoichiometry, and choice of fuel and oxidizer."

"Stoichi-who?" Foster said.

Jack's eyes fixated on Harritt.

The professor sighed as he looked away from Foster.

Harritt said, "Never mind. I now direct your attention to the most important formula of the day, and a reaction by which the explosive is produced."

"You lost me at nano." Foster scratched his head.

"Understanding comes with time and intense study. Science isn't intuitive for most, you know." He pointed to a reaction on the board: $2Al + Fe_2O_3 \rightarrow Al_2O_3 + 2Fe$ (molten iron). "Make sense?"

"Clear as mud," Foster said.

"Good." Harritt leaned on the table. "Any questions?"

Jack said, "Has this type of explosive ever been used?"

"Not outside a laboratory in Moscow, as far as we know."

"Who invented it?"

"I did, along with a colleague from Cambridge. We published our findings last month in an issue of *Popular Mechanics* and documented use of thermite in the demolition of Skyride Tower in Chicago and the dome of the German Reichstag, but there has been no recorded and confirmed use of nano-thermite for commercial, scientific, or military purpose."

"Will your invention allow us to rescue my son?"

Foster's eyes jetted at the scientist.

Without delay Harritt said, "That's the plan, but you'll need a prolific swimmer to assist in deploying the waterproof explosive. Otherwise, the invention is useless."

Jack turned to Foster.

A confident man knows what to say.

Foster replied, "That won't be a problem. Our asset is an Olympic swimmer who won three gold medals in Rio."

## 24

It was not quite morning yet.

Musandam Peninsula lay still as a sleeping babe illuminated by ambient light from an early sun. East of the sea route, barren hills of Minab and Qeshm rose in the horizon.

A duo of wet suits shimmied in light from a half moon that lingered in a cloudless sky. Suri held a fist to her lips and whispered a prayer for strength. Ari clinched the Star of David in one hand while the other pointed toward heaven. He nudged a button on his timepiece. Its face illuminated the local time: 0600.

It was for a mission such as this that they had trained. Suri holstered a ray gun and tossed her backpack aside. Head nod, fist bump, night vision goggles on.

They entered the Strait north of Dubai and reviewed a checklist again: welder's mask, check; fire resistant gloves, check; nichrome bridge wire, check; laser pulse, check; and, lest they forget, a hundred kilos of nano-thermite.

Suri dove in first.

*Splash!*

Fluorescent dials on her compass and pressure gauge twinkled as she jetted out from an embankment in the international port. A drone raced over them from the west, hovered a moment, and then proceeded toward Qeshm Island in southern Iran.

Chinook helicopters with standby mercenaries roared overhead. Spotlights converged on Suri a hundred meters below. Ari caught up with her fast. They glided smoothly through the hypertonic water.

Another drone arrived. By now sunrise had come.

Abu Dhabi was saturated with reporters from all over the world. From there, mass media would unleash real-time video to cover events of the day. Commentary would follow as information was made known.

A propulsion vehicle loaded with explosive payload met them two hundred meters from shore. The duo rose to the water's surface. Ari popped open a hatch. Flotation devices skidded next to the vehicle as it bobbed in the Strait of Hormuz. The vehicle was directed via remote control operated by Foster in Tel Aviv.

As the propulsion vehicle approached the freighter, Suri's face turned to stone. She exchanged a signal with Ari as a twin sharing identical DNA. They edged close to the freighter as a drone equipped with a high-def camera hung overhead.

Suri descended.

Ari watched as she dove headfirst.

They went deep into water next to the vessel's hull. In an instant, they were directly against the ship, swimming faster and deeper into the water.

Foster locked the propulsion vehicle without delay.

Suri laced opposite sides of the vessel with the explosive. She drew a continuous vertical stream of nano-thermite on the hull in a straight line bisecting the ship. Ari applied bridge wires to the hull while Suri bound and attached them underneath the ship's stern. Suri inspected her handiwork on the eastern side of the vessel.

The threat of electrostatic discharge required careful handling of the explosive. Once ignited, the sticky dust would morph into a continuous line of heat that would instantly reach 2000°. The reaction would last no more than a second. Only time would temper the blaze. Anyone observing the blast without protective eyewear would immediately lose sight.

The assets swam away from the vessel. A helicopter raced in from the west.

Suri reentered the propulsion vehicle. A cable lifted it a hundred meters into the air. The Chinook moved southwest toward Oman.

Ari watched as Suri engaged the drone. He gave a signal with a neon light that queued Suri to power on the ray gun. She rested the gun on a shoulder and adjusted a lens. One peek through the tactical riflescope revealed bright red crosshairs and the target located three hundred meters away. One wrong move and the children would disappear into oblivion. Suri thought of Nathan and other innocent children on board the cargo ship. The world awaited their rescue, let alone their horrified parents.

Jack and Carmen observed a telescreen with Captain Lou. A drone operator remained engaged in his work on a computer in an adjacent room.

All eyes were on Suri, who gave the signal to dispatch the Phantom drone.

Gut check. Crunch time.

Suri lifted the ray gun. The pressure gauge beeped once and her shoulders froze. In a sober breath she whispered, "One thousand one, one thousand two . . ."

With utmost precision, she pointed the beam of radiation at a lock on the ship's door and gently squeezed the trigger. She rotated the ray gun back and forth, peering continually through the scope.

A microscopic beam of radiation raced left and right over the lock. Immediately, the door swung open.

The Phantom drone raced into the ship, down a flight of stairs, through a narrow hall, and into the bowels of the massive ship, where a few dozen children were held. A spotlight clicked on as the drone spun 360°.

Still, there was no sign of Nathan.

A girl awoke and scurried toward the bow.

"Help! Please! Somebody!"

Outside the ship, Suri fired another beam of radiation to ignite the explosive. The weapon heated up in her hands. A thin line of smoke appeared on the ship, singing the bridge wire traversing its hull. Suri watched the vessel crack open like a fresh-laid egg.

A child's hysterical scream pierced the air. The voice sounded like Nathan's.

Panic spread like wildfire as the Goldwyns watched with Captain Lou.

"My son!" Carmen shrieked. Jack squeezed her arm and prayed. Her muscles buckled as she lowered her head and prayed.

The Phantom drone zoomed in close.

Rauf and Ali ran for the stairs, eyes bursting from their sockets as they realized the ship would go down.

"There's got to be a way out!" Ali shrieked.

Rauf didn't answer. His ribs rose and fell with the urgent rhythm of each desperate breath. He spotted scuba gear stowed deep in the hull. The anointed one clutched his chest.

Ali peeped through a periscope. Warm Gulf waters washed over the deck. The scene inside the *Maersk* was pure chaos. Ali turned and slipped on the floor. His head slammed into a fire case, shattering its cover into a thousand tiny pieces. Fear in Rauf's mind grew into rage as the probability of his demise came into view. He was facing certain death, along with Ali, and dared not to pray. Auwal Masjid was a lifetime away. So were countless fatwahs and ancient verses from the Qur'an.

"Imam, they're coming! What should we do?"

The anointed one didn't answer.

"Imam, it's over!"

"Allahu Akbar!" shouted Rauf. "Allah is with us! Are you not ready to die?"

Suri boarded the freighter seconds after the blast. She worked smoothly and without delay. Not a move was wasted, even on the shifting deck. Ali appeared in view of the Phantom's camera.

"Rauf! They've got us!" he screamed.

The children grew more restless. Panic was stuck on every face.

Ali ran across the room.

From a speaker on the drone, a voice said, "Where is Nathan?"

At once, a laser beam cased over Ali. He shivered and fell to his knees, pointing a half-bent finger at a closet door.

"Open the door," the voice said.

Ali didn't budge.

"Now!" the voice commanded.

The children's screams intensified as Ali turned the knob. The next moment, Nathan and another child appeared with skin ecchymotic and pale.

"Help!" Nathan implored.

"Nathan!" the Goldwyns screamed.

A voice from the Phantom drone said, "Children, follow me."

The children raced upstairs.

A laser beam cased over Ali.

"Don't shoot!" he exclaimed.

"Say hello to your virgins, bitch."

Ali turned, his eyes wide and frightened.

The first shot from the drone passed through his neck and into a gas line close to the stern. In less than a minute, the freighter would blow.

Ali fell hard when the second bullet penetrated his skull.

The Phantom showed it all in perfect view.

Rauf crouched on a stairwell. He sensed that his breaths were numbered.

Suri spotted him, then raised her weapon and said, "Say your prayers, holy man. Not even Allah can save you now."

Rauf shut his eyes. With hands raised, he shouted, "Allahu Akbar!"

A rifle bullet exploded his chest.


"Suri!"

Nathan's eyes dripped tears of joy as his arms extended to greet her.

Adrenaline pumped through her veins.

"Nathan!"

She lifted the boy high in the air.

"I'm so happy to see you! Are you okay?"

"I want my mummy!"

A voice crackled through the drone. "Nathan! I'm here!" Carmen cried. "We'll see you soon."

The drone caught the boy's smile.

Captain Lou peeped at Jack. He nodded and said, "Two down, one to go."

Suri's mission was not yet done.

Nathan stepped out of a tub on the *Royal Flush*. Carmen wrapped a warm towel around him. He peered tenderly at his mother.

"Mummy, I want to sleep."

She hugged him and said, "You can sleep as much as you'd like."

"But I'm afraid," he said.

Carmen's eyes welled with tears as she kneeled to embrace her only son. She regained her composure and said, "Don't be afraid. You're safe now."

"Will those men on the boat ever come back?"

Standing in the doorway, Jack locked eyes with his wife.

"No, son. Those men are dead," Jack said.

Nathan's eyes shifted between his parents. Pulling back from Carmen, he said, "Mummy, I love you."

"I love you too, Nathan. Let's get ready for bed."

## 25

The manhunt lasted a week.

Asram was losing time. Sirens wailed in the distance. A policeman on Büitengracht Street activated emergency lights atop his SUV. Horns from a line of approaching squad cars screamed louder. A swat team surveyed Bo-Kaap from a helicopter as it hovered close to Signal Hill. A sniper adjusted his tripod on the roof of ABSA Bank.

After hiding in an abandoned flat without food or water for two days, Asram dressed and prepared to leave. He packed a few items in a duffle bag: a compass, two sacks of rice, three bottles of water, a knife encased in its leather sheath, and, of course, the Qur'an.

"Why me?" he said aloud. "Why did Allah allow this to happen?"

Asram moistened his lips. Vitriol pumped in his veins. *Then again, why not me?* he thought.

An oscillating fan whirred on a table at the center of the room. Its blades were caked with thick grey dust. He relived the dirty village in Yemen where he was raised: polluted water, crowded streets, a scarce food supply, endless misery that accompanied life in Sana'a. That was all he remembered of his childhood home.

Auwal Masjid was starkly different from places where he had lived as a boy and man. Holiness was in a mosque, a pristine white turban, the call to prayer reverberating through narrow streets of Bo-Kaap. Islam was a welcome alternative to a broken spirit and troubled mind that obsessed about his past. His heart was recalcitrant to love. Harmonious words projected from stylish architraves at Auwal Masjid were no longer heard. The mosque had been an accessible haven for troubled souls like his.

But the Masjid had been overtaken by infidels.

Stealthily as a leopard, Asram leaped off a balcony onto a sidewalk where his motorbike was hiked on its kickstand. He donned a silver helmet, fastened the chinstrap, and turned the key. The fuel gauge read a quarter of a tank. He walked the bike a few paces back and wound the motor to full throttle. His chest pulsed with a fury he had never known. The smell of burning oil wafted through an alley that led to Dorp Street.

*Vroom! Vroom!*

His tepid eyes peered up and down the minaret at Auwal Masjid. He remembered the muezzin's last call to prayer and paused to hear the bellowing voice again in his head. His boyhood in Sana'a shrunk to a faint memory. Imam Rauf was nowhere to be found. Inspiration from Tuan Guru seemed a lifetime away—the holy prophet had left him too.

Asram raced his motorbike past shops and vendors on Longmarket Street. He cleared the city limits and sped along M2 toward rolling hills in the Eastern Cape. The road curled between piggeries and wetlands as wide as the sea.

Suri waited motionless on a hilltop at woods' edge. The sound of the bike's engine sharpened. A long straightaway came into view as he rounded a curve. Asram felt a glimmer of hope.

*Vroom!*

Suri peered through a high-powered lens and calmly pulled the trigger. Two sharp reports from the rifle rang out. *Ka-pop! Ka-pop!* The second shot was true. A plume of blood burst from Asram's chest. The back of his flaxen robe was soaked in an instant. He arched leftward in pain. The bike jerked into the opposite lane, and then spun madly out of control. Blood spurted from the wound on Asram's chest and onto the steaming road. He kept the speeding bike on course for a thousand meters as the bumpy road drew next to a farm.

Asram's face twisted with pain as he reached for the bleeding gash. "*Arrrr!*"

The bike slowed, wobbled, and then pitched violently back and forth before it careened off the highway and into a pile of burning brush. Moments later he was back on his feet. He spotted a farmhouse at several hundred meters from the road. His legs grew weaker as blood oozed from the wound. He trotted with great effort until his pace slowed, then stumbled but somehow recovered and pressed on through an open field, lurching, cursing, enduring the pain. His trek toward the farmhouse was no more than a primitive flight response. Instinct spurred him. His gait slowed to an awkward trot. The next moment he fell to his knees and crawled under a gate.

Asram stepped clumsily in front of a door. He twisted the knob right and left, but it didn't budge. Asram turned in a fit of rage and stumbled again.

He rounded a corner of the house and spotted a shed with a fenced enclosure. With every step labored, he steadied his gait with a metal rail. He vomited as inertia carried his body over the fence. Thick mud softened his fall. His torso wriggled back and forth.

Consciousness wavered as he wallowed in a shallow pool near the center of a swine pen. He rolled onto his back. It was then that his breaths turned lighter. He could go no more. His arms were limp and spent. His pale face sunk below the surface of the stinking pool. As summer's hottest sun blazed in a cloudless sky, his body writhed as a vermin approaching its fated end.

Asram lifted his head. A hog snorted beside him. His face was caked with mud infused with putrid waste. With his chin planted in fetid slop, he heard the muffled sound of a woman's voice and opened his eyes. His face splashed into the shallow pool from which he was too weak to escape.

Anxious pigs grunted as they circled him in the mud and dung. One of them squealed excitement. Asram lifted his head in the muck and came face-to-face with a snorting hog. He turned his mud-caked face and Suri met him with a loaded Glock.

"No!" He beckoned the only will that remained. "Please!"

His pants turned into gasps that soon became faint and slow. There was nothing more he could do. This was the end of his jihad: he had not the strength even to hate.

Suri stood with arms extended. She adjusted her aim, then pulled the trigger.

*Boom!*

Her slender wrist jolted slightly, absorbing the powerful recoil.

Lanky arms flailed out from his body. His neck jerked violently back and forth as the pistol fired again. A crimson rivulet flowed into the shallow pool from Asram's forehead.

Foster stood beside her. He said, "The cleanup men will take it from here."

Suri was quiet.

The only sound was oinking pigs routing around the shallow pool and the jihadist who lay dead under an eternal sky and light from a thousand suns.

## 26

A few weeks passed without a peep from the mysterious man. Suri assumed he was gone.

A double-decker bus swirled into a roundabout. The tour guide said, "No list of lively world cities is complete without Cape Town. Mother City offers boutique shopping, jazz clubs, trendy wine bars, and a night life with never-ending thrills."

The bus driver shifted gears and straightened his bowler hat.

"Did you know the King Protea is the national flower of South Africa? It blooms in late spring with marvelous pink and red colors. The giant protea resembles an artichoke and is native to many regions of the Western and Southern Cape, where it may be admired in Cape Point as well as Somerset West."

A spraying fountain cleansed grubby wings of a seabird at the center of a roundabout, and the double-decker went by with its bold façade advertising wine and spirits from around the globe. Malay children played on a sidewalk as the tour guide gave her speech. You heard the children's laughter and thought of crayons, a blackboard, dusty chalk scattered on a pencil rest. A scent of baking pastries wafted through the morning air.

In Cape Town, one observes freedom *in situ*. Mother City is replete with vibrant sights and sounds: eclectic locals smartly dressed in business attire, a steady hum of conversation in quaint wine bars with open windows and hanging plants, rattling manholes covered by a company's metal logo, booming industrial sites with thick columns of smoke reaching toward an infinite sky, a locomotive blowing its horn, parking meters that flicker 'Empty' at the end of a productive day, stoic policemen keeping watch on a corner.

A regal mountain reigns over all.


Bascule Bar came alive with music and drink. Aromas of cherry-garnished cocktails and foaming beers passed through the air. Indulgence was all around: in champagne and Ossetra caviar, prized Cabernets, a bouquet of impala lilies, and hip tunes playing overhead.

> *Daddy works a long day*
> *He be coming home late*
> *and he's coming home late*
> *And he's bringing me a surprise*

A bartender wiped a pint glass.

"I'd like to send a martini to the brunette sitting at the corner table," the mysterious man said. He peered at Suri across the bar. "Extra olives, please. Tell her it's from the man sitting alone."

His instruction came with an air of self-assurance, his courage emboldened by a shot of Jäger.

"Right away, sir." The bartender interrupted his cleaning and went for a glass.

The mysterious man dropped a thousand rand into a tip jar.

Time moved with the slowness of a well-poured drink. The man's physique emitted a sense of triumph. His voice was strong and daunting. Puffs of smoke from his perfecto brought an ethereal aura to his face. The next move was hers to make. The mysterious man took a sip of his drink. He folded his hands on the bar and waited.

Cheerfully, and with a hint of surprise, the young woman received her cocktail. Passion moved at its own pace, a heated game of chess. The first pawn was advanced with a strategy in mind. Both players were experienced enough, in leisure games and romance too. Rules of engagement were universal and adhered to by those concerned. The young woman smiled and crossed her legs. The match could take hours yet, and still no winner would have to be declared. Perhaps the contest would last all night and end in a draw, necessitating a rematch the following day. Her dainty hand hovered over the board. The mysterious man paid her no mind as he listened to a Mozart sonata played on a grand piano—or was it Brahms?

He shifted his hips on the barstool. What would become of his advance? How had it been received? The pianist touched another note and paused, only to start again after a moment's delay. He bobbed an olive-laden toothpick in a glass filled with too much ice. Music enlivened his soul, and so did London's driest gin.

Did the young woman have a proven strategy, a method of her own?

A gentle breeze soothed his sunburned face. Suddenly, he felt more at ease.

"Is this seat taken?" Suri asked. She stood close to him and stirred her drink. Her nails were freshly polished. She drew her silky hair to one side and tucked it crisply behind one ear. Attraction was evident as her eyes darted back and forth across his chest, then over his shoulders in a fit of anticipation she could not tame. Ari's soul lit with a feeling his mind could not recall. Passion rushed in his cheeks before spilling into his heart and pumping out again.

"No, it isn't," he said, a fresh cigar between his teeth. His timepiece glistened in a ray of sunlight. He reached for a box of matches and put forth an open hand.

"I'm Suri."

They shook hands.

Her eyes rushed over his face. She smiled at him again. A famed sonata came to its climax as the Whitsun sun began to set.

"Lovely piece," Ari said. The Bösendorfer was perfectly tuned.

"Indeed," Suri replied.

Their conversation continued without much effort and the bartender refreshed their drinks. Suri's face was ripe with structure. High cheekbones, a classic nose, and lips that were full and cherubic made for a countenance that was strong and bright, and her demeanor was equally engaging.

He blew a ring of smoke and ashed his cigar. His eyes were drawn to a cable car in a little nook near the crest of Table Mountain. They moved here and there over his irresistible company.

Suri's mug held the impression of an era from long ago. Elegance was spread on her face. Modernity had attempted to stamp out her kind, but the breed lived on in full breasts and tempting curves, flowing locks of jet-black hair lifted by a gentle breeze. She crossed her legs and went for a glass of rum.

"You look like someone who might have voted for Bernie Sanders," the man said.

She turned. "I'm sorry?"

"You heard me. Or was it Barrack Hussein. You voted for him too, didn't you?"

The voice sounded familiar, but his cropped hair and sunshades made him almost impossible to recognize.

"Not this chick."

"What about Crooked Hillary?"

"What about her? And what about Bush and Cheney? That's who stirred up the hornet's nest in the first place."

"I thought it was bin Laden," the man said, "but my boss says the Ayatollah is to blame."

"You have a boss?"

"Don't we all?"

"Yes, I suppose."

"You're Jewish, no?"

"Jesus, Abraham, Mohammed, Lord Shiva. What's the difference?"

He swigged a beer.

"Depends on who you ask."

"I don't get religion," she said. "What's the point?"

A frosty mug thawed in his hands.

"Harmony with your fellow man, a peaceful means of maintaining control."

"Oh, really?" she said. "More people have been killed in the name of God than for any other reason."

"Clearly, I've touched a nerve."

"You can have your religion. Just leave me the hell alone."

He cornered her with a practiced grin. "You sound like a libertarian."

"Maybe I am."

Again, he swigged his beer.

He said, "Did you hear the one about the Jew, the Christian, and the Hindu who died and went to heaven?"

"No," she answered.

"Three men arrived at the gates of heaven and Saint Peter asked, 'What's your religion?'

"'Jewish,' the first man said.

"Saint Peter looked at his list of souls and said, 'Room Two. Be quiet as you pass Room One.'

"Another man stood at the gates of heaven. 'Religion?' Saint Peter asked.

"'Catholic,' the man said.

"Saint Peter referred to his list. 'Room Three. Be quiet as you pass Room One.'

"A third man stood at the pearly gates. 'Religion?' Saint Peter asked.

"'Hindu,' the man replied.

"Saint Peter said, 'Room Four. Be quiet as you pass Room One.'

"And the Hindu said, 'Sir, I understand there are different rooms for different religions, but why must I be quiet when I pass Room One?'

"Saint Peter said, 'The terrorists are visiting from hell and they think they're the only ones here!'"

Suri giggled and sipped her drink.

"What's your name?" she asked.

Table Mountain loomed in the distance, an ever-present observer keeping watch over predator and prey.

"Are you a sultan?"

The mysterious man peeked at his timepiece. His face held no emotion.

"No, I'm a surgeon." His breath was imbued with ale.

Suri's head tilted. Merriment beamed from her face. Her eyes held on a bit longer than the moment before. His features were as handsome as the ones she recalled. She fingered her hair seductively as her eyes cased back and forth over the mysterious man.

An awkward silence fell between them.

Her puckered lips stopped him cold. "Tell me your name," she commanded.

"My friends call me Ari," he said.

Low clouds over Table Bay receded. Nothing but possibility as far as the eye could see.

"No, they don't."

Passion emanated from her cheeks and eyes. It radiated from her soul as boldly as the first time she saw him at Bascule Bar.

"What's your name? Where are you from?"

"I told you."

She rested an elbow on the table.

"What brings you to Cape Town?" she asked.

"Adventure," said the mysterious man.

She had a vision of him alone in bed.

Silence came and went. She wondered why he had not called.

"Do you enjoy living in Cape Town?"

"Beats the hell out of Sana'a."

"You've been there?" Her face teamed with interest.

"Yes, unfortunately, I have."

She repositioned her hips as a favorite tune played in the bar.

*All the other kids with the pumped up kicks*
*You'd better run, better run, outrun my gun*
*All the other kids with the pumped up kicks*
*You'd better run, better run, faster than my bullet*

"I've thought of settling in Windhoek," he said.

"So have I."

"You look stunning," Ari said. He sipped his beer and studied her face.

"A drunk man says what a sober man thinks."

"Perhaps I've had too many."

Suri's eyes were poised and still.

He said, "Life is uncertain nowadays, I mean with the holy war and all."

"It's not a holy war," she said.

"That's true," the mysterious man agreed.

"War is never holy." Suri sipped her rum. "Even a jihadi knows that."

27

It was Monday in Washington, the first of April, and cherry blossoms dotting the capital were in full bloom. Dogwoods, kayakers, and picnics along the Potomac River heralded a resurgence of spring. To the west, a twin-engine Gulfstream went airborne from Dulles and soared over a cesspool of corrupt politicians and sneaky bureaucrats. One gazed at the aircraft as it flew south along the River and marveled that genius minds that designed such a fine machine could once have germinated in a country now riddled with endless rules and regulations that make technological advance virtually impossible in the present day.

A hearing was led by the chairman of the Middle East and North Africa Subcommittee on Foreign Affairs in Longworth House Office Building. Testimony from an independent auditor extended into the afternoon.

Congressman Montgomery spoke with a polished southern drawl as he adjusted his microphone.

He said, "Moving into the third hour of testimony, Mr. Kimball, I want to thank you for your patience. Now, regarding items 17, 47, 53, and 80 of the Special Investigator's Report, I will refer to sites of indoctrination and abuse collectively as 'the orphanages.'

"Accounts for more than 100 itemized social service programs in Egypt were frozen at the dawn of the Arab Spring in March 2011. According to Secretary Rodham's plan, and this appeared to be one of many hasty decisions she made prior to leaving office, not a single program was required to reapply for funding, but were allocated funds in January 2013 that lasted through the end of the fiscal year. Total funds sent to the orphanages were $350 million. Were operations at the orphanages verified before allocation of funds?"

Leyton Kimball was close to retirement and known for brevity under oath. Concision in discourse is a public servant's essential virtue. He said, "I did not find evidence of verification from interviews at the State Department or the Embassy in Cape Town."

The congressman pressed him further.

"So, it is reasonable to conclude that imams and clerics, who held extremist views about Islam, petitioned the State Department for $350 million of federal assistance and Secretary Rodham granted the request. Do you agree?"

"Sir, I'm not prepared to comment on the Secretary's private conversations with any cleric or imam."

"You report that all of the orphanages were closed or relocated as of March 2015, but State Department memos do not say when the orphanage at Auwal Masjid was closed. Why were those specific dates omitted?"

"I can't say."

Congressman Montgomery leaned back in his chair.

"What information do you have about that particular orphanage which is not in this report?"

"My associates and I conducted a series of extensive interviews. We believe children who were held at the largest orphanage in

Sana'a were moved to the mosque on Dorp Street in Cape Town during May 2011."

The congressman eased forward.

"That's about the time $300 million in foreign contributions were contributed to Secretary Rodham's presidential campaign."

The room was quiet.

"Peculiar timing, don't you think?"

## 28

Except for the most critical memoranda, the library at Mossad Headquarters had been purged of all sensitive files collected since the agency's inception. The few that remained were duplicated electronically and stored in encrypted software.

Foster cleared the way for Jack's helicopter to land at midnight. He watched him enter the building on real-time video, and then rebooted the security server.

He greeted Jack in a corridor.

"Thanks, Dellon. Where to?"

"The lift is this way."

The billionaire still had manners. "After you."

"I'll get fired for this if they catch me."

"Oh well," Jack said, "at least you have options."

They had discussed formation of an international security firm on numerous occasions, and the possibility of Foster taking charge.

Jack exited the lift and went immediately to the library on the second floor. He snatched a folder that Foster had concealed in an atlas and made his way to a cubicle. One memo, dated 10 September 2001, caught his eye.

Conspiracy theories mix blatant facts with subtle falsehood, thereby distorting truth.

"Captivating, isn't it?" a voice said.

Jack's chest buckled. He slammed the atlas shut.

It was Reuben. A moment later, he stood beside the cubicle.

"Welcome back."

"Thanks, Abel. It's good to see you."

"Conducting research?"

"Just reading a memo."

"May I see?"

"It's your library. Do as you please."

Reuben scanned the first line. "Ah, yes. The September 10 memo from Washington's trusty CIA."

"Numerous warning signs were flatly ignored."

"No doubt. The system was blinking red," the director replied.

"Any chance the attacks were an inside job?"

"No. Bin Laden was determined to strike the United States. The president's daily brief on August 6 said as much."

Reuben sat in a chair.

Jack said, "America's political class perpetuates the greatest scam in the history of mankind."

"How so?"

"They feign public disagreement only to collaborate behind closed doors, all while living off fruits of the world's highest corporate tax rate."

Reuben nodded. "Nothing more important than preserving the status quo."

"Power thrives off uncertainty. What better way to justify sacrifice of freedom than with a promise of security?"

"It's true. How else would Congress get away with spending half a trillion dollars on national defense every year?"

"All in the name of peace."

"Correct."

"What a farce," Jack said.

Reuben agreed.

Jack said, "America's military-industrial complex is the most advanced on Earth, and yet terror abounds. Why?"

"National security be damned. It's an exercise in profiteering for defense companies and contractors."

"What use is a powerful military to an administration hell-bent on avoiding conflict?"

"Point taken."

"Meanwhile, evil lurks at every turn."

"Perhaps more than ever. It's civilization versus barbarism." The director's face was more animated. He said, "World leaders aren't bold enough to take action. Only a man like you can stamp out terror."

"What do you mean?"

"Policy gets in the way. Government can't get the job done. Bureaucrats serve only to fuel problems through endless negotiation and lack of focus."

"I understand."

"Terrorists win when we play nice." Reuben paused and looked at Goldwyn.

"You'll hear no argument from me."

The director gazed through a window. He paced back and forth and said, "You need a plan, Jack, a strategy."

Goldwyn nodded. "Any thoughts?"

Reuben responded with conviction. "The answer isn't in that atlas or any other book. Rather, your answer lies in the most basic concept of war."

"And that is?"

"Deception."

Reuben stood calmly.

Jack crossed his arms.

"War is an expensive game with even higher stakes. You win through deceit, by appearing weak when you are strong. Victory emerges after your foe's self-defeat. Excellence consists of breaking the enemy without casting a blow."

"Sun Tzu."

"Indeed, *The Art of War*." Reuben sat in a chair. "You see, Jack. A noble multibillionaire is freedom's only hope. You have resources necessary to purchase terror's defeat. Money buys peace. Isn't that how you rescued Nathan and the rest of the kidnapped children?"

"I suppose."

"What conclusion can you make?"

"Terror is a business. Anyone who attempts to crush it must approach the problem as such."

"Well said."

"Paying rogue nations to be good doesn't work. At best, funds are embezzled. At worst, they're funneled to terrorists themselves."

Reuben agreed. "Now you're speaking my language."

"For more than a millennium, jihad propagated through Islam as a means to an end, a worthy pursuit exploited by imams for political and economic gain. But still an important question remains."

Reuben raised an eyebrow.

"What properly executed strategy will allow us to end terror?"

Jack Goldwyn spoke with Foster inside the *Royal Flush*'s saloon.

Nathan and his mate played chess on the flybridge while Carmen and Captain Lou led Jonas to the saloon.

"Honey?" Carmen said.

Jack stood at the sight of Jonas' familiar face.

"Hello, Jonas." Jack offered a hand.

"Good afternoon, sah."

"You're one of us now."

"Thank you, sah." The boy smiled. "It's an honor to be here."

"We're glad to have you."

Humility overcame him. Jonas asked, "Why are you so kind to me?"

"You helped us locate Nathan, remember?"

"Yes. I'm glad he's safe."

"So are we."

Jonas peered through a bay window. Arching dolphins came into view.

"Would you like something to eat?"

"Yes, please. Then I must check on my brother and report to work. So says Captain Lou."

The boy grinned and made for the galley.


Foster perched on the upper deck.

Jack approached and gazed over his private island.

Foster said, "A man could get used to this."

Jack sat on a stool. "You're welcome anytime, Dellon. Stay as long as you would like."

"Don't you love watching scumbags go down the hard way?"

"Of course," Jack replied. "Especially when politicians watch with envy."

Foster chuckled. Sunlight flickered through a cloud as he sipped a beer.

The billionaire spoke with obvious fervor. "We need a means of stepping in when governments can't or won't."

"You mean an option outside the political realm?"

"Yes, Dellon. World leaders fail us every time."

Jack Goldwyn had a plan. He rested his glass of sherry on a table. "What would it take?" he said.

"For what?"

"To rid the world of terror."

"By take, you mean . . ."

"Cost."

"Not sure."

"Throw out a figure."

"My guess is five hundred mil."

Jack's eyebrows rose. "Is that all?"

Foster grinned. "That's pocket change for you."

"A small price for the end of terror."

"You could probably do it for less."

"Half a billion, eh?"

"I'd say, give or take."

"How long would you need?"

"Six months, maybe less."

Foster set his beer aside.

Jack sipped his sherry.

Behind them, a door opened. A host of trained assassins marched out, all confident in their ability to execute a vital scheme.

A shiny chopper waited on the helipad. Inside, Ari closed a briefcase stuffed with a million dollars. A dozen others matching it were stowed next to his rifle case.

Slowly, rotor blades started to turn. Suri waved from the pilot seat.

Jack stood on the upper deck. He said, "You'd better go, Dellon."

They shook hands and Foster departed.

As a brilliant sunset threw its last rays over a private island on the first of May, Jack Goldwyn lounged on a balcony of his megayacht and gently puffed a stogie. His wicker chair creaked as a plume of smoke wafted up from a battle-worn face.

The chopper roared to life.

"Heaven help us," he mumbled.

Carmen appeared in a doorway.

"What did you say?"

The billionaire peeked at his Rolex.

"Time is wasting."

## About the Author

Starner Jones is an award-winning author and physician. His novella, *Purple Church*, won the 2011 George Garrett Fiction Prize. *Mother City* is his debut novel.

# Questions for Reading Groups

1. How does the novel's unique setting enhance the story?

2. What are the novel's most important themes and motifs?

3. Who are the prominent characters in the novel?

4. What are the major conflicts and how do they arise?

5. How do protagonists and antagonists change or grow throughout the novel?

6. Do characters seem real and believable?

7. What role do fate and chance play in the novel, and how is their importance presented in the plot?

8. Does the novel cause you to reconsider the importance of diplomacy in world politics?

9. Does the novel make you feel uncomfortable? If so, why?

10. Does reading the novel result in a deeper understanding and awareness of implicit dangers in today's world?

11. How would you react in a similar situation faced by Jack and Carmen?

12. *Mother City* focuses on the interplay between politics, economics, and religion. Does the novel change your impression of certain world leaders or political agendas?

13. What does the plot and how it unfolds tell us about the author's world view?

14. Why is the conflict between Prime Minister Reznik and Suri left unresolved?

15. What role do children play in the novel?

16. What emotions do you feel after reading *Mother City*?

17. Discuss religion as it relates to main characters and how they evolve.

18. What is the significance of Jack and Carmen's final exchange?

19. What does *Mother City* teach us about a multibillionaire's role in society?

20. What do you perceive as the author's motivation for writing the novel?

 WORLD AHEAD *press*

Authors welcome! Publishing your book with us means that you have the freedom to blaze your own trail. But that doesn't mean you should go it alone. By choosing to publish with WORLD AHEAD PRESS, you partner with WND—one of the most powerful and influential brands on the Internet.

If you liked this book and want to publish your own, WORLD AHEAD PRESS, co-publishing division of WND Books, is right for you. WORLD AHEAD PRESS will turn your manuscript into a high-quality book and then promote it through its broad reach into conservative and Christian markets worldwide.

## IMAGINE YOUR BOOK ALONGSIDE THESE AUTHORS!

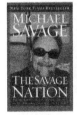    

We transform your manuscript into a marketable book. Here's what you get:

**BEAUTIFUL CUSTOM BOOK COVER**
PROFESSIONAL COPYEDIT
**INTERIOR FORMATTING**
EBOOK CONVERSION
**KINDLE EBOOK EDITION**
WORLDWIDE BOOKSTORE DISTRIBUTION
**MARKETING ON AMAZON.COM**

It's time to publish your book with WORLD AHEAD PRESS.

Go to www.worldaheadpress.com for a Free Consultation

CPSIA information can be obtained
at www.ICGtesting.com
Printed in the USA
BVOW08s0518201017
498039BV00001B/7/P